# LARISSA'S BREADBOOK

## Baking Bread & Telling Tales with Women of the American South

## LORRAINE JOHNSON-COLEMAN

### ILLUSTRATED BY KATHERINE SANDOZ

RUTLEDGE HILL PRESS®
Nashville, Tennessee
A Thomas Nelson Company

Published by Rutledge Hill Press, a Thomas Nelson Company, P.O. Box 141000, Nashville, Tennessee 37214.

Book design by Design Press, a division of the Savannah College of Art and Design.

**Library of Congress Cataloging-in-Publication Data**

Johnson-Coleman, Lorraine, 1962–

   Larissa's breadbook : baking bread and telling tales with women of the American South / Lorraine Johnson-Coleman.

   ISBN 1-55853-845-3

   1. Women—Southern States—Fiction. 2. Reminiscing in old age—Fiction. 3. Southern States—Fiction. 4. Women cooks—Fiction. 5. Aged women—Fiction. 6. Baking—Fiction. 7. Bread. I. Title

PS3560.O38685 L37 2001

813'.54—dc21                                        2001019029

Printed in the United States of America

1 2 3 4 5 6 7 8 9—06 05 04 03 02 01

*To my husband, Lance;*

*my children, Larissa, Lauren,*

*Lance, and Latrice; and last, but not least,*

*Amy Parks, my executive assistant,*

*whose many contributions were invaluable*

# CONTENTS

# First, a Note from
# *Larissa's Mama*

I've been thinking lately, and that can be a dangerous thing, let me tell you. But every once in a while, I just have to—think that is, otherwise I begin to engage in other dangerous activities like sneaking potato chips (plain, not Ruffles) into my bedroom and wolfing them down one handful after another. No, there is no doubt about it, thinking is a much safer activity, at least for the sake of my thighs. And I've decided that if, indeed, there is any true justice in the world, then every woman over the age of thirty-five should automatically be granted certain rewards, just for having the good sense to survive the challenges of day-to-day living.

Really and truly, it shouldn't just be *one* reward; after all, thirty-five years is a long time. And if you throw in a house that needs to be cleaned, a husband who expects at least some of your attention, and a couple of children who ask for things like food, shelter, and clean clothes, well the thirty-five years get longer by the day. So I think that in exchange for such sacrifice, we women should just get certain blessings automatically, really, without even asking.

I figure the goodness should just kind of come down from the Lord's pearly gates in certain intervals, reminding us that bit by bit and day by day, we, the mamas of the world, are ever earning our place in heaven—where there will never be another dirty dish or inevitable dinner dilemma of how to fix the chicken in a way we've never fixed the chicken before. I sincerely believe that the kitchen gods should take mercy on us and send us down those keys of domestic wisdom, so that we can automatically possess necessary solutions instead of having to search through tedious helpful-hint columns, women-can-do-it-better articles, or endless self-help books that really and truly reveal absolutely nothing. No, after the age of thirty-five, I believe that we've paid all the dues we need to, and somebody ought to go ahead, take pity on us, and simply make this kitchen thing easier.

I want all the answers, and I want them right now. But alas, it doesn't look as if when the disciples put together the Good Book, they included in their many promises for happiness, assured domestic bliss. So I guess like most women, I'm on my own, and I better go ahead and get the wisdom any way that I can.

Well, in this instance, the wisdom did eventually arrive. Wisdom about the beauty, diversity, tasty nature, and history of Southern breads—the staple of the diet for all those folks who live below the Mason-Dixon line. Yes, the South has many delicacies, but none as wonderfully significant as bread. I, of course, never took the time to associate the various breads of the region with the many immigrant cultures that exist in the South. Unfortunately, I just looked at all that delicious bread merely as bread, but I have learned that it is so much more than that. It is the remnant of an incredible story—a story that tells the world that the South was never only black and white but was always a rich rainbow of ethnic groups that came in all colors in-between.

Most folks came to the South with very little in the way of belongings, but they did bring their hearts, their souls, and their very special way of doing things. Because they did, they never became one big melting pot of sameness but rather one big stew with all kinds of different flavors rubbing up next to one another and seasoning each other. So now at almost forty years old, I've finally learned that Southern bread is *not* just Southern bread, but that it pays tribute to some pretty awe-inspiring folks. The worst part is, I didn't even learn all of this by myself. No, my thirteen-year-old had to be the one to enlighten me (and if you have ever had teenage children yourself, then you know that they are the last ones you want to bring you the lesson, because they never let you forget it). Well, in all fairness I have to give her a chance to tell you her story, which is really quite wonderful. Truthfully, this book is more about her than it is about me. I'm just along for the ride, and that's okay. Sometimes great learning is revealed most clearly from the back seat, and, yes, at times the young can indeed lead us.

So sit back and enjoy Larissa's tale of courage, adventure, and eventual discovery. After a while, we will get to all those great recipes, but Larissa is a storyteller just like her mother, and she wouldn't dream of letting you get to point B (the recipes) without beginning at the beginning and telling you in stunning detail just how she got to where she needed to be. She is her mother's child, after all, and like me she absolutely loves a captive audience.

This all began with a school project, and that's all I'm going to tell you, but I couldn't resist giving you a little hint on what the story is about. However, that school project gets mighty interesting. Larissa not only learns a great deal, but she also makes some loving friends along the way whom neither one of us will ever forget.

So, without further delay—Larissa, baby, you're on!

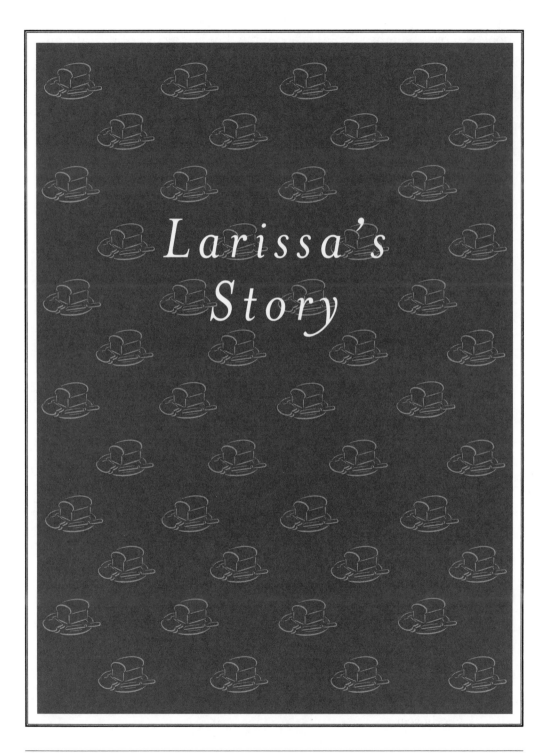

# Larissa's Story

This whole adventure (you know, the one that I'm going to tell you about) started this past Tuesday. What's funny is that I always seem to get my most important news on Tuesdays. It was on a Tuesday that I found out that I was getting a baby brother. (I admit that I didn't care for him at first, but he quickly grew on me and now I think he's the bomb!) And it was on a Tuesday that I found out that my dad had been given a promotion at work, so we had to move to a brand-new town. I missed my old neighborhood at first, but I love our new house and I've already made lots of friends.

So you see, there just seems to be something special about Tuesdays. It's at the point now that I wake up bright and early on Tuesday mornings, and I can't help but wonder what the day has in store for me. At one time I used to worry about it all, but I've learned that even though my Tuesday news may seem troublesome at first, it usually does work out for the best. That's why I wasn't too worried about this latest Tuesday news. Even though I had just been given a new (but somewhat tedious) responsibility, I was fairly certain that I could do a good job.

It all started when Miss Jones, my eighth grade teacher, announced in class that the school was going to try to raise money for some brand-new library books. Well, I love to read, and in the year that I have been at H. B. Suggs Middle School, I have already read my way through all the very best stories. Why, the last time that I stopped by to see Miss Williams at the media center, I told her then that there wasn't too much left for me to discover in that little blue section along the far right wall that she created for the seventh and eighth grade readers. We simply needed more books and we needed them quickly. Spring break was right around the corner, and I depended on my library books to get me through those occasionally boring, or sometimes rainy, vacation days. So you can just imagine how happy I was to hear Miss Jones announce that our class would be responsible for this library fund-raiser. If we simply tried hard enough, I was sure that we could raise enough money to keep me, and others just like me, knee deep in books all the way until summer. Now, that was a possibility worth working for.

Everybody seemed to have a different suggestion as to what we ought to do to raise the much-needed dollars. Alma DoLittle (a very appropriate name, too, since she always said a whole lot, but in the end usually did very little) suggested a car wash. No one liked that idea, however, because it had been chilly as of late, and the last time that the school had a car wash while there was still a nip in the air, everybody caught a cold and then ended up sneezing their way through the entire spring break. Another car wash? I didn't think so.

Little Lauren Simpson (we call her that because she's the smallest girl in the class) suggested a garage sale, but Nina Brown (our dress-up-every-single-day-no-matter-what, pain-in-the-neck, class princess) quickly knocked down the idea because she thought that it would be too messy. She claimed that the stuff the people always brought in to sell, somehow or another, usually managed to get everything and everybody around it all dirty. After the last one the school had, Nina's brand-new dress was ruined and she had to throw it away even though she'd only worn it one time. A filthy garage sale? "Out of the question!" screamed one prissy Nina Brown.

Finally our teacher, Miss Jones, made a suggestion no one had a problem with—a bake sale. Our class would be in charge, and she would be giving each of us an important assignment. I couldn't wait to get mine. As I've already told you, I am really quite responsible, a born leader so to speak, so any assignment of mine was certain to be completed promptly and efficiently. Miss Jones would not have to worry about me, that was for sure.

Alma DoLittle was given the task of gathering together the paper goods. She would have to stop by each of the parent volunteer's homes and collect a different item from each; napkins, paper cups, paper plates, and plastic forks were just some of the things we would need. Well, surely that wouldn't be too difficult. I figured, even a do-little like Alma should be able to manage that small chore.

Little Lauren Simpson was given the responsibility of heading the decorating committee. Six students were chosen to be a part of that group, and it would be up to them to make sure the cafeteria looked festive. "Festive" always puts folks in a buying mood, and that's the kind of feeling you want at a fund-raiser. It would take a great deal of work, but there was no need for concern. Lauren was a creative genius when it came to this kind of thing. At our holiday party last December, Lauren managed to make hallway ornaments from nothing more than scrap paper, rubber bands, beads, and white glue. By the time Lauren and her crew were finished, that plain old cafeteria would say "party time" to anyone who cared to stop by.

Nina Brown was given the job of hostess—a perfect job for a little girl who thought she was a dress-up doll. She would be responsible for meeting and greeting each and every customer who came in the door. She would be required to smile, say "welcome," and then hand them each a price list. Knowing Nina, she would probably come decked out in a ball gown on the big day. As expected, she started grinning the moment Miss Jones announced her job. Well, at least she wasn't on a committee. Now perhaps she would stay out of the way and maybe even manage not to get on anybody's nerves. We could only hope.

Miss Jones then worked her way through the rest of the task list and made all the necessary announcements. Eric was put in charge of the cookies. (I was, however, a little worried about this particular arrangement because as of late Eric seemed to be going through some kind of supercharged growth spurt and was currently eating anything that didn't eat him first. We would all just say a prayer that the cookies he collected actually made it to the bake sale.) Billy was chosen to make the lemonade, and Carlita would make the tablecloths out of crepe paper. Lucy and her gang of four would pick up the pound cakes from Miss Whatley's bakery, and Miss Jones promised to make two pans of brownies. Miss Williams, our media specialist, promised to make cupcakes, and Mr. Limster, our principal, was going to bring in a triple-layer chocolate cake. Everybody, it seemed, had something special to do except for me—the most efficient and reliable one of the entire bunch. Surely there had to be some mistake.

I was just about to stand up and point out her oversight when Miss Jones looked over at me and said, "Oh, and you, Larissa, are in charge of the bread.

I saved the absolute best for last." Bread? I wondered. What was so exciting about bread? Yes, you do bake it, so technically it does qualify as a bake sale item, but it was certainly nothing to get worked up about. Miss Jones then continued, "The ladies over at our brand-new senior citizens center have graciously volunteered to make us some homemade bread that we will then be able to sell at the bake sale. They will be baking it on Tuesday afternoon so that it will be fresh for our Tuesday evening event. They want you, Larissa, to get there early in case they need help. You should be there no later than four o'clock, so I will be excusing you from any homework given that day in order that you may give this assignment your complete attention. Do you have any questions?"

Questions? Who could possibly have questions about bread? It seemed, after all, to be a fairly basic idea, so I shook my head no to indicate that I did indeed have a grasp of this relatively simple concept.

Oh well. I vowed that I would do a good job even if it wasn't the best assignment given that day.

Finally, it was the end of another Tuesday. I let out a great big sigh. I was trying not to be disappointed about the way things seemed to have worked themselves out, but it sure wasn't easy. I had been hoping for a job that was a great deal more interesting than bread, but I should have known better. After all it was Tuesday.

As I walked home, I let out yet another sigh, this one even longer and sadder than the last. This Tuesday I had been made a bread monitor. Next Tuesday I would be a baker's assistant to a group of older ladies that I didn't even know. Maybe the following Tuesday I would just stay in bed with the covers pulled up over my head.

On Friday I decided to stop by the public library on the way home from school to see if perhaps there was a little something about this bread thing I just might be missing. I believed strongly that there must be some level of preparation for any and all new responsibilities, no matter how small or how boring. Besides, I was hoping that maybe they had gotten in some new mysteries since the last time I had been in, and if so, I would be able to pick up something great to read over the weekend.

Our library is a small brick building on the corner of Main Street and Fifth Avenue. In the front there are six big cement steps that you have to climb in order to get to the door, but once inside you are greeted by a colorful lobby and a sometimes pleasant receptionist. Today she was obviously in a good mood because when I explained to her what I was looking for (info on bread, remember?), she smiled and cheerfully pointed me toward the cookbooks located in the back corner of the reference section.

I was surprised to see so many books on something as simple and as easy to understand as food, but here they all were, dozens and dozens of them. I picked out four that seemed to be pretty good. These were easy to read and they had pictures too. I sat down at an empty table and started to flip through the various bread sections. You wouldn't believe what I discovered.

Bread! Bread! Bread! Everywhere and every way. You could bake it, sop it, drizzle it, dunk it, smother it, or stuff with it. You could eat it at the beginning of a meal or as the last delicious drop to finish a good one off. But no matter what you did with it, no real meal, it seems, was complete without it.

In those bright and colorful cookbooks I found cornbread, French bread, fry bread, and Italian bread. There were also hoecakes, hush puppies, rolls, and biscuits. Thankfully, all kinds of people had come to the South to make it their home, and they had each brought their different foods, especially their breads, right along with them.

Maybe, just maybe, this bread monitor position wouldn't be such a boring job after all. I mean who's to really say what a couple of senior ladies might just cook up once they get going? With choices like these, I thought to myself as I put the cookbooks back on the shelf, we could very easily have the best table at the fund-raiser.

The following Tuesday flew by in what seemed to be no more than a blink of an eye. The morning was devoted to math, science, and music. Lunch was even good. We had sloppy joes and French fries, two of my favorites. It was raining, though, so my friends and I stayed inside the cafeteria and giggled over silly stories. (Mine was the most ridiculous, as I was, and continue to be, the school's champion of tall-tale telling.)

The afternoon included free reading, a social studies lesson, and a geography review for an upcoming test. Miss Jones had excused me from any homework, so I left for the senior center as soon as the three o'clock bell rang, signaling the end of a rather nice, believe it or not, Tuesday. (Just when you think you've got this Tuesday thing all figured out, it up and changes on you. Go figure.)

The senior center was not too far from the school, so just as I expected, it looked as if I would be at least thirty minutes early. I was glad about that, too, because this meant that I would really have an opportunity to see some of the bread in the making. I could hardly wait.

I walked along Main Street, made a left at Mr. Sam's candy store (resisting the temptation to go in and take a peek at the new and expanded bubble gum section), crossed at the light, and then cut through the alley behind the hardware store, thereby delivering myself at the senior center in exactly twenty-two minutes. That had to be some kind of record, I was sure of it.

Even before Miss Mary Sims opened up the door, I could smell something good cooking inside. So many fabulous aromas mingled together on that beautiful Tuesday afternoon that I couldn't resist taking in several good whiffs before Miss Sims waved me inside.

Inside the building was a large bright kitchen at the end of the hallway. When I walked inside, there were baking pans and working hands everywhere. Some of the ladies must have brought toaster ovens from home in order to handle all the baking that needed to be done. There were six of them lined up along the counter next to the two large wall units.

One of the ladies was singing what sounded like a pretty nice little song, but I couldn't make out the words because not too very far away, two angry women were shouting at one another over an open oven door. Uh-oh, I thought. This must have been what Grandma meant when she said that only confusion cooks when one too many women attempt to share a kitchen space. But luckily for all of us, the argument ended as quickly as it had begun, and all that remained were the sounds of folks who were happily at work.

I put my knapsack in the corner, out of everyone's way, and then wandered over to observe Miss Bessie. I knew her from church, and Mama always said that she was, without question, one of the best cooks in town. Miss Bessie reminded me of a large gingerbread cookie, and I just loved looking at her. She was the color of pretty brown cinnamon, and she was kind of round and curvy everywhere.

Today she was wearing a red calico apron, and according to my list, she was making biscuits. I figured that if, perhaps, I watched her ever so carefully I might be able to pick up some pointers. Biscuits were some of my favorites, especially the big ones made with cheddar cheese, or better yet, the delectable little sweet potato ones. Yum! Yum!

"Hey, Miss Bessie," I called out. "I got here early so I could watch you make biscuits. You got a recipe, Miss Bessie? Because according to all of those cookbooks I found in the library, you got to have a recipe. Where's yours, Miss Bessie?"

Well, she didn't answer me at first. Instead she just looked at me as if I had suddenly and quite miraculously grown an extra talking head. "Honey," she said to me when she finally spoke, "I have never, ever used a recipe." Her voice was very firm on the matter. "Why I have been making these biscuits the exact same way for over sixty years. I learned how to make them from my mother, and she never used a recipe either." Miss Bessie then stopped talking long enough to reach underneath the sink and get out one of her baking pans. She rubbed oil all over the inside of it.

"I learned to cook the way most black women do—by watching. Pull up a stool, hush, and pay attention. It wasn't always easy, but my mother did manage to teach me a thing or two. She's gone now—died about ten years ago and I sure do miss her, especially when I make these biscuits."

"Well, if you don't have a recipe, how are we going to make the biscuits? I'd like to help, but I don't know what to do."

"Girl, reach in that flour canister, get you two handfuls of flour, and throw it down on that little wooden board." Well, that hardly seemed scientific to me. I was expecting to measure everything out ever so carefully and then level it off just so with a butter knife. I knew for sure that those cookbook experts I'd read about in the library wouldn't have approved of any of this, but I wasn't about to utter a single word. Miss Bessie didn't look to me as if she was in the mood for a whole lot of discussion about her special way of making biscuits, so I decided to just do as I was told.

"Now add some water," she directed. Some? How much was some? I didn't know so I just kept adding it until she yelled, "Good gracious, honey, that's enough! You want the dough to be mushy but not soggy." Next a "pinch" of baking soda went in, "two fingers of butter," and finally a "reasonable amount of sugar." We then "worked it," a term Miss Bessie used to mean "mix thoroughly until the dough had an even consistency." Once we rolled it out so that it resembled one big pancake, it was then time to cut out the biscuits.

"Do you have biscuit cutters in all different shapes and sizes that we can choose from?" I asked. I remembered that one of the cookbook authors had a variety available to her when she made biscuits. Well, Miss Bessie didn't answer me right away. First, she gave me that look again, you know the one where she stands and stares at me for a moment as if I've grown that extra talking head. I was beginning to fear that Miss Bessie didn't think of me as being very bright. Still, if I wanted to learn, then I had to ask questions. I would just try not to ask any more than necessary.

"Honey, reach up in that cabinet and get hold of one of those drinking glasses." I did as I was told and used the top of the glass to cut out a dozen little circles that would hopefully become beautiful biscuits.

"Is the oven preheated so that we can be sure that it is hot enough?" I inquired.

"Open up the oven door," Miss Bessie instructed rather matter-of-factly. "Now stick your hand in there—just a bit. Ease it in real careful-like. Well, is it hot?"

I nodded yes, my hand stinging slightly from the prickly heat.

"Then go ahead and put that pan on in there." I did it without question, but I couldn't help wondering exactly how long it would take for all those white dough balls to become beautifully brown biscuits. What we needed was a timer to help us count the minutes away. I decided to ask Miss Bessie if she had one. When I asked the question this time, Miss Bessie didn't give me that look, you know, the two-headed one. She just smiled. I figured out for myself that I was probably starting to grow on her, and she couldn't help but begin to love me as time went on. I am a pretty lovable kid, if I do say so myself.

In response to my request for a timer, Miss Bessie declared that we would not need one. We would simply have to wait a few moments. She would know when the biscuits were ready, and she would be sure to let me know when the time was up. So we just stood there and waited. Miss Bessie hummed an old church hymn which made the waiting that much nicer. After a short while, she directed me to open up the oven door and look inside. The biscuits looked great.

"Go ahead and take 'em out," Miss Bessie told me. "They're done." And as we waited for the biscuits to cool down a bit (I couldn't wait to taste), Miss Bessie and I finally had a moment to catch our breath and to just talk.

Miss Bessie decided to sit on a high wooden stool. It took her a little while to get all the way up there, though, and another moment or two to get completely settled. The way she had to move around trying to get comfortable did make me a little nervous, and of course, I said so. When will I learn to keep my big mouth shut?

"Now, girlie, I ain't now nor have I ever been that old or that unsteady," she replied with warm laughter. "I've been climbing up on stools like this one for as long as I can remember. So don't you worry about me none. Miss Bessie has been taking care of herself for a long time."

I took a seat on a footstool not too far away. There was another high stool in the area, but I decided to pass. The last thing I needed at that moment was to fall off one myself after so foolishly worrying about Miss Bessie. A footstool seemed a whole lot safer anyway, so I pulled it over and sat squarely upon it. Now that Miss Bessie and I were finished with our own bread, I finally had the time to just enjoy all the sights and smells. Briefly I considered helping out one of the other ladies, but I noticed quickly that they all seemed to have things well under control.

"Boy, it sure smells good in here, Miss Bessie," I said, and my stomach grumbled in agreement. Miss Bessie must have heard it, too, because she offered me a piece of the fried chicken she'd prepared earlier and one of our biscuits that were now ready to eat. I hated to see her have to climb down off that stool after she'd spent so much time getting up there, but I was pretty hungry.

You know what I admired most about Miss Bessie? It was the fact that she could move around so quickly in a kitchen, but she still managed to talk all the while.

"Honey, there isn't another place in the world as wonderful as a Southern woman's kitchen. Head into one of our kitchens, and you'll notice right off that this here isn't just working space. It's the place where we laugh together; talk over a long, long day; cry on each other's shoulders; and pass down hard-earned traditions." Miss Bessie paused long enough to wipe the crumbs off the counter.

"Go into a Southern kitchen, and you will quickly discover that it smells good, too. Yes, there are the fragrances of the day, but there are also the lingering ghosts—those aromas that still hang around from some long-ago celebration, the ones that simply refuse to roll over and die. In my kitchen at home you can still sense the presence of the fried chicken and collard greens I made this past Sunday." Miss Bessie quickly finished wiping away crumbs, and was now busy washing a sink load of dishes. It seemed to me as if Miss Bessie never ever sat still for very long. There always seemed to be that one more thing to do that was sure to keep her on the go. It was amazing to see how much she could get done in a relatively short period of time.

"My mother used to say that if you wanted to know about a woman, go into her kitchen. It will tell you more truth about that woman than she ever will. I've discovered, too, that those words are as right today as they ever were yesterday. The place where a woman shelters her morsels speaks volumes about who and what she happens to be. Taste a woman's cooking and there are memories there, histories and traditions in each and every bite. Every single woman here today is different, not just because we are all unique individuals, but also because we come from such different cultures. Now you take Miss Elise over there," Miss Bessie pointed to a pretty older woman wearing a colorful scarf wrapped around her neck. "Her people are

Cajun, straight from the Louisiana bayou. She's making her famous plantation French bread today. And Chepita over there wearing the vividly colored skirt is Mexican and her people come from Texas. Of course, her food has a strong Spanish influence. She even puts jalapeños in her cornbread. Girl, wait until you taste it! It's spicy but good!" Miss Bessie looked over at me then to see if I understood what she was trying to tell me. I nodded my head yes to indicate that indeed I understood every word. Amazing! Even Southern black folks weren't all the same. Just like other people, we, too, were a product of those very distinctive places where we have either been ourselves or where our people come from. My history books at school had never made mention of anything like this, that was for sure.

"Yes sir, we are all from different cultures. Now you take Mrs. Cohen over there. That woman is one proud Jewish lady who is Southern all the way down to her toes. She told me once that her people have been living in the South for over two hundred years! They come from somewhere around Savannah, Georgia, or maybe it was Charleston, South Carolina. That mandelbread she's making has been a Passover family favorite for generations. I know that because she told me so."

"And that pan of garlic sticks Mrs. Morelli is making has graced her Italian family's table as long as they've been Italian. Dip them into some olive oil and you have something good in your hands, let me tell you!" Miss Bessie pointed to the back of the room. "Now look way in the back there," she directed, "and you'll see Mrs. Tell—a perfectly lovely Cherokee woman from the western mountains of North Carolina. The Cherokee Indians were there long before anybody else and they are committed to keeping their traditions intact. Why, every fall they have a big powwow celebration, and Mrs. Tell goes back home for it. She's making bannock bread today. She says it tastes best when it's cooked in a hearth over an open fire, but we don't have anything like that around this place, so she'll just have to make do with these new-fangled ovens we do have." Miss Bessie chuckled, and now that she was finished washing, wiping, and drying, she sat down once again.

"Baby, we've got hoecakes, spoonbread, loaves of bread, rolls, and bread pudding thanks to these ladies here today. But it's not just bread that they are giving you. They are each giving you a piece of themselves in the process." I was now finished with my fried chicken and biscuit and really needed to use the rest room, but I sensed that Miss Bessie had a little more to say and I didn't want to miss a single word, so I stayed right where I was. I was correct, too, because after just a moment Miss Bessie continued on.

"There has been way too much said in this country about the South in terms of black people and white people only. But Southern folks are so much more than that. We are as diverse as people anywhere else; it's just that other folks plain refuse to see it. That's why I love coming to this center—because I get to meet so many different kinds of people. You see, when I was a little girl, the South was a very segregated place. Everybody kind of stayed with their own, but, thankfully, now it's a brand-new day, and I finally have friends of all kinds." Miss Bessie stopped talking again, and I was sure she was finished this time with the storytelling because she soon announced to everyone that it was time to get all the bread together and pack it up to go on over to the school gym. There was an oven in the teacher's cafeteria to heat up whatever we needed to. I reminded Miss Bessie of that convenience, so she wouldn't worry unnecessarily about the bread that had gotten cold. I was so excited. As I raced to the ladies' room, I was grinning from ear to ear. What a bake sale this was going to be!

When we arrived at the gym, things were pretty much as I expected them to be. Little Lauren Simpson had done a fantastic job with the decorations, Eric was complaining of a stomachache from eating too many cookies, and Nina Brown looked like the Good Witch of the North in a green satin dress with big puffed sleeves.

Everybody else was busy setting up their tables, and a quick glance around the room told me we had the best selection of baked goods. I expected that we would make a good bit of money that evening, and I could already see those bookcases filled with new library books for my vacation enjoyment.

It didn't take but a moment to set up our space because I had six senior helpers from the center that really knew their way around a table. Within minutes the room was filled to capacity with eager bake sale buyers. Folks bought our breads as fast as we could heat them up, and we were moving pretty fast. In the end, it was announced that we had raised over five hundred dollars for the library. Everybody clapped at the good news and some people whistled. What an incredible Tuesday!

The next day Miss Jones asked each of us to write a brief report about our individual experiences with the bake sale. Mine was longer than anyone else's because I included the bread recipes and stories from each of my new senior friends that I had collected the day before. I called it *Larissa's BreadBook,* and it contains both recipes and stories from some of the best Southern ladies anywhere.

At the very end of my report, I concluded that if you truly want to learn about the South, you simply have to start with the food, and if you truly want to learn about the great Southern people, then all you have to do is take the time to break a little bread with them. There's no better fellowship anywhere, at least none that I can think of, and I'm pretty smart about these things, I can promise you that.

# *Another Note from Larissa's Mama*

(I know, I know. Some folks just don't know when to hush.)

I can't tell you what a joy it has been for Larissa and me to have had the opportunity to get to know all of these marvelous women. The recipes, of course, will be the treasures that will forever remind us of the experiences, but it will be the stories of these ladies and their lives that ultimately will be the most significant. Sadly, despite all of the sharing, it still just doesn't seem to be enough. I want more and I'll bet you do, too.

Let's face it, Larissa and I had limited time. The breadbook report was due almost immediately after the bake sale, and it just couldn't be late. But I sense that our ladies have a great deal more to say, and I think we ought to let them say it. So, at this point the story takes an interesting turn as we move our mamas front and center. They have a story to tell, and I promised them they could take their time and tell it. Now, don't worry, we are about to get to all those recipes you've been waiting for, but really, who in the world wants a recipe without a really good story to go along with it?

Enjoy!

## A Note about the Recipes

Some recipes are more difficult than others, so follow the signs so you don't end up in over your head.

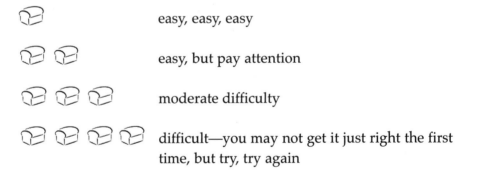

easy, easy, easy

easy, but pay attention

moderate difficulty

difficult—you may not get it just right the first time, but try, try again

# Miss Bessie

M iss Bessie went from a peaceful slumber to a rudely imposing reality in a matter of minutes. She had been awakened (at least she figured she was awake, it was hard to tell with all this darkness) by a strange feeling that was settling itself rather comfortably in the pit of her stomach. She reached up and tried to touch her eyelids. Instead she poked herself right in the eye and concluded painfully that, yes, she was, indeed, awake. It was obvious that she was staring, even if she couldn't see anything yet. She waited a moment and her eyes adjusted to blackness. When her rightful vision returned, she allowed her eyes to sweep across the little space she called a bedroom. Everything seemed to be just fine, and judging by the way the moonlight was now peering through the small window, and by the way the crickets chirped nosily in the bush, Miss Bessie figured it must have been somewhere between eleven o'clock at night and five o'clock in the morning. This was the time that all God-fearing, hardworking, and somewhat sensible people were supposed to be snoring, instead of staring into the night rubbing a lead belly.

She had been so whipped when she lay down that she was sure that, despite her usual restlessness and her never-ending nervous stomach, the long, tiring day coupled with the warm tea at bedtime would ensure her a good night's sleep. She had waited as long as she possibly could to finally lay her weary body down deep beneath her new sheets, hoping that the late hour would guarantee she would sleep through the night, but here she was—wide awake. She knew what was wrong. The signs had been there all week. First, there had been that whistlin' woman that had crossed her path on Tuesday, the fly that had been pestering her on Wednesday, and finally, that snake she saw slithering 'cross her porch on Thursday. If all that hadn't been bad enough, the Devil had to bring himself to poor Sister Mabel's funeral yesterday. There they all were, the Good Samaritan Sisters, all dressed in their beautiful blue dresses, white satin aprons, and set to proudly put away one of their own. She had been chosen to be the lead Samaritan, so it was up to her to carry the little wooden arch that each of the women would have to pass through on their way to the service. It was supposed to be just so. It sure wasn't supposed to go down the way that it did.

The sisters had come to get Sister Mabel ready. They had laid her out so pretty, too. Her house had been cleaned special. They had put her in the parlor so people could file past her easy and then take their seats in the front room for the service. It was going fine, too—that was 'til Sister Chattie got there, late as usual. Then she had had the nerve to push her way past Sister Bezza just so she could get her "the first good look." Didn't even have the decency to ask if she could look, just pushed her way straight on to the lookin'. Everybody knows that you got to ask first. That's just the way things are done proper. You got to get permission. Well, 'course Sister Bezza had to go to pushin' her back, and one thing 'bout Sister Bezza, she push hard, too—so hard 'til Sister Chattie fell all the way forward, knocking over poor Sister Mabel so that she rolled right smack onto the floor. Then the little wooden coffin flipped up, breaking not one, but two of the carefully covered mirrors (covered so that Sister Mabel wouldn't be too busy lookin' at herself that she forgot to be getting' to where she needed to go).

Well, after the breakin' of the mirrors, the casket landed right on top of Sister Mabel, but not before her dress had rolled clean up to her waist, revealing a beautifully brown, but totally naked, behind. Somebody must have forgot to put her drawers on when they had so carefully dressed her the day before. Now, there was Sister Mabel, a decent Christian woman who boasted on more than one occasion that her husband had never, ever even seen her bare feet, and there she was layin' face down and butt up in the middle of her living room floor. The preacher 'bout choked on his chicken, Li'l Boy Luther commenced to snickering, and Miss Clara and her silly self just kept yellin' "Oh my God!" over and over again, like the Lord hadn't heard her the first time. Well, it had taken the entire Good Samaritan group to get things back together, and in a few moments, things were the way they were supposed to be. Even Sister Shug had scrounged up some drawers for Sister Mabel. (Lord, let's hope that they weren't Sister Shug's. Mercy, that would be about as bad as the bare butt disaster. It just wouldn't be decent, nope, not decent at all.) Of course, Sister Chattie and Sister Bezza wouldn't let their little cat fight die a natural death, so Miss Bessie had to step in and threaten to send them both back home if they didn't begin to act like good little Samaritans. After a while, they did manage to get themselves together, but oh Lord, what a day!

Now Miss Bessie's daddy had always tried to teach all his children the ways of the world. From the time Miss Bessie was knee high to a grasshopper, he'd told her how the Lord had given black folks all the signs. "You learn how to read the signs," he said, "and you can find all the truths you are looking for." Well, let's see now. Her gut was burning, her left foot was itching, and her right foot was twitching. Add that to the whistling woman, the pestering fly, the slithering snake, the feuding Samaritans, and the butt-naked Miss Mabel, and what do you have? That's right, nothing but trouble, and today she sure didn't need any trouble.

Later this morning it would be her turn to make the biscuits for the homeless at the shelter downtown. They would need at least eight dozen and they would just have to be perfect—those down-and-out folks deserved at least that much. Good, good folks with so very little. It was a darn shame, that's what it was. It reminded her of her childhood days—those tough times she sometimes tried to foolishly bury, but no matter how hard she tried, those memories always rose on back up again, like a sore that stubbornly refused to heal. Truthfully, those early days weren't without their own brand of blessings. Sister Bessie liked to say that back then the loving was easy; it was just the living that was so hard.

Little Larissa from the middle school had asked her to share her story and a few of her recipes. For Miss Bessie, talking about herself wasn't easy. There were places she'd been that she really didn't want a whole lot of people to see, but the child had asked so sweetly, Miss Bessie had no choice but to say yes. So she had gone back, way back to another time and place, and reluctantly she had shared. Her mama always said that the truth shall set you free. Miss Bessie sure hoped that she knew what she was talking about.

Miss Bessie lay in bed a while longer and watched the dawn roll in slowly. She knew there was no point in trying to go back to sleep. It wasn't long until she was far too restless to stay put so she got up and put the coffee on. She said her prayers and read her selected Bible verses—same as she did every day. She must have gotten lost in her thoughts, though, because somehow the early morning hours managed to slip away without her even noticing, and soon it would be time for her to go.

Miss Bessie lingered over her coffee a moment longer, and then suddenly she looked up and saw that it was almost eight o'clock. Glory! She had to get going. There were hungry mouths to feed and she was just the one to feed 'em.

# Miss Bessie's Story

## From the Very Beginning

I WAS BORN THE FIRST OF THIRTEEN CHILDREN IN A SHARECROPPER shack not too far from Snowhill, North Carolina, in a tiny, tiny little place called Tin Tub. Now, usually not too much happened around Tin Tub. Tin Tub was the "colored" side of the creek that had officially belonged to the darker Chapmans since the Civil War changed the face of the nation many years before. Unofficially it had belonged to them since old man Joseph, head of the white Chapman family, set up his slave mistress out there, way out of the way of his wife, but still close enough to be convenient. That woman was my grandmother. And even after the old man died, my grandmamma stayed right where she was, stating quite clearly that she had something powerful for anybody who was crazy enough to even think about removing her. So where she had been put was exactly where she stayed, and didn't nobody say another thing about it.

Now, when I was little, there was only about forty-eight people in the entire community (and that was because Sister Sal lost the twins she was carrying and luckily Mr. Lee held on past his bout of pneumonia). Forty-eight folks. And since my mama and daddy had thirteen children, we was most of 'em. At the top of the area's twin hills (nicknamed the Holy Tits and shaped, believe it or not, just like Miss Sue's oddly shaped bosom), there were two churches—one too many, for sure, for so few folks, but Reverend James just couldn't seem to convince nobody that you couldn't increase nothing by dividing on it. Across from the churches there was a barber shop run by Mr. J. T. (the Negroes had to have their own 'cause the white folks wouldn't cut the Negroes' hair unless they paid double and allowed the white folks to anoint their heads with holy water and search their scalps for horns). Then there was Mr. George's general store (and thank God for him, too, because that man would carry your credit until it became just too burdensome to bear). And finally there was about twelve sharecroppers' shacks (most of 'em ready to tumble right where they was at), a couple of chicken coops, a tobacco barn, a mill, and a ramshackle mess of old cemetery plots, kind of sprinkled throughout (most of which cradled folks whose names had long since been forgotten, but the hospitality committee laid wreaths on 'em just the same, each and every Memorial Day, to ensure that they still felt a part of things).

Most times the black folks didn't cause any real trouble, well no more than would be considered fairly ordinary. There had been that time when Sister Mims had gotten mad as a wet hen at that trouble-making man of hers and hit him over the head with a frying pan, then dragged him down to the creek and tossed his butt right on in the icy waters. Luckily the shock of the frigid temperatures served to wake him 'bout soon as he landed, so he didn't actually have time enough to drown. Truthfully that didn't count as no real trouble either because all the harm that come to Brother Mims that day amounted to no more than some hurt feelings and a slightly lumpy head.

Nope, trouble didn't come around too often, partly because of a particular understanding that had planted itself into the land a long time ago. Everybody knew exactly where they were supposed to be, and for the most part they stayed there, too. The black folks held on to the south-side piece, and the white folks took up the north, while the Indians grabbed what little they could at the far west corner of the county, where they couldn't get into nobody's way and couldn't nobody get into theirs. Of course, each group was free to cross over the creek as they saw a need to. After all, living was a practical thing and couldn't nobody really find all that they required in that limited space they each called home. So back and forth across the creek they went. The white folks stepped south to mess with the black folks (especially the women), or else they came around to have some work done that couldn't nobody else do. Sometimes they would even take to creeping around places where they clearly had no business being, just so they could be privy to all the black folks was up to. The black folks ventured north to work, to shop, or to travel even farther north, some of 'em destined for that promise land and determined to never, ever look back. The Indians, however, pretty much stayed to themselves, figuring out correctly that neither the whites or the black folks meant them one bit of good.

The white folks' side of the creek really wasn't much different from the black folks' side, and those rascals could stir up a hornet's nest quicker than you could say, "Mercy, there's a fly in the buttermilk!" They lived in neat little gray row houses built at a time when old Mr. Chapman discovered that he needed lots of help working his business and keeping his Negroes in their proper place. The dogtrot homes were built facing south just so the white over-seers could do the watching and the black folks could know that they were being watched. In exchange for their assistance, old man Chapman kept them white folks well fed and gave them a roof over their head and enough leeway in handling the Negroes to provide the appointed vigilantes with ongoing entertainment. And so the watchmen watched, sometimes getting carried away with their work, and that was when the trouble usually got started.

But despite the difficulties of that place, it was home, pure and simple. It was the place where Daddy and the old cotton-picking men sat on the porch and sipped whisky in cracked coffee cups and told one big lie after another. It was the place where Mama could feed a family for a week with a shelf full of nothing and a little imagination, and it was a place that Santa passed right by. It was where ring games were sometimes the only fun we had, where people worked too hard for far too little, and where many younguns never had a chance to be young. But the love was there, and prayers were life's saving grace. It was pain and it was joy, and you didn't understand until much later in life that you would never, ever be able to look back at that place and feel one without the other. And it was the place where a warm biscuit and a good cup of coffee was a meal fit for a queen, and that still hasn't changed.

# Miss Bessie at Her Soulful Best

*As you have already heard, it is hard for me to share a written recipe because I have never done a whole lot of measuring. But for that sweet child, Larissa, I took some time and took careful note of how I make my favorite baked goods. Now, if you just do what I tell you in the next few pages, your bread, starting with this cornbread, will be as good as mine, I can promise you that!*

## MISS BESSIE'S CORNBREAD

**I cup sifted all-purpose flour**
**I½ tablespoons sugar**
**2½ teaspoons baking powder**
**½ teaspoon baking soda**
**½ teaspoon salt**
**I cup yellow cornmeal**
**2 eggs**
**I½ cups buttermilk**
**¼ cup melted butter**

Preheat the oven to 425°. Sift together flour, sugar, baking powder, soda, and salt. Add cornmeal. In a medium-sized bowl, mix together eggs, butter-milk, and butter. Add flour mixture. Mix just enough to moisten. Pour into a greased 8-inch square baking pan or a 12-muffin tin. Bake for 20 to 25 minutes (15 to 20 minutes for muffins) or until golden and firm to the touch in the center. If using a square pan, cut cornbread into squares.

Yields 12 muffins or 12 squares of cornbread.

*My mama told me that this recipe was so named because the slaves used to mix up the batter, clean off the hoes they used to ready the field, and bake the bread right there on the hoe under the hot blazing sun. Now we use a skillet. It sure is a great deal easier that way.*

## HOECAKE

**I cup cornmeal (plain or**
**  self-rising)**
**¼ cup chopped onion**
**¼ cup chopped green pepper**
**½ teaspoon salt**
**2¼ cups boiling water**

In a small bowl, mix the cornmeal, onion, green pepper, and salt. Pour boiling water over the meal mixture and let stand a few moments. Drop by the tablespoon on a hot, generously greased skillet or griddle. Turn over once when nicely browned. Drain and serve piping hot.

Yields 8 servings.

*I remember that my granddaddy used to have a big helping of spoonbread and a tall glass of buttermilk each and every morning before he headed out to the fields. He claimed it was the perfect way to start his day.*

## SPOONBREAD (A FAMILY FAVORITE!)

**1 quart milk**

**1 cup white cornmeal**

**¼ cup butter or margarine**

**4 large eggs, lightly beaten**

**¼ cup sugar**

**2 teaspoons salt**

Yields 6 servings.

Preheat the oven to 350°. Heat milk in a small saucepan over low heat for 10 minutes or until almost boiling. Stir in cornmeal. Cook over low heat, stirring occasionally for 5 minutes or until thickened. Stir in butter. Remove from heat and beat with a wooden spoon for 1 minute.

Stir one-fourth of hot mixture into eggs; add to remaining hot mixture, stirring constantly. Stir in sugar and salt. Pour into a lightly greased 2-quart baking dish. Bake spoonbread for 1 hour.

*I can eat a pan of buttermilk biscuits all by myself. I love them with homemade jam or molasses. Baby, my mouth is watering just writing down the recipe.*

## BUTTERMILK BISCUITS

**2 cups sifted**
**  all-purpose flour**

**½ teaspoon baking soda**

**½ teaspoon salt**

**2 teaspoons baking powder**

**⅓ cup shortening**

**⅔ cup buttermilk**

Yields 12 to 15 biscuits.

Preheat the oven to 450°. Sift flour again with baking soda, salt, and baking powder. Add the shortening and rub with your fingers until the mixture resembles small crumbs. Stir in enough buttermilk to make soft dough.

Place the dough on a floured surface and knead slightly about 10 to 12 times. Roll out ½ inch thick and cut with a small, floured cookie cutter or glass. Bake on an ungreased baking sheet for 12 to 14 minutes.

*If the way to a man's heart is through his stomach, then these muffins must have been one of the reasons my husband said that he fell in love with me at first sight. I served these the first time I made him dinner, and we were together from that moment on, until the day he died fifty years later.*

# BASIC SWEET MUFFINS

**1½ cups all-purpose flour**

**½ cup sugar**

**2 teaspoons baking powder**

**½ teaspoon salt**

**1 large egg**

**½ cup milk**

**¼ cup vegetable oil**

Yields 12 muffins.

Preheat the oven to 400°. Stir together first four ingredients in a large bowl; make a well in center of mixture. In a separate bowl, stir together egg, milk, and oil until blended. Add to dry ingredients, stirring just until moistened.

Spoon batter into lightly greased muffin pans, filling two-thirds full. Bake for 18 to 20 minutes. Remove muffins from pans immediately.

*Basic muffins are great, but a little variety every now and again is a welcome change. These sweet potato muffins are a little extra work, but, baby, are they worth it!*

# SWEET POTATO MUFFINS

**1 sweet potato, peeled**

**1 tablespoon unsalted butter**

**Pinch of salt**

**½ cup milk**

**2 eggs, well beaten**

**2 cups flour**

**1 teaspoon baking powder**

Yields 12 muffins.

Boil the sweet potato until done. Preheat the oven to 350°. Mash the sweet potato very well. Pass through a sieve to free all lumps. Add the butter and salt and whip well. Add the milk and eggs. Combine the flour and baking powder. Add enough of the flour mixture to the creamed mixture to make a soft batter. Bake in a lined muffin pan for about 30 minutes.

When I was growing up, every Friday evening was fish fry night. Everybody would gather together as soon as the sun set, and in a big pot over an open fire, Mama would fry the fish Daddy had caught that afternoon. Well, anybody knows that you can't have a fish fry without hush puppies, so try these anytime you are planning a special seafood meal.

## HUSH PUPPIES

**2 cups cornmeal**
**I teaspoon baking powder**
**½ cup flour**
**I teaspoon salt**
**I onion, grated**
**¾ cup milk**
**I egg**
**Oil for frying**

Yields 24 (1-inch) balls.

Combine dry ingredients and onion, mix well, and make a hole in the center. Add egg and milk to make a stiff dough. Shape into 1-inch balls and drop into hot oil. Fry until golden brown.

Every fall in communities throughout the South, folks got together for hog-killing time. It sounds like a strange reason for a celebration, but it was one of the grandest times of the year. It was like one big party and cracklin' bread was one of the treats I looked forward to at that time. It is an old-fashioned favorite, but it's as good now as it was then.

## CRACKLIN' BREAD

CRACKLIN'S
**I pint water**
**5 pounds pork fat, diced**

Yields 5 pounds.

Place the water and pork in a deep black iron pot. Place over medium heat. Cook for about 1 hour, or until the water has evaporated and the fat has fried tender, brown, and crisp. Drain. Store in a covered jar. Eat as a snack or with grits, or use in cracklin' biscuits or cornbread.

## CRACKLIN' BREAD

**1 medium sweet potato**

**2 cups cornmeal**

**1 cup cracklin's**

Yields 10 to 12 patties.

Preheat the oven to 400°. Peel the potato and cut into small pieces; boil until tender. Remove the potato; reserve the cooking water. Combine the cornmeal and cracklin's in a mixing bowl. Pour enough potato water into the cornmeal mixture to form a batter. Add the potatoes and fold twice. Form large patties. Bake on a cookie sheet for 35 minutes, or until done.

*We didn't just get good cracklin's from all those good old hog killings. We got good sausage, too. These next two recipes are so wonderful, they'll make you want to slap somebody.*

# SOUTHERN SAUSAGE MUFFINS

**2 pounds pork sausage, hot or mild**

**⅓ cup green onions, finely chopped**

**1½ cups Bisquick baking mix**

**1½ teaspoons brown sugar, packed**

**½ teaspoon dry mustard**

**¼ teaspoon ground red pepper**

**⅔ cup milk**

**½ cup finely grated cheddar cheese**

Yields 12 muffins.

Preheat the oven to 400°. Grease bottoms only of muffin pans. Crumble sausage in skillet; add chopped onion. Cook until sausage is done. Stir to keep sausage in small pieces. Drain well. Combine baking mix, brown sugar, dry mustard, and red pepper in medium bowl. Stir in sausage mixture. Add milk and cheese; mix until just blended. Batter will be a thick consistency. Fill muffin pan about two-thirds full, spreading batter to edges of cups. Bake 20 to 25 minutes or until golden brown. Cool slightly before removing from pan. Serve warm.

## SAUSAGE CORNBREAD STUFFING

**1 (16-ounce) package Jimmy
Dean Sage Sausage,
cooked, drained, and
crumbled**

**½ cup butter**

**1 large red onion, diced**

**1½ cups celery, chopped**

**6 cups day-old cornbread,
crumbled**

**⅓ cup water**

**2 teaspoons dried thyme**

**1 teaspoon salt**

**1 teaspoon pepper**

**1 can (approx. 10 ounces)
condensed cream of
mushroom soup (optional,
for making a casserole or
stuffing peppers only)**

Melt butter in large saucepan Add onion and celery; cook until soft. Add remaining ingredients and mix well.

For casserole or peppers: Pour mixture into dish or divide among bell pepper halves; cover and bake at 400° for 30 minutes.

To stuff turkey: Fully cool mixture and then stuff turkey. Cook turkey according to package instructions.

Yields stuffing for a 12- to 14-pound turkey.

*My favorite auntie always had something or another to say about food. Here are some of her favorites:*

> *A half a loaf is better than no bread at all.*
> *Don't let your eyes get bigger than your stomach.*
> *Don't borrow or lend salt because it's bad luck.*
> *Those that eat can always say grace.*

*And finally: Don't invite silly folks to dinner because they just eat up all your food and wear out your sitting chairs.*

## SALLY LUNN BREAD

**2 cups sifted flour**
**3 teaspoons baking powder**
**½ teaspoon salt**
**I egg, beaten**
**I cup milk**
**¼ cup shortening**
**¼ cup sugar**

Preheat the oven to 375°. Sift flour with baking powder and salt. Combine beaten egg and milk. Cream shortening and sugar. Add flour alternately with liquid mixture. Place in a greased loaf pan or muffin pan. Bake for 30 minutes.

Yields 1 loaf or 12 muffins.

*Any good bread can use a little extra every now and again. Try any one of these as a tagalong for sliced bread, rolls, muffins, or my famous cornbread.*

## MILK GRAVY

**I pound hot sausage**
**½ cup flour**
**½ teaspoon salt**
**½ teaspoon pepper**
**I¼ cups milk**

Yields 2 cups.

Crumble sausage in pan. Cook until done, about 8 minutes. Remove from heat and drain on paper. Reserve 8 tablespoons of fat. Put fat back on high heat and add flour, salt, and pepper. Stir until golden brown. Add milk, stirring until thick. Stir in drained sausage. Cook until hot. Serve hot with biscuits.

## APPLE BUTTER

3 quarts unsweetened
   applesauce
2 pounds sugar
I pound brown sugar
¾ cup apple cider
I tablespoon cinnamon
1½ teaspoons ground cloves
½ teaspoon allspice

Mix together the applesauce, sugars, and cider in a large glass baking dish, and cook in a 325° oven for 3 hours, stirring occasionally. Add spices and return to oven to cook for 1 hour more. Apple butter requires long, slow cooking.

Yields 8 cups.

## RASPBERRY BUTTER

½ cup margarine or
   butter, softened
½ cup raspberries, crushed
I tablespoon sugar or ¼ cup raspberry jam

Beat all ingredients together.

Yields 1 cup.

## CINNAMON HONEY BUTTER

2 sticks plus 3 tablespoons
   butter (room temperature)
¾ cup margarine
⅓ cup honey
2 teaspoons cinnamon
I teaspoon vanilla
½ cup brown sugar

Mix all ingredients with a mixer until blended. Makes 3 half-pound units of spread that can be frozen if necessary.

Yields 2 cups.

# Miss Martha

The old country diner looked fairly out of place next to the brand-new strip mall that had rudely planted itself without warning less than spitting distance away. It was an odd-shaped little place—just like a good diner was supposed to be. It was kind of long and narrow, and the outside was tacked over in dingy tile with ugly gray trim. There was a black-and-red rooftop that would have looked out of place anywhere else and stainless steel railings that wrapped themselves strangely around the place in a way that, if you thought about it, served no real purpose at all. The front door creaked loudly when you opened it, and several of the windows had broken during the last big rainstorm. Rather than replace them, the owners had simply taped them back in place with wide strips of silver duct tape. There were never any tablecloths, but Miss Millie, the waitress, would gladly give you a piece of the day's newspaper if you just had to have a little covering to rest your plate on. No, this here sure wasn't one of the fanciest places in town, but it was Miss Martha's absolute favorite, and there wasn't a single Wednesday morning when she couldn't be found sitting at the same small table by the kitchen, starting her day the way a woman was supposed to, with a big bowl of grits and a good cup of strong black coffee.

Miss Martha checked her reflection in the glass door before she went in. She was a youthful-looking woman for her seventy years and took great pride in her appearance. She knew Mr. Sam, the cook, cast sly little glances in her direction when he thought she wasn't looking, and who could blame him? Her carefully dyed blonde hair was always swept neatly into a severe twist so's to show off her delicate ears (her most ladylike feature according to her mama) and her violet eyes. Her face was too long and narrow, and in truth, her skin was far too white, but there were clever ways to compensate for such shortcomings and she made sure she took full advantage of them—a swoop of hair across the forehead and something called a bronzer that you powdered all across your face to look tan. All in all, there was really no good reason that a woman need not look her best. With all the new-fangled things in the department store, for just a few dollars and a little effort, anybody could at least look presentable. It was too bad Millie didn't feel the same way. Martha took one look at her as she walked in and just shook her head.

Millie didn't bother to do the least little bit to fix herself up, but that was just Millie, and it wasn't likely she was going to change anytime soon. She was sixty years old and was mighty set in her ways. Martha had known her for over thirty years and she was the same as she had always been—settled and satisfied with little or nothing. Today her stringy hair was fast escaping from its bobby pins in droopy little sprigs that sagged pitifully behind her ears. Sadly, the image reminded her of some woman she'd known a long time ago and had almost forgotten. Millie's lipstick had bled all over her mouth, so she looked more like Bozo than anyone else. Also, her eye makeup had blurred again under the weight of perspiration and she looked like a raccoon. But Millie was a good woman and an even better friend.

Millie didn't take to too many people, so she spent a great deal of time at home alone with her cat. Martha had tried time and time again to get her to come to the senior center to meet all the other ladies and maybe find a little companionship, but Millie had always refused. Oh well, at least Martha had tried.

Miss Martha looked around the diner. It wasn't too crowded today. In fact, there were really just three of them in the entire place—all of them regulars. Lost in her thoughts and her delicious breakfast, Martha hadn't even realized that Millie was going on about something or another. Lord, could that woman talk and it didn't take much to get her going either (maybe it was an overcompensation for all that time with her cat). She was steadily slurping her way through a cup of coffee, but it didn't slow the flapping of Millie's gums, that was for sure!

"I'm telling you that the Yankees are coming, and it won't be long 'til they get here neither." Millie stopped talking for a moment, took a long, loud slurp, and then continued on, "I figure any day now them Northern folks gonna take this city like Sherman took Richmond. Why, I was looking at the weather channel this morning, and ain't a thing happening up north but gloom and doom. It won't be long now 'til some of them folks get a notion to take leave of them gray skies and head down south where the gardens are blooming and the waters are warming." Miss Millie was leaning on the counter and resting on her elbows now. She was even pointing her finger to punctuate every word. "Y'all just give it a good week or two and them Yankees, or as the Mayor likes to call 'em, tourists, will be swarming around here like ants on a good country biscuit. Now, it isn't like they ain't sweet at times, and I like company like anybody else, but it seems like 'fore they get here, they ought to take a li'l time and learn something about what all they're getting themselves into. I declare some of 'em come in here and ask for the most foolish things. Like the other day, this woman sat right there," and Miss Millie pointed to the table where Martha was sitting, "and she asked me for honey and cinnamon so's she could sweeten her grits. Sweeten grits! Who in the world wants to sweeten their grits? I just looked the other way and acted like I ain't even heard her." Miss Millie was finished with her coffee and was now clearing dirty dishes from the counter. "Then yesterday, I had a man ask me what kind of meat we use to make the stew. Well, I didn't know. Heck, knowing Sam, it could be anything from beef to whatever was running around his yard the day before. I reckon that's why he calls it stew surprise. Well, when I told that man that I didn't know, do you know what he did? He just got up and walked out. He didn't even say good-bye. I'm telling you, them Yankees are heading here fast and they gonna turn this place upside down for sure."

Miss Martha suppressed a laugh. Millie was on a roll this morning, but then that was why Martha came here, for good grits and even better company. She'd have to be on her way soon, though. She was due at the senior center by ten o'clock. It was her day to lead the craft circle, and today she was going to teach them a quilt pattern her mama had taught her many years ago.

Her mama. Lord, she missed her still, and the woman had been gone for years now. There wasn't a day that went by that Martha didn't think about her, but it wasn't too often that she got a chance to talk to anybody about her and she was glad little Larissa had given her that chance. She had told her story, she had shared her recipes, and she'd been glad to do it, too. It had allowed her to talk about the greatest woman she had ever known, her mama, Lucy Lee Jones.

# Miss Martha's Story

### And, of Course, Her Mama's Story, Too

In the far end of a southeastern North Carolina county, way out of the way of all that was citified and civilized, there was a place that the old folks love to call Cracker Barrel. Wasn't too much to the place really, stretching on for no more than maybe a good country mile, but it rolled on across some of the best tobacco land anywhere, and that was the reason that we was there. We were white tenant farmers who worked the land for little more than it took just to stay alive. I think the only folks worse off than us was the black sharecroppers that stayed 'cross the ditch, but we didn't have a whole lot to do with them so I can't say too much about their particular way of living. No, on our side was all poor, poor white folks. That's why they called our section Cracker Barrel. I guess we should have been offended that the rest of the community considered us no better than poor white trash, but my mama used to say that "labels was for canned goods, and she sure didn't bring us into this world to set on nobody's grocery shelf." So we didn't much trouble ourselves about what folks said; we had bigger headaches than that, that was for sure.

It's always been amazing to me that folks have such strange ideas about the South. I meet so many people that think that back in the good

old days, all the black folks was poor and all the white folks was rich, living in big white houses and sitting on the porch all day sipping sun tea. Well, our house wasn't no big white nothing. I suppose, though, that you could call where we lived "a house," if you're real generous about what you get to calling "a house." In my mind, the place was little more than a shack that was a devil's breath from falling down all around us. It was unpainted, unscreened, with two rooms, a little narrow hallway, a kitchen, and eight folks all crowded up in it trying their best not to sit right on top of one another. Back then, there was me, my mama, my daddy, and five sisters and brothers, but somehow we made it. I still don't know how we did it, but we did.

That house wasn't even ours. It was given to us by the landowner, who, in truth, didn't live much better than we did. Most times his place leaked, and the steps were rotted clear way through, so maybe that was why we didn't even know how bad off we was, because he wasn't doing much better than us. But make no mistake about it, he might have been poor as dirt, but he held the purse strings. You see, we worked the land all year, and what the boll weevils, the floods, the droughts, or the storms didn't kill, we used to settle up with the boss. He added up all he had loaned us throughout the year for supplies and such and then added up what our crops was worth. Well, we never came out ahead. We always ended up owing, so each and every year we started out a little more in debt than we was the year before. We figured we was being cheated, but there really wasn't too much you could do about it, except maybe pull up and move on to somewhere else the very next year. I remember that there were some weeks right after settling time that you could barely see the dirt on the road 'cause of all the wagons on it heading to who knows where. All they knew was that they was going, and wherever they ended up had to be better than where they had just been. I heard from my daddy that even we moved four or five times before I was three, most times not even finishing out the season. Then we settled in Cracker Barrel, and that's where we stayed put until I was a young woman of marrying age.

Most of the women did what they could to keep their looks up, but it was hard, that kind of tough living. Most of 'em had no time for primping, and stringy bits of drab hair often escaped from the day caps they wore, rudely showing themselves from time to time and reminding each of us that a trip to the beauty parlor was a fantasy that existed a million miles away. Those women back then didn't wear makeup, and most of the time day dressing was no more than a worn and faded something or another that had sure 'nough seen better days. They all had shoes in the winter, but in the summer they was just plain unnecessary. The men didn't look much better than the women, all of us looking 'bout raggedy as a scarecrow, but we was what we was, and there was no sense in sitting around trying to figure the fairness of it all.

Mama was different, though. Oh, she was as poor as all them others, but she was a prideful woman. She was petite and pretty, and she had taught herself how to do her own hair so it always fell in long, black waves clear down to her shoulders. She made all of her own clothes, and once a week she did the wash for this rich woman who generously gave her leftovers and leavings that Mama could piece together into something wearable and wonderful. She would listen to how the rich folks talked, too, and she would come home and practice saying what they said, just the way they said it, too, and she made us do it right along with her. That's why I don't sound like poor white trash today. There's a little betterment in my speech, and I'm darn proud of it.

Mama was small and she was so sickly. Since I was the oldest, I helped out as much as I could. I was more mama to my five brothers and sisters than a sister, but that was okay. We're a lot closer now than we used to be, and we comfort one another quite a bit in our old age. None of us moved too far away, so we get to see each other at least a couple of times a year. Mama would have been happy about that.

I married the very first man that could get me off the farm. I was seventeen years old, so young that I really wasn't too sure about it at the time. But Mama could see into people's hearts, and she assured me that he was a good one. He was tall, twenty years old, gawky, and built like his body wasn't made to go together, but he was handsome to me and he had kind eyes and warm hands. I guess that's what I loved most about him. Well, he was a fisherman, and even though he spent more time with his boat than he did with me, we did manage to learn how to love each other and love each other we did for more than forty years. We was never blessed with a child, but he used to tell me that he was needy enough himself for any two or three good younguns I might of had. He did need a lot of looking after, but I didn't mind. I just seem to be made to be looking after somebody or another. I guess that's why life sometimes seems so empty now. There ain't nobody that needs my looking after. But thank you, Jesus, I do have Millie and I do have my friends at the senior center, so life ain't nearly as bad as it could be. And I am still blessed enough to be among the living. As Mama would say, if you can't be grateful for another thing, at least be grateful for that!

# Miss Martha's Favorite Recipes

*I remember one time when one of our neighbors was getting married, Mama made her bread as a gift. She also included a little note. It said*

> *The Bride*
> *Be to her virtues very kind.*
> *Be to her faults a little blind.*

*I guess really this advice was more for the groom than the bride. I sure hope he used it.*

## APPLESAUCE BREAD

2 cups all-purpose flour

¼ cup dark brown sugar

1 teaspoon baking soda

¾ teaspoon salt

1 teaspoon ground cinnamon

½ teaspoon ground nutmeg

1 teaspoon vanilla

1 stick butter, softened

1 cup applesauce

2 eggs

1 cup raisins

½ cup walnuts

Preheat the oven to 350°. Combine all ingredients except raisins and walnuts. Mix well until blended. Stir in raisins and walnuts. Pour into a greased and floured 8x4x3-inch loaf pan. Bake for 60 to 65 minutes.

Yields 1 loaf.

*Just like that little verse about the bride, Mama loved pretty sayings. She didn't have any kind of real education, but she did know how to read and write, and every once in a while she would come across something nice in a newspaper somebody had thrown away. She would clip it out and hang it up somewhere in the house. Well, in one of the Wednesday afternoon lady pages, they had this recipe and a pretty little poem. I figured I'd go ahead and stick it in, too, since it did come out with the recipe.*

> *They talk about a woman's sphere as though it had a limit;*
> *There's not a place on earth or heaven,*
> *There's not a task to mankind given,*
> *There's not a blessing or a woe,*
> *There's not a whisper, yes or no,*
> *There's not a life or death or birth,*
> *That's not a feather's weight of worth without a woman in it.*
> *—Anonymous*

*I don't know why whoever wrote it didn't put their name to it. If I had written something so pretty, I sure would have, but maybe some are just shy about some things.*

## Shortening Bread

**4 cups sifted flour**
**1 cup light brown sugar**
**2 cups butter**

Yields 1 pan.

Preheat the oven to 350°. Mix flour and sugar, and work in butter. This will be very stiff. Put it in a pan wide enough to permit the mass to be patted down to about ½ inch thick. Bake for 30 minutes.

*We only made this bread when company was coming because it cost quite a bit to fix. So when we smelled it cooking in the oven, we knew somebody special was sure to be resting their shoes underneath our table 'fore long. Usually it was the preacher's wife stopping by on an occasional Wednesday morning to see how Mama was making out. With so many of us, you never did get more than a single slice, and I could make mine last sometimes a whole hour just by taking little itty-bitty bites.*

# RAISIN BREAD

**1 cup applesauce**

**¼ cup melted butter**

**1 egg, beaten**

**½ cup granulated sugar**

**¼ cup brown sugar, packed**

**2 cups all-purpose flour**

**2 teaspoons baking powder**

**¾ teaspoon salt**

**½ teaspoon baking soda**

**½ teaspoon ground cinnamon**

**1 teaspoon grated nutmeg**

**¾ cup raisins**

**¾ cup chopped walnuts**

Yields 1 loaf.

Preheat the oven to 350°. Combine applesauce, butter, egg, and sugars in a bowl. Blend well. Sift other dry ingredients, including cinnamon and nutmeg. Add raisins and chopped nuts. Turn into a well-greased 9x5x3-inch loaf pan. Bake for 1 hour, or until edges shrink away from the pan and the bread is nicely brown. Serve plain or toasted with butter or cream cheese.

*Mama got this recipe from Miss Wills, who ran the only country store for miles around. She ran it for her husband, but let me tell you, she was the boss of that place. She was a nice woman, too, but she didn't allow no nonsense—no drinking or carrying on, no cussin', no fightin', and no spittin'. Folks said she was trying to be uppity, but I don't think so. She was just trying to have her a decent place, and what in the world is wrong with that, I ask you?*

*Boy, did I love that store. It sat at the crossroads, and it was the gathering place for everybody in the county. It was built sort of like a barn with a thick wooden frame, and it had these little add-ons that had just been stuck hither and yonder as they needed more room for things, and they always needed more room 'cause that place had everything: tobacco, axle grease, hats, gloves, and groceries, you name it. If they didn't have it, you didn't need it.*

*Mama and I would go there and flip through the Sears catalog, or the one from Montgomery Ward, and we would wish for things. Only every once in a while did we ever get to order. After we had looked our fill, we'd pick up the few things we could afford and head back home.*

*Lord, I miss that place—them men sitting outside over a game of checkers, the women in the corner whispering about things they had no business even speaking on, and old lady Mae Rae, who would come dip her snuff and spit anyway. She never did mind anybody else's rules. She was old and she just didn't care no more. I remember I even heard her cussin' a time or two. Yes sir, that little place was something, and Miss Wills ran it like a place ought to be run. She was a heck of a cook, too, and she probably passed this recipe out to every woman who came in.*

## NUT BREAD

**3 cups flour**

**3 teaspoons baking powder**

**I tablespoon lard**

**I cup chopped nuts**

**I½ cups milk**

**I teaspoon salt**

**2 tablespoons sugar**

Yields 1 loaf.

Preheat the oven to 400°. Mix together all ingredients in a large mixing bowl. Place in a well-greased loaf pan and bake 50 minutes.

FOR DATE NUT BREAD: Add 1 cup chopped dates, 1 teaspoon nutmeg, and ½ teaspoon allspice.

*You know, when I was a little girl, there was a black family what lived the next farm over. My mama didn't hold color over nobody's head—she said it didn't have a thing to do with a person's heart, but my daddy was different. He was as mean as anything the Lord put a gut in. Anyhow, the black woman and my mama used to meet at the ditch every once in a while and talk. Well, one day Mama invited her over to see some hats she had crocheted, to see if the woman wanted to buy one. Sad to say, Daddy came in while that black woman was trying on a hat that was way too small. Before the woman could take it off and try on another, my daddy yelled out 'bout rude as could be, "Nigger, you done bought that hat. Don't nobody want a hat that been on no colored woman's head." Well, I tell you, that woman didn't say one word, not one, just went and reached in her pocket and pulled out a dollar. To this day, I can still remember watching her fade away as she walked on down the road, getting smaller and smaller, with her head held high and that silly little hat setting right on top of it. Well, she was the one who gave Mama these two biscuit recipes, and every time I bake 'em, I think about her.*

## SOUR CREAM BISCUITS

**2 cups self-rising flour**
**½ teaspoon salt**
**12 ounces sour cream**

Yields 16 to 18 biscuits.

Preheat the oven to 450°. Combine all ingredients. Mix until a ball is formed. Turn out onto a floured surface. Roll out and cut with 2-inch cutter. Bake 12 minutes or until browned.

## SOUR MILK BISCUITS

**4 cups flour**
**1 tablespoon salt**
**1 teaspoon baking soda**
**2 cups buttermilk (or 2 cups milk mixed with 1 table-spoon vinegar)**
**1 tablespoon Crisco**

Yields 16 biscuits.

Preheat the oven to 400°. Sift the flour with salt and baking soda. Flour or butter a baking pan, and see that the oven is hot. Wet the flour mixture with milk, using enough to make a soft dough. Add 1 tablespoon of Crisco by chopping it into the dough. Shape the biscuits quickly, put them into a muffin pan, and bake for about 20 minutes.

*I think that for just about every Southern girl, making bread was the first thing you learned 'bout the kitchen. It was a kind of rite of passage. You were on your way to womanhood once they let you make a part of the supper meal. I remember oh so well how proud I felt my first time, and these here drop biscuits became my specialty after that.*

# DROP BISCUITS

**4 cups flour**

**3 teaspoons baking powder**

**I teaspoon salt**

**I heaping tablespoon of butter**

**2 cups milk**

Preheat the oven to 400°. Mix all ingredients together in a large mixing bowl. Drop biscuits onto a buttered pan or baking sheet, not too close together. Bake for 20 minutes.

Yields 16 biscuits.

*Mama loved to make dumplings. She said, "Them suckers just plop on in the gut and fill you up for a good while to come." Sometimes we had chicken with our dumplings, and other times things were really bad and all we had was broth.*

# DUMPLINGS

**2 cups flour**

**4 teaspoons baking powder**

**I teaspoon salt**

**I tablespoon lard**

**⅔ to ¾ milk and water (half water, half milk)**

Sift together flour, baking powder, and salt in a large bowl. Cut in lard with two knives or a pastry blender. Add liquid gradually. Drop by large spoonfuls on top of boiling stew pot. Cover quickly and do not open for 20 minutes. Serve at once.

Yields enough dumplings for 2 pots of chicken stew.

*Once during the height of the Depression, the mayor's wife (who had never been forced to scrape together a meal from leftovers and leavings or go to bed hungry a day in her entire life) decided that we so-called poor and ignorant white women desperately needed someone to teach us how to better manage our kitchens. So she invited some fancy-dancy-looking expert from the city of Atlanta to teach us all a class at the new city hall building.*

*In truth, most of us knew how to manage our kitchens just fine—if we had enough food, we fed everybody without a problem, and if we didn't, we pieced together a meal the best way we knew how. During them tough times, there weren't too many choices—either you had what you needed or you didn't, and all the management techniques on God's green earth wasn't going to change that reality. Still, Mama and I decided to go. I was a little bitty thing then, but the thought of a trip seemed kind of exciting so I couldn't wait to go. So off we went, each of us dressed in our one good dress and decent pair of shoes, for an exciting afternoon of domestic learning.*

*Well, it turned out that the woman talked through her nose, used a whole lot of words that couldn't nobody make any sense of, and surely didn't have the good sense the Lord gave a guinea hen. The whole day would have been a complete waste of time, except that she did give us these great recipes to use at holiday time. Before that class, we never did have anything quite this fancy to go with a turkey. Heck, we was glad just to have the turkey. But these dressings gave that poor table a touch of class. Christmas during the Depression usually didn't have too much in the way of extras, but Mama always made sure that the meal was a celebration no matter how tough times were.*

## FANCY-DANCY CORNBREAD DRESSING

CORNBREAD
**2 cups self-rising cornmeal**
**1 cup self-rising flour**
**1 teaspoon baking powder**
**2 teaspoons sugar**
**1 cup milk**
**2 eggs, beaten**
**3 tablespoons oil or melted**
   **shortening**

CORNBREAD: Preheat the oven to 450°. Mix all ingredients and place in a greased 10-inch pan. Bake for 30 to 35 minutes or until lightly browned. Cool; crumble cornbread into a large bowl.

## DRESSING

**3 celery ribs, chopped**

**I large onion, chopped**

**2 tablespoons butter or margarine**

**I recipe cornbread**

**¼ pound saltine crackers, broken**

**2½ to 3 cups hot chicken broth**

**½ teaspoon salt or 2 chicken bouillon cubes**

**½ teaspoon pepper**

**2 eggs, beaten**

DRESSING: Preheat the oven to 450°. Sauté celery and onion in butter until tender. Combine cornbread, crackers, celery, onion, broth, salt, pepper, and eggs; mix well. If dressing doesn't seem moist enough, add more broth. Spoon lightly into a greased 13x9x2-inch baking pan or casserole dish. Bake for 25 to 30 minutes or until lightly browned.

Yields 1 pan of stuffing.

# TURKEY STUFFING

**¼ cup olive oil**

**I shallot, finely chopped**

**I large onion, finely chopped**

**1½ cups celery, finely chopped**

**12 cups ½-inch stale bread cubes**

**2 tablespoons ground sage**

**½ teaspoon ground thyme**

**½ teaspoon celery seed, ground**

**½ teaspoon paprika**

**Pepper to taste**

**2¼ cups strong vegetable stock**

Heat the oil in a heavy pot, and add the shallot, onion, and celery. Sauté until the vegetables begin to soften, then add bread cubes, sage, thyme, celery seed, paprika, and pepper to taste. Mix well. Cook, stirring frequently, for 5 minutes over medium-low heat.

Add hot vegetable stock to pot and mix well. Cover and cook over low heat for 30 minutes or longer, stirring frequently, until bread cubes have broken down.

The secret to good stuffing is in the slow cooking and the frequent stirring.

Yields stuffing for an 18- to 20-pound turkey.

## APPLE-PECAN STUFFING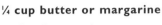

¼ **cup butter or margarine**

⅔ **diced cup onion**

⅔ **cup diced celery**

3 **cups diced day-old bread**

3 **cups diced apples**

I **teaspoon salt**

½ **teaspoon pepper**

⅛ **teaspoon sage, ground**

⅛ **teaspoon marjoram, ground**

⅛ **teaspoon thyme, ground**

½ **teaspoon dried parsley**

½ **cup chopped pecans**

½ **cup water**

Melt ¼ cup butter or margarine in skillet. Add onion and celery, and cook until tender. Add this to the bread. Mix in apples, salt, pepper, sage, marjoram, thyme, parsley, and pecans. Add water and mix thoroughly. Makes enough for a 10-pound turkey.

Yields stuffing for a 10-pound turkey.

## CHESTNUT STUFFING

3 **cups chestnuts**

½ **cup butter, divided**

⅓ **teaspoon salt**

¼ **cup cream**

I **cup cracker crumbs or**
    **grated bread**

Shell and blanch chestnuts, and cook in boiling salted water until soft. Drain and mash with potato ricer. Add half the butter, salt, and cream to the chestnuts, and mix with a hand mixer. Melt remaining butter and mix with crumbs. Add this mixture to the chestnut mixture.

Yields stuffing for a 10- to 12- pound turkey.

# RICE DRESSING FOR TURKEY

**I quart hot cooked
  rice (dry)**
**3 eggs, well beaten**
**½ cup chopped white onion**
**½ cup chopped green
  onion tops**
**I teaspoon pepper**
**I teaspoon salt**
**I cup crumbled fried sausage,
  if you have some left
  over from a meal**
**Finely chopped giblets (optional)**
**I cup brown turkey gravy**

Mix together rice, eggs, onion, onion tops, pepper, salt, sausage, and giblets in a large bowl. Add turkey gravy to rice mixture and place in a deep skillet on medium heat, stirring constantly until well cooked. Do not bake.

Yields 7 cups.

# Lady Patricia

I t was still early; actually it was too early, but Lady Patricia got out of bed anyway and headed into the bathroom. The reflection in the brightly lit mirror revealed tired brown eyes, but the rest of the face, Patricia noticed, looked pretty darn good. As well it should. The facelift had cost her a pretty penny, and whenever she spent that kind of money for anything, she expected nothing less than the best. In this case she had gotten just what she wanted. Not only had the surgeon managed to pull the once-sagging skin up just enough so that it was now taunt and tight, but he had also thrown in a few extras. He had given her cheekbones—the very ones she had always wished for—the kind that added just a bit of an angle to a slightly round face, but they weren't those pointed ones that made the face sharp and hard-looking. Also, she now had a new pouty fullness to her bottom lip. Yes, it was a little too sexy a little too late, but what the hell? Finally she had the aristocratic face she deserved. She'd always had the lineage, and now she had the look—what else could a woman ask for?

The kitchen was already brightly lit, thanks to the generous sunlight streaming in through the windows. Through the glass sliding doors, Lady Patricia caught a glimpse of a newly blooming azalea bush, "the first sign of a Southern spring," her mother used to say. And oh, how her mother loved a spring garden—a massive, well-manicured, colorful one. She was absolutely convinced that no good Southern woman could exist without one, but Lady Patricia had recently discovered that a woman could do just fine with no more than a few azaleas, a rose bush or two, and a few impatiens here and there. In truth, Lady Patricia had found that a good Southern woman could do without a great many things that her mother had found to be so essential. Maybe that was because the South was such a different place now than it used to be. Lady Patricia wondered whether her mother would have even survived all the changes had she lived long enough to see them, but there was no telling. Sometimes even her mama managed a surprise or two.

But there was no question that Lady Patricia's mama would *not* have understood her great-granddaughter Linda's choice of a mate. Why just last week Lady Patricia had traveled all the way back to Birmingham for the sole purpose of meeting her granddaughter's intended. Well, Lady Patricia had suggested one of the city's finest restaurants as a meeting place, but the young couple wouldn't hear of it. They'd suggested a coffee shop instead and promised faithfully that the place would have tea for her as well. Lady Patricia hadn't known what to expect, but she certainly hadn't expected to end up in a dark, dingy hole sipping coffee that was way too strong for her delicate system, with so much caterwauling going on folks couldn't even talk to one another. Worse yet, some fool was sitting in the back smoking so many funny little cigarettes that Lady Patricia was forced to cough like a truck driver in between sips of the very nasty brew. It was simply too dark in there for Lady Patricia to see who was who or she'd have seen to the matter herself. It was obvious that no one else in the place was the least bit concerned.

Unfortunately, it wasn't *too* dark to see quite clearly the young man who was trying to marry himself into her family. From what she could make out, he had two-toned blonde hair that spiked out from the top of his head in new and strange directions so that he looked kind of like an alien on one of those science fiction TV shows. She couldn't tell what color his hair was on the sides of his head because it was shaved clear down to the skin. He obviously wasn't a natural blonde, because his eyebrows were jet black and they had grown together until they met up in the middle of his face. He also had a tattoo on his left arm that said "whatever" (it wasn't a complete thought, so if there was a message there, Lady Patricia missed it) and a pierced tongue with a little purple stud stamped in it that sparkled brightly under the neon-colored lights. Lady Patricia found it quite difficult to concentrate on one thing the young man was saying with that art deco tongue darting in and out with each and every word. Worse yet, the young man came from one of the finest families in Birmingham. It used to be that you could tell who was who and what was what just by looking at people, but now, who knows? Today, your city councilman might very well look like one of those men you used to hide your purse from, and the ax murderer might come a-calling in a suit. But it was a new day, her granddaughter reminded her, and this was a new South. "It would be best," the lizard-looking young man said to her that day, "if the old folks could start getting used to it." What nerve, Lady Patricia thought to herself. The two of them had made her feel like an old pair of shoes nobody had use for anymore. But she had to admit one thing: things were certainly different than they used to be.

This new South—what an interesting blend of contradictions and complexities! Now it seemed as if people were trying to find a way to make old ways lie peacefully next to new ones, but unfortunately some things simply weren't made to be put up next to one another. These new Southerners, they wanted growth—they just didn't want it too fast. And they wanted to appear as sophisticated as Northerners with all of their new-fangled ballet centers, but yet they weren't quite ready to give up the magic of a good storytelling on a rickety old porch. There were still the good old barbecue stands in all the familiar places, but now there were sushi places right across the street. And yes, folks did recognize that it was now the twenty-first century, but they still refused to excuse some young upstart from a polite "yes ma'am" or "no sir."

No, Southern folks were not easy people for outsiders to understand, Lady Patricia reflected as she put on the coffee, at least not these days. In all fairness, there were things that did need changing and most good folks knew it, too. It's just that Southerners tend to move slowly with just about everything, and working around the past to make a decent future wasn't going to happen overnight, no matter what them other folks said. Look at how long it had taken her to come around and understand some things, and still she had a great deal of learning to do. Sometimes Lady Patricia felt like she had one foot planted in yesterday and the other one in today, and Lord, if she didn't learn how to balance herself soon, she was sure to fall on her face.

Like last week at the tea party she sponsored at the senior center—she had said the word "colored" instead of "African American" at least three times (she thought that maybe "black" was okay, but she really wasn't sure about that one either). And then when Miss Bessie had risen to her feet to pour herself a cup of tea, Lady Patricia had unthinkingly waited for her to serve her as well. Well, when Miss Bessie had realized what she was waiting for, she had graciously poured her a cup, but Lady Patricia couldn't help feeling like she owed the woman an apology. She had treated Miss Bessie the way her mama had treated "cook"—the black woman had served their family for years, yet her mama had never even bothered to learn her name. She had just called her "cook" and then sat there day after day waiting for "cook" to take care of her. Mama probably hadn't meant any harm; she simply didn't know that there was any other way that things could be. She had taught Lady Patricia what she herself had been taught to be true—that everybody had a place and as long as everyone understood their place, the world was destined to remain a mighty fine place. But in the last thirty years, places and spaces were changing mighty darn fast, and sometimes Lady Patricia felt like you needed a score card to keep up with it all.

Today she was giving yet another afternoon tea at the senior center. She was going to try it again, and this time Lady Patricia was determined to get it right. She knew that the ladies at the center hadn't quite accepted her yet; women of her social status didn't usually spend their days at a community-run senior citizens center. She had met them when her bridge club helped out at a clothing drive sponsored by the center. The ladies had all made the long day pass ever so quickly with their witty stories and wonderful laughter. Lady Patricia had not wanted the day to end. Well, that good time may have ended, but now there would be many more. Lady Patricia loved the center and she loved the ladies. Yes, they were different from the women she had known in the past, but she was anxious to be their friend all the same. It would just take time, she vowed, and Lady Patricia had plenty of that.

At three o'clock this afternoon, Lady Patricia would sit down to have tea with women she would have never had the pleasure of knowing four or five decades ago. She had very carefully planned the menu—tea, sandwiches, and scones—and she was even bringing her mama's antique tea set to donate to the center so that the ladies could have their own tea parties anytime they wanted to. Lady Patricia smiled to herself as she imagined her mother looking down from the heavens and watching Miss Bessie or Sister Friday sipping tea from her very best set. Well, it was time. Hell, it was past time.

Lady Patricia had invited Larissa to the tea party, and the sweet girl had seemed so excited. Larissa had never been to a tea party, she'd told Lady Patricia, and Lady Patricia had responded that it was high time that she went to one. Not only was she going to allow her to take tea with the ladies, but she also promised Larissa that she would teach her all the ins and outs of giving a proper afternoon tea. Lady Patricia also promised Larissa that after the tea party she would spend some time with her, sharing more of her life stories and favorite recipes. She was a little nervous about the life stories part, though. It sure wasn't going to be easy to tell a little black girl what things were like in the Birmingham, Alabama, that Lady Patricia had grown up in. Worse yet was the fact that her family hadn't helped things much. In fact, in many instances they had made things worse. But the child deserved the truth, and no matter how ugly it was, it needed to be told. Lady Patricia would simply have to find the courage to tell it.

# *Lady Patricia's Story*

## *A Life of Southern Splendor*

I was born during the height of the Depression, the youngest of three daughters. Unfortunately for my daddy, he never had a son, but I was such a tomboy I did my best to make up for it. Now, the Depression tore the city of Birmingham to pieces; folks that never ever had to even think about money suddenly didn't have any. Some managed to cut back enough so that they could still make it and keep up appearances, but others just lost it all and they never did fully recover. Well, we survived without too much hardship. I tell people honestly that although my daddy walked around like some kind of Southern gentleman, he was really a hustler at heart. He had his hands in more stuff—from gambling to real estate and a few other things—that I probably really don't want to know anything about.

My daddy was certainly something else—a great big man with a head full of black hair. He had a mustache, too, and he trimmed it every single day. He was a dapper dresser; it didn't matter where he was going—but he looked good getting there. He also talked a lot—a whole lot. I think he imagined himself to be some kind of reincarnated Thomas Jefferson, and he used to walk around giving these long speeches about citizenship, responsibility, and the danger of big government. It got so bad that when people saw him coming, they'd do their best to hide just so's they wouldn't have to listen to him. The only time he got quiet was when he was full of good bourbon, so we did our best to keep him just this side of drunk most of the time. That was the only way that we could be spared the rhetoric. Lord, could that man talk! And he talked all the way up to the minute he died, still telling us all what we needed to do. But for all that bluster, I miss him and there are days I'd give just about anything to hear one of those long, tedious speeches just one more time.

Daddy took good care of us, though. We lived in a great big colonial house that was built by my great-grandfather and miraculously survived the Civil War. Oh, it was a beautiful home with a lavish entranceway and a stairway that swirled up so high, I declare, it looked like it was going to reach clear up to heaven one day. I remember, too, that we used to have a great big porch that wrapped all the way around the house, but it started to rot and Daddy had it all torn down, all of it except for the very front part. That was where we sometimes entertained friends. Mercy, there sure was nothing prettier than that little piece of porch under a starlit sky. We had some really good times there.

Mama and Daddy were not very close. Sometimes I wondered why they even bothered to get together, but I reckon Mama thought he was a good catch so she caught him. He complained that Mama was an awfully prissy and particular woman, but he made sure she had anything and everything she wanted, and she spent just about every waking moment telling him exactly what that was. Other than that, I don't believe they had a whole lot to say to each other. My uncle James told me that once upon a time they loved each other a great deal, but Daddy had some kind of indiscretion with a black woman who worked for them when I was a baby, and that was it between him and Mama. Uncle James said, too, that he believed that Daddy had children with the woman, and I believe it because I saw Daddy one day standing next to this black boy who looked just like him. But we were raised to stay out of grown folks' business, so I never asked him one thing about it.

Well, if Daddy did have himself some black children somewhere, it sure didn't soften his heart toward black folks any. I was a young woman in the

1960s, already married and out of the house at the time, but I remember all that race stuff like it was yesterday. Worse yet, my daddy was right smack in the middle of it. I declare, if it had been left up to him, I believe he would have had black folks still slavin' on the plantation today. I remember that he went to every city meeting they had on all that civil rights stuff, and he would go and make these long speeches about the superiority of white folks and the lowly place that needed to be set aside for the black folks. I didn't believe he was right about that, and one time I said so. Glory, I'd never seen him so mad, so I never mentioned it again. I just watched all the going-ons from afar and waited to see what would be what when it all shook itself out. Now that I'm older, I'm sorry that I didn't do more, or at the very least do something, but things are better for black folks now, and I am glad about that.

My daddy didn't live to see how it all worked itself out. He died before the walls separating blacks from whites came tumbling down. I remember clearly standing in the center of town one day and watching folks take down all those "white only" signs, and I know for sure Daddy was gone by then. If he hadn't been, he probably would have cried. But you never know. I saw some white folks come around years later who I thought would never accept those kinds of changes. Maybe Daddy would have been one of them. I'd like to think so.

Well, things are different now for me and for the South. I've left Birmingham, divorced my husband, had a facelift, and bought a dog. I've got some new friends at the senior center (well, they're almost friends), and life is looking mighty darn good. Like my granddaughter and her young man so graciously reminded me, I haven't figured out this new thing completely, but I'm a quick study and I'm mighty determined. In my mind, all the dust still hasn't settled around here yet, but I sure would like to be around long enough to see how it all, or at least most of it, ends up.

# *Lady Patricia's Teatime Favorites*

*The mint julep is one of those wonderful nostalgic reminders of the good old days. It is really nothing more than a little liquor, simple syrup, mint, and ice. Now, you can fancy it up with rum, fresh fruit, or peach brandy, but I like mine made the old-fashioned way. Somebody once said that the mint julep is "all delight—nectar to the Virginian, mother's milk to the Kentuckian, and ambrosia to Southerners anywhere." Honey, now that's a man who knows what he's talking about!*

## MINT JULEP

**½ lump sugar**
**1 tablespoon water**
**1 mint leaf**
**Crushed ice**
**Bourbon whiskey**
**Mint sprig**

In a silver goblet, dissolve the sugar in the water. Bruise the mint leaf between your fingers and drop it into the dissolved sugar. Stir well and remove the mint leaf. Put the sugar mixture into a goblet. Fill with crushed ice. Add bourbon whiskey to the top. Garnish with a mint sprig. Let goblet stand until frosted. Serve immediately.

Yields 1 serving.

*I understand that iced tea was introduced in 1904 at the St. Louis World's Fair by a tea plantation owner. Originally he had planned to give away free samples of hot tea to the visitors. But when a heat wave hit, the folks weren't interested, so he dumped a load of ice into the brewed tea and served the first iced tea. Well, I thank the man for creating such a wonderful beverage, but it seems such a shame that it had to come about on Yankee territory. Anyhow, this is the way that I make iced tea, and there's none better anywhere.*

## SUN TEA (THE HOUSE WINE OF THE SOUTH)

**3 tea bags**
**1 quart cold water**

Put the tea bags into a clear glass quart jar filled with water. Set in the sun for several hours.

Yields 1 quart.

*A tea party simply isn't a tea party without wonderful sandwiches, but a sandwich is only as good as the bread that you start with. Here are a few of my favorite bread recipes. They are easy and delicious. Any one of them would make a great beginning for a marvelous tea sandwich.*

## Basic White Bread

2¼ cups warm water

2 packages active dry yeast

3 tablespoons sugar

6½ cups all-purpose flour

3 teaspoons salt

2 tablespoons shortening

Yields 2 loaves.

Pour water into a large mixing bowl. Sprinkle yeast on top of water and wait 5 minutes. The yeast will activate during this time. Stir yeast into water. Add sugar and half the flour to the water mixture and stir. Stir in salt and shortening. Beat this mixture for a couple of minutes, and then beat in remaining flour. Cover with a towel and let rise in a warm place until dough has doubled in size. Beat down and divide dough between 2 loaf pans, smoothing the tops. Let rise in pans until doubled in size.

Preheat the oven to 375°. Bake for 40 to 50 minutes or until done. Remove from pans and cool on a wire rack.

## Excellent Graham Bread

2 cups whole wheat flour

½ cup flour

1 teaspoon baking powder

½ teaspoon salt

¼ cup sugar

1 teaspoon baking soda

4 tablespoons melted Crisco

1½ cups buttermilk (or 1½ cup
   milk with 1 teaspoon vinegar)

Yields 1 small loaf.

Preheat the oven to 325°. In a medium-sized mixing bowl, sift flours with baking powder, salt, sugar, and soda. Add Crisco and milk. Mix and turn into greased and floured cake tin, and bake for 50 minutes.

## Whole Wheat Gingerbread

**2 cups flour**

**2 cups whole wheat flour**

**3 tablespoons candied**
**lemon peel, chopped**

**½ cup seeded raisins**

**½ cup chopped nuts**

**1 teaspoon ground ginger**

**½ teaspoon ground mace**

**1 teaspoon ground cinnamon**

**½ teaspoon salt**

**½ cup Crisco**

**1½ cups molasses**

**4 tablespoons sugar**

**2 eggs**

**1 teaspoon baking soda**

**¼ cup milk**

Preheat the oven to 325°. In a large mixing bowl, combine regular and whole wheat flour. Add lemon peel, raisins, nuts, spices, and salt. Melt Crisco, molasses, and sugar over medium heat, and then cool. Add well-beaten egg and soda mixed with milk. Mix well; then combine with flour mixture. Fold into a cake pan that has been greased and floured. Bake for 1 hour.

Yields 1 large loaf.

## Honey Bread

**2 cups rye flour**

**2 cups white flour**

**¼ cup brown sugar**

**1 teaspoon baking soda**

**1 teaspoon salt**

**1⅓ teaspoon ground ginger**

**2 cups honey**

**2 egg yolks**

**water (optional)**

Yields 2 small loaves.

Preheat the oven to 400°. In a large mixing bowl, sift the rye flour and wheat flour several times with brown sugar, baking soda, salt, and ginger. Mix in the honey and egg yolks, adding a little water if the honey is too thick. Knead the mixture to make a medium-soft dough. Spread the dough evenly, about 1 inch thick, into two shallow buttered cake tins and bake for 45 minutes to 1 hour. You may want to line buttered tins with foil.

NOTE: You may also want to add a little anise seed and cardamom, or you may add some finely chopped almonds and raisins.

*"Cook" taught me how to make these rolls when I was a young girl. She knew how much I loved having them at my tea party, and she wanted me to be able to have them anytime I wanted, even if she wasn't around. I tell you, the first time my mother saw me in the kitchen cooking, I thought she was going to have a heart attack. But she did stay and watch, and when the time came, she even helped me roll them out and get them into the oven. I don't believe that I saw my mother cook before that day or since. I guess that's one of the reasons these rolls are so special to me.*

## SWEDISH TEA ROLLS

**2 cups flour**
**4 teaspoons baking powder**
**½ teaspoon salt**
**I egg, slightly beaten**
**¾ cup milk**
**3 tablespoons shortening,**
  **melted**
**Sugar**
**Cinnamon**
**Dried currants**

Preheat the oven to 375°. In a medium bowl mix together flour, baking powder, salt, egg, and milk. Spread and roll out, long and narrow. Sprinkle dough lightly with shortening, sugar, cinnamon, and dried currants. Roll the dough like jelly roll and cut in slices ¾ inch thick. Set these on a greased shallow baking pan. Bake for 20 minutes.

Yields 24 rolls.

*With rolls and wonderful breads like these, you simply can't serve regular old margarine. Pick one of these fancy butters to serve, and give that bread an extra touch of class.*

## CRANBERRY BUTTER SPREAD

**I cup sugar**
**½ cup water**
**I ¼ cups cranberries**
**½ cup butter, softened**
**I tablespoon powdered**
  **sugar**

Yields 1 cup.

Bring sugar and water to a boil in a small saucepan over medium heat, stirring until sugar dissolves. Stir in berries; bring to a boil. Reduce heat and simmer, stirring occasionally, for 10 to 15 minutes or until thickened. Remove from heat and cool.

Press through a fine mesh strainer and discard solids. Beat butter at medium speed with an electric mixer until fluffy; add powdered sugar and cranberry mixture, beating until blended.

## APRICOT BUTTER

½ cup butter or
  margarine, softened
¼ cup honey
¼ cup finely chopped
  dried apricots
½ teaspoon grated lemon rind

Beat butter at medium speed with an electric mixer until fluffy; add remaining ingredients, beating until blended. Chill if desired.

Yields ¾ cup.

## HERB BUTTER

1 pint heavy cream
1 teaspoon chopped fresh
  chives, parsley, and dill,
  combined
¼ teaspoon salt

Place cream in a mixing bowl and beat with electric beater until water separates from a solid mass. Pour off the liquid, season the butter with herbs and salt, and spoon into a decorative dish.

Yields approximately 8 ounces.

*This spread is good on just about anything. It can even make slightly stale bread taste good if you put on enough of it, but don't tell anybody I said that.*

## OLD-FASHIONED CHEESE SPREAD

8 ounces packaged cream
  cheese, softened
½ cup sour cream
1 envelope Italian-style salad
  dressing mix
1 cup (4 ounces) shredded
  cheddar cheese

Yields 1½ cups.

Beat cream cheese at medium speed with an electric mixer until fluffy; add sour cream and salad dressing mix, beating until blended. Reserve 1 tablespoon cheddar cheese; stir remaining cheddar cheese into cream cheese mixture.

Spoon into a bowl, cover, and chill 2 hours. Sprinkle with reserved cheddar cheese and serve over hot breads or crackers.

*I think the hot, humid weather has a great deal to do with truly understanding who Southern folks really are. You see, we figured out a long time ago that after it gets so hot, there is no need to be hurrying around. The hotter it gets, the slower we move and the longer it takes us to say a single word. Well, when it got hot, hot, I didn't want anything heavy on my stomach, so I'd settle for a light sandwich instead—the cucumber and tomato ones were my favorite.*

## CUCUMBER SANDWICHES

2 large cucumbers, peeled
   and finely grated
1 tablespoon salt
1 rounded tablespoon
   mayonnaise
1 rounded tablespoon sour
   cream
1 rounded tablespoon cream
   cheese, room temperature
⅛ teaspoon green onion
   flakes
⅛ teaspoon dill
Dash of pepper
1 small onion, finely chopped
1 loaf sliced white bread, crusts removed

Combine the cucumbers and salt in a bowl and chill for a few hours. Wring the moisture from the cucumbers with your hands. Chop the cucumbers. Mix the mayonnaise, sour cream, and cream cheese with the cucumber in a medium bowl. Add the green onion flakes, dill, pepper, and onion. Cut each slice of bread into quarters. Spread the cucumber mixture on each quarter to make an open-faced sandwich.

Yields 20 to 24 servings.

# A Tasty Tomato Sandwich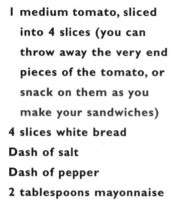

**1 medium tomato, sliced into 4 slices (you can throw away the very end pieces of the tomato, or snack on them as you make your sandwiches)**

**4 slices white bread**

**Dash of salt**

**Dash of pepper**

**2 tablespoons mayonnaise**

Yields 8 small sandwiches.

Place 2 slices of bread on a plate. On each slice of bread, place 2 slices of tomato side by side. (You may want to use a paper towel to dab away any moisture on tomato slices—otherwise you will have a soggy sandwich.) Sprinkle with salt and pepper. Spread mayonnaise on the other 2 slices of bread and place them on top of the tomatoes. Cut each sandwich into 4 equal pieces.

TIP: Sprinkle bacon bits on tomato slices for added flavor.

VARIATION: Instead of mayonnaise, use a flavored butter. Try basil butter, garlic butter, or herb butter.

*Now, if you want to add a little heat to that tomato sandwich, horseradish will do the trick just fine. Be careful, though, because horseradish has quite a kick.*

# Tomato and Horseradish Sandwiches

**1 tablespoon Crisco**

**¼ cup grated horseradish**

**¼ cup mayonnaise**

**2 or 3 tomatoes**

**Salt and paprika to taste**

**20 slices bread**

**Butter**

**Parsley**

Yields 10 sandwiches.

Mix Crisco, horseradish, and mayonnaise together in a small bowl. Slice tomatoes. Sprinkle tomatoes with salt and paprika. Spread thin slices of buttered bread with Crisco mixture and put sliced tomatoes between bread slices. Cut sandwiches into fancy shapes and garnish with parsley.

*In truth, I didn't start eating a lot of turkey sandwiches until I got old and found out how healthy they were—my doctor recommended them. Of course, he didn't mention anything about smothering them in honey mustard butter or cranberry spread. I came up with that on my own.*

## TURKEY TEA SANDWICHES

**2 (8-ounce) packages petite dinner rolls, split**
**Honey mustard butter or cranberry butter spread**
**I pound thinly sliced cooked turkey, cut into 2-inch squares**

Spread cut sides of rolls with spread of choice. Place turkey evenly on bottom halves and cover with tops.

Yields 12 to 16 small sandwiches.

*A regular old ham and cheese sandwich doesn't seem very special, but cut it into tiny pieces and suddenly that sandwich is elegant and beautiful. These are easy to make and go a long way.*

## TINY HAM AND CHEESE SANDWICHES

**I package of cream cheese, softened**
**¾ cup sharp cheddar cheese, shredded**
**1½ tablespoons mayonnaise**
**Dash of garlic salt**
**¼ teaspoon salt**
**Dash of pepper**
**4 dozen rolls, homemade or prepackaged**
**I pound sliced cooked deli ham, cut into 2-inch squares**

Beat cheeses, mayonnaise, garlic salt, salt, and pepper all together. Slice rolls in half. Spread ½ teaspoon of cheese mixture on the top half of each cut roll, and place sliced ham on each bottom half. Combine into sandwiches and serve immediately.

Yields 48 sandwiches.

*The graham bread is the key to this sandwich. I've given you a wonderful recipe so you can make your own. These sandwiches are reason enough to give that recipe a try.*

## PIMIENTO CHEESE SANDWICHES

**I cup diced cheese**
**2 tablespoons Crisco**
**I teaspoon cornstarch**
**6 tablespoons milk**
**I teaspoon salt**
**Paprika to taste**
**I can pimientos**
**Butter**
**50 slices graham bread**

Put cheese into double boiler. Add Crisco, corn-starch, milk, salt, and paprika to taste. Stir and cook until smooth; then add pimientos cut into small pieces. Spread between buttered slices of graham bread.

Yields 25 sandwiches.

*When I was a little girl, we had tea each and every afternoon at four o'clock. It was all very British, and I loved the pomp and circumstance of it. When Mama was too busy to join me, I would have tea with my stuffed animals. I used to pretend that they were all of my closest friends coming to visit. We had some wonderful conversations and some very good times. But no tea was complete without a tray of scones, some cream, and a little jam.*

## CLASSIC SCONES

**2 cups all-purpose flour**
**I teaspoon cream of tartar**
**½ teaspoon baking soda**
**Pinch of salt**
**¼ cup (4 tablespoons)**
  **unsalted butter, chilled**
**2 tablespoons sugar**
**½ cup milk**

Yields 12 scones.

Preheat the oven to 425°. Sift the flour, cream of tartar, baking soda, and salt into a medium bowl. Cut butter into flour mixture with pastry blender until the mixture resembles coarse crumbs. Stir in sugar and enough milk to mix a soft dough.

Turn out onto a floured surface, knead lightly, and roll out to 3/4-inch thickness. Cut into 2-inch rounds and place on a lightly greased baking sheet. Brush with milk to glaze. Bake for 10 minutes, remove from baking sheet, and cool on a wire rack. Serve with butter, jam, or clotted cream.

*I made these scones on special occasions, like my son's birthday. I declare, he ate them two at a time.*

# HAZELNUT CHOCOLATE CHIP SCONES

**2 cups all-purpose flour**

**⅓ cup firmly packed dark brown sugar**

**1½ teaspoons baking powder**

**½ teaspoon baking soda**

**¼ teaspoon salt**

**6 tablespoons unsalted butter, chilled**

**½ cup buttermilk**

**1 large egg**

**1½ teaspoons vanilla**

**1 cup semisweet or milk chocolate chips**

**½ cup toasted hazelnuts, chopped (optional)**

Yields 8 scones.

Preheat the oven to 400°. In a medium bowl, stir together flour, brown sugar, baking powder, baking soda, and salt. Cut the butter into ½-inch cubes and put in flour mixture. With a pastry blender cut the butter into the mixture until it resembles coarse crumbs. In a small bowl, stir together buttermilk, egg, and vanilla. Add this mixture to the flour and stir. Add chocolate chips and hazelnuts (if desired). Dough will be sticky.

Drop by large tablespoonfuls onto a lightly greased baking sheet. Bake for 17 to 19 minutes, or until top is lightly browned and a toothpick inserted into the center of a scone comes out clean. Remove from baking sheet and cool on a wire rack. Serve warm or cool. Store in an airtight container or plastic bag. May be frozen.

VARIATIONS: Omit chocolate chips and hazelnuts; add ⅔ cup raisins or any other dried fruit.

# Sister Friday

Sister Friday looked directly at the devil tree that stood not very far away. Funny that despite its impressive size, compelling legend, and close proximity to the senior center, she had rarely given it a second thought until recently. In the daylight it didn't look so frightening, but last night when she'd snuck out of the house to examine it more carefully, it had very nearly scared her to death. Basking in the moonlight the unusual grim gray color of the trunk seemed to take on a gruesome glimmer in the midst of the darkness. Even its gnarled branches seemed to come alive.

Legend had it that the tree was brought out of Africa by white slave catchers over two hundred years ago. Intrigued by its appearance, and not realizing its spiritual significance, they had moved something that clearly had no business being moved, and now folks were in real danger as a result. The black folks in town believed that a demon lived in its core, and the only way to confine it to its rightful place was to salt down the base of it, but as of late, nobody had taken up the task. Annie Williams had told her that now the demon was on the loose and she had seen it. She'd warned everybody that there was no telling what the thing was capable of, but nobody knew what in the world to do. Once upon a time, some of the local men had tried to cut the tree down, but the sucker just wouldn't budge. Mr. Williams said that they were going to try it again, though, because as long as the devil tree stood, that demon was a threat. At the very least, the boo-hag needed to be rounded up and put back where it belonged.

Well, if that be the case, then Sister Friday was just the one to do it. She had been born with a caul over her face and a single tooth in her mouth. The moment her mama had seen her, she knew that Sister Friday would be special. That caul meant she would be able to see and hear the spirits and she would have the power to chase away the hants. Sister Friday had not disappointed either. In the last seventy years, she had chased away more devils than a preacher could shake a stick at, and her work was far from being through. Not that any of it was easy. Each case required its own special handling, and Sister Friday had the gift to know exactly what to do each and every time. Now there was a she-devil on the loose (and the thing was definitely female), and it was up to Sister Friday to take care of it. Would salting it be enough, or would she need a little graveyard dirt too? Well, Sister Friday was trying to figure out which remedy was needed when Larissa walked up and stood right next to her.

"What you doing, Sister Friday?" Larissa wanted to know.

"Lookin' for a demon."

Larissa wondered what she meant by that. Everybody said that Sister Friday was special and took care of stuff that other folks didn't begin to understand, but demons? Nobody had ever said anything about demons. Why would anyone *want* to find one?

"I see," Larissa responded. But in truth, she really didn't see at all. She had the feeling, too, that Sister Friday was in no mood to explain it either, so she decided to change the subject. "I want to thank you for those latest recipes you gave me. Mama and I have already tried them out and they are great!" Well, it was obvious to Larissa that Sister Friday wasn't listening to a word she was saying—she had a demon on her mind and Larissa certainly couldn't compete with that. With a quick good-bye Larissa moved up the steps to the center. Today was the day she'd promised to help clean the windows.

Sister Friday hated that she couldn't spend a little time with Larissa, but that child sure could talk! A conversation with her could last over an hour. She seemed to have so many questions, and Sister Friday had already shared her entire life story and most of her best recipes. The only thing left was idle chitchat, and chitchat had no place on a day like today when there was a boo-hag on the loose.

A cool wind suddenly surrounded the tree, and a chill ran straight through Sister Friday. *She* was near. Sister Friday could feel it. She was just about to reach into her pocket and pull out the salt when she spotted Estella Mae out of the corner of her eye. Judging by the look on the woman's face, she was having problems with that man of hers again and was coming to Sister Friday for help. Obviously, there was more than one demon running wild on this day. Knowing that man of Estella Mae's, he was out there somewhere and up to no good. She had already told Estella Mae more than one time that there were just some dogs you couldn't keep on the porch, and it was best to let those go. But sad to say, Estella Mae just wouldn't listen.

It seemed to Sister Friday that if love was all the whispered promises of wonders yet to come, then heartache must have been the splintered remains of things hoped for but sadly never meant to be, or so Sister Friday concluded as she looked into the sad eyes of one Estella Mae. At least the years had been good to her, even if her men never were. Estella Mae was more than fifty years old, and her skin still shone like black rain, her full lips and beautiful white teeth could still give way to an incredible smile, and those slanted jezebel eyes still hinted of mischief and smoldering sensuality. Her hair was covered with a colorful and elaborately tied silk scarf, somewhat out of place against the rather plain white dress, but on Estella Mae it worked. On Estella Mae, everything worked.

"Sister Friday," she began breathlessly. But before she could even get it all out, Sister Friday interrupted her.

"Honey, I know why you here and I don't know what else to tell you. Dat man of yours ain't never gonna settle down. Oh wait, dere is one more thing you could try. It's de last thing I know. Dere ain't many dat escape my powers, but dis one, I jus' can't figure." She paused for a moment before continuing on. "Go get you some scissors, and den find a pair of yo man's drawers. Cut dem suckers in all de right places, and you won't have no mo' problems out of him." Of course, Estella Mae started grinning immediately. "I'll do it, Sister Friday. I sure will. I'll do it and thank you." As she ran off Sister Friday smiled to herself. If the woman really wanted that scissors thing to work, she would need to do the cuttin' when that man was in the drawers, but that was not for Sister Friday to say. It was time now to get back to that other demon at hand.

A moment later there was a subtle flicker of leaves on some of the bottom limbs, and Sister Friday knew right then that she had her—the boo-hag was back and she was as good as done for. Sister Friday pulled out the salt and sprinkled it as fast and furiously as she could, yelling "Jesus" all the while. Within minutes the breeze was gone, the chill had disappeared, and the flickering ceased. The deed was done.

Yes, it took a special woman to be able to use the power of Jesus and the magic of charms to set things back to the way they were supposed to be. No, there was no doubt about it, there were times you needed just the right woman. There were times you needed a Gullah woman, and nobody knew that any better than one rather extraordinary Sister Friday.

# Sister Friday's Story
### Tellin' de Truth and Shamin' de Devil

*If you head to that beautiful piece of coastline that runs from the very northeastern tip of South Carolina and straight through Georgia, you'll come to a land where there is water, water everywhere, Gullah is the language of the local black folks, and moss hangs down from great big trees like the thick, long, tangly locks of an old gray head. Little islands dart in and out of the endless blue horizon, and the remnants of once-thriving rice plantations can still be seen throughout the countryside. Here Africa still lives on in a wonderfully peculiar way, and if you listen to the tales of Miss Friday Brown, the oldest lady at the senior center, you can't help but feel like you're right there—moss trees, sea breezes, and all.*

I was born on a li'l island way out in de middle of nowhere. Folks called us de Gullah. De *buckra*\* brought us dere two hundred years ago and dey ain't had a whole lot to do with us since. Well 'cause of dat, you know us not mixing it with de *buckra*, us had our own way of doin' things dat was kinda a cross betwixt African and American. Us made sweet grass baskets like we did back home, and we even kept hold of some native words dat we put with de English ones. Other folks sometime couldn't make out exactly what we was sayin', and I still laugh at de way some of dem looked when us opened our mouth and started talkin'. I reckon dey musta figured dat dey somehow or another landed on another planet.

Yes sir, us held on to our African selves and I sure am mightily proud 'bout dat. My name is proof of what I been tellin' you, too. You see dey named me Friday 'cause of course I was born on an early Friday mornin'.

---

\**buckra:* a Gullah term for white people

Just like in Africa, dey named me after de day I came into dis world a kickin' and screamin' all de while. Folks say dat's basket namin' when you do dat. I remember, too, dat my granddaddy was called Christmas 'cause him came jus' like Jesus did on December 25. And him wasn't by heself neither; a whole lot of my people got 'em some strange names. Some of 'em was named after places or foods or even de months of de year. I got me a cousin named Thin Gravy, and one dat lived way out in de country named Possum Trail. Chile, with names like dat, you ain't gonna hear yourself comin' and goin' real regular, I can promise you dat. See, I don't want me no name dat's so ordinary dat you can jus hear it any old where. I'm special and I want me a name dat's special. Dat's why I love my name, Sister Friday.

I was my mama's oldest, but dat didn't mean I had her complete attention. Her watched over a whole lot of babies, mostly for de womens dat worked on de mainland. But no matter how many babies her had, she cared for 'em good. She didn't throw away none of dem likes dese young gals do today— jus' put 'em aside when dey gets tired of 'em. No, Mama wrapped them little ones in love. Her played with dem, stretching dey little arms and legs, and she sing to 'em, too.

> Go to sleep, li'l baby,
> 'Fore de booger man get hold of you.
> Go to sleep, li'l baby,
> Mama went away and she told me to stay,
> So here I am,
> Taking care of dis sweet li'l baby.

From de time it seemed like I could walk, I been workin'. When I was li'l, I helped in de fields, watched de other li'l children, or swept out de yard. Dere jus' always seemed to be so much to do and not enough folks to do it. 'Cause I was de oldest, I didn't get to go to school past de age of ten. I can read and figure numbers, so I get by, but I do wish I had me some more schooling. If I was a young gal today, I would get me all de learnin' I could, but some of 'em jus' too busy being fresh tails to do what dey need to.

My mama and daddy were righteous people, and dey raised us up in de way we was supposed to go. We went to de prays house at least twice de week—usually on Tuesday and Friday. My daddy, he teach us how to sing, how to pray, and how to shout. Up until a few years ago you used to see prays houses all over de place, but now when I go home, I can barely find one. See, de prays house is different from de church. It was de place you went to learn, to train, to get ready to go into de church. It was de meetin' place. See, you go dere to testify. When you went dere, dere was always a man to give us de Bible words so dat we could find our way to de Lord. Den on another night de women would sing and talk 'bout de goodness of Jesus. While dey was praisin' we would listen and sometimes clap.

Used to be, you could go to de church and tell de saints from de sinners. De saints sat up in de front and de sinners sat in de back. Even after I was baptized, I couldn't sit in de front. Couldn't sit dere 'til one of de saints led me dere and let me sit dere. Now you go to church and you can't tell de devils from de righteous. It ain't right, I tell you. It jus' ain't right.

Now I'm many a mile from home, but I done held on to my religion. My husband and me, we both go to church every Sunday, and when we's feelin' really good we makes it out to pray on Tuesday nights, too. I tries not to wear my religion too heavy 'cause it ain't everybody that love Jesus likes I do, but even at de center, every once in de while I jus' got to say how good de Lord done been to me. I guess dere ain't a whole lot left for me to hope for. I done been loved by a good man. I done seen my children growed and takin' care of theyselves, and I done got to know Jesus for myself. All I wants now is a place in de heavenly skies to lay dis weary head and to hear de Father say, "Well done."

# Good Gullah Cooking

*I can tell you us Gullah folks is some mighty interestin' people. Us was brung here as captives from West Africa to slave for de buckra. Dey brought us here to grow de rice, somethin' us knew a whole lot about since dat's what us grew back in Africa. Now, where I come from, de coast of South Carolina, de land may set down low, but de humidity runs mighty high, and between de heat and de mosquitoes, de buckra. run out of dere like from a house afire. Well, dey put my people on dese isolated islands to work as slaves, but for de most part dey left 'em alone, so my people was able to hang on to a lot of de African ways. Well, us grew a whole lot of dat rice, so we figured out how to use it every way dere was. Dese recipes here are some of what we come up with. I hope you like 'em 'cause I know I do!*

## RICE MUFFINS

**I cup cooked rice**

**I teaspoon salt**

**I tablespoon sugar**

**2 eggs, well beaten**

**I tablespoon melted butter**

**I cup flour**

Yields 12 muffins.

Preheat oven to 400° and place greased muffin pan in the oven while preheating. Rub cup of rice with a fork until well separated. In a bowl mix together rice, salt, sugar, and butter. Beat this mixture to a creamy consistency. Add eggs and flour and beat thoroughly. Bake for 15 minutes in the hot greased muffin pan. These should be eaten right away from the oven.

## RICE WAFFLES

**2 eggs, separated**

**I cup cooked rice**

**2 tablespoons unsalted butter, melted**

**2 cups flour**

**2 heaping teaspoons baking powder**

**I teaspoon salt**

**Milk, if needed**

Yields 6 to 8 waffles.

In a large bowl, beat the yolks and add the rice, butter, flour, baking powder, and salt. Add a small amount of milk if batter is too thick. Beat the egg whites until stiff peaks form, and fold into the batter. Cook batter on a waffle iron.

# RICE SANDWICHES

½ cup uncooked rice

1 sprig parsley

1 blade mace

1 strip lemon peel

2 tablespoons chopped cooked liver

1 tablespoon Crisco

2 tablespoons chopped cooked ham

Salt and butter

10 bread slices

Boil rice in plenty of boiling salted water. Add parsley, mace, and lemon peel (the parsley, mace, and lemon peel can be placed in cheesecloth for easier removal). When quite tender, strain off water and take out parsley, mace, and lemon peel. Stir in liver, Crisco, ham, and seasonings. Spread mixture on 5 slices of bread. Top with remaining slices; trim and cut into diamond shapes.

Yields 20 sandwiches.

*Us was so poor dat de children had to learn how to entertain theyselves. Well, us had dese plays, or games as some folks call 'em. Some plays was jus' a song you had to sing, and some of 'em had somethin' you had to do—like run 'round in a ring, clap yo' hands, or shake yo' bottom. De bottom-shakin' ones was my favorite. Well, jubba was one of dem plays dat was a good one. It's old, too—real old. I know 'cause my grandma, she say her played it, too, when she was a girl.*

*Now, if you listen, you can hear dat jubba is really 'bout slavery. Back den, de slaves didn't get no whole lot to eat. Those ole masters would jus' sometimes take a whole lot of mess and mix it together, and then feed it to 'em. Dat's what jubba means—de ends of things. Leftovers and leavin's dat wouldn't nobody else even touch. Well, de master, him take dat mess and pour it in a great big trough like you feed a hog or a dog. Anyhow de slaves sang about it, like dey did all dem other miseries dey couldn't do nothin' 'bout, and jubba was one of dem songs. It go like dis:*

> Jubba *dis and* jubba *dat*
> *(A little of this and a little of that)*
> *And* jubba *killed a yellow cat.*
> *(That means it would have killed dem white folks if dey ate it.)*
> *You sift de meal, and give me de husk,*
> *You cook de bread and give me de crust,*

*You fry de meat and give me de skin,*
*And dat's when Mama's trouble begin.*
*(Dat's what Mama wishes her could give she babies but to do dat,*
*her would have to steal and dat's when de trouble gonna start.)*
*Now you jubba up and den you jubba down,*
*Den you jubba all over town.*
*Jubba for yo' ma, jubba for yo' pa,*
*Den jubba for yo' brother-in-law.*
*(The rhyme was the fun part 'cause dat's when you get to*
*shake yo' bottom—the best part of the play!)*

*Well, now us got all de meat and us got all de bread we want, and I sho am glad about dat.*

## BACON MUFFINS

**4 cups sifted pastry flour**

**1 teaspoon salt**

**4 teaspoons baking powder**

**1 tablespoon sugar**

**2 eggs, beaten**

**6 tablespoons lard, melted**

**1½ cups cold water**

**2 tablespoons crisp bacon,
   diced**

Preheat the oven to 400°. Sift flour once and then measure; add salt, baking powder, and sugar, and sift three times. Put flour mixture in mixing bowl and add well-beaten eggs, melted lard, and water, and beat hard. Lastly, add bacon. Bake in muffin pans for 25 to 30 minutes.

Yields 48 muffins.

*I'll bet you didn't know it, but two hundred years ago, most of de black folks come here by way of de South Carolina shore, even when dey was eventually shipped off to other places. Dem other folks mighta come here lookin' up at Miss Liberty, but when my people come, de first thing dey saw was de sunlit marshes of de South Carolina coast.*

*You know, I remember dat when I was a little bitty thing, my mama used to tell me dis story 'bout de flying Africans. Later on I told it to my children. Dere sho are some times, when life gets troublin', dat I wish I, too, could jus' fly, fly away.*

*Now de way de story goes is dat one day, de slaves was workin' out in de fields. Well, all of a sudden dey all got together and started movin' 'round and 'round in one big circle. 'Round and 'round dey went, faster and faster. Den one by one dey started to rise up, take wings, and fly jus' like a bird. De overseer heard all dat noise, and him come out jus' in time to see de slaves rise up and fly back on to Africa. Him run den, and him manage to catch de last one by de foot as him was 'bout to fly off. But dat slave was gonna get back home one way or 'nother. So he let out dis loud, hard laugh, and den shook his foot 'bout fast as he could and knocked dat overseer clean to de ground. Dem slaves took off for home and dey ain't looked back since.*

*You know, I think of dat story every time I make dese* **benne** *wafers because* **benne** *is de African word for sesame seeds. When I was li'l, I used to pretend dat de* **benne** *had magical powers and if I sprinkled dem 'cross my toes, dey would carry me away from my troubles like dem flyin' Africans done. But I don't need to tell you dat it ain't never happened. All I managed to do was get seeds stuck between my toes, and what a devil of a time I had gettin' 'em out. But it sho was fun to pretend. I suppose* **benne** *will always be special to me 'cause I'd like to believe dat some of my people got away from dey troubles one way or another.*

# BENNE WAFERS

**I cup firmly packed brown sugar**

**½ stick (4 tablespoons) unsalted butter or margarine**

**I egg, lightly beaten**

**½ cup flour**

**¼ teaspoon salt**

**⅛ teaspoon baking powder**

**I cup toasted *benne* (sesame seeds)**

**I teaspoon lemon juice**

**½ teaspoon vanilla**

Yields 50 wafers.

Preheat the oven to 325°. In a medium bowl combine brown sugar and butter; beat until creamy. Stir in the egg, flour, salt, and baking powder. Stir in sesame seeds, lemon juice, and vanilla. Drop by teaspoonfuls on greased cookie sheet, 2 inches apart. Bake for 15 minutes or until wafers are lightly brown around edges. Remove from oven.

NOTE: To toast sesame seeds, preheat the oven to 425°. Place sesame seeds in a shallow pan and put in oven. After 5 minutes check on seeds. They should be the color of butterscotch and have a delicious toasted smell. If not, shake the pan and return to the oven for another minute. Be sure to watch carefully; they burn easily.

*I ain't too big on bakin' no bread. It take too much time and it seem like I got me too many other things to do. But when I do some bakin', dis here pecan loaf and peanut butter bread are two I jus' love.*

# PECAN LOAF

**2 cups grated breadcrumbs**

**2 cups pecans**

**2 grated raw apples**

**½ cup celery, finely minced**

**2 tablespoons sugar**

**2 teaspoons baking powder**

**2 tablespoons flour**

**Milk**

Preheat the oven to 350°. In a large bowl, mix together the breadcrumbs, pecans, apples, celery, sugar, baking powder, and flour. Add enough milk to make a soft dough. Pour into a greased 8x4x3-inch loaf pan. Bake for 30 minutes.

Yields 1 loaf.

# PEANUT BUTTER BREAD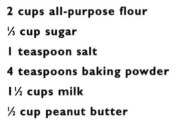

**2 cups all-purpose flour**

**⅓ cup sugar**

**1 teaspoon salt**

**4 teaspoons baking powder**

**1½ cups milk**

**½ cup peanut butter**

Preheat the oven to 375°. Combine dry ingredients. Add milk and peanut butter. Pour into a greased 8x4x3-inch loaf pan. Bake for approximately 50 minutes.

Yields 1 loaf.

*I ain't never throwed nothin' away, not even stale ole bread. I figured out how to use everything, and dese here muffins are a great way to use up leftover bread or old dried up breadcrumbs.*

## CRUMB MUFFINS

**2 cups stale breadcrumbs**

**1¼ cups milk**

**1 cup flour**

**2 teaspoons baking powder**

**½ teaspoon salt**

**2 eggs, beaten**

**1 tablespoon shortening, melted**

Preheat the oven to 375°. Soak breadcrumbs in cold milk for 10 minutes. In a separate bowl, sift together flour, baking powder, and salt; add to breadcrumbs. Add well-beaten eggs and melted shortening; mix well. Half fill two greased muffin tins with batter, and bake 20 to 25 minutes.

Yields 24 muffins.

*When my husband and me was first married, him used to run de ferry boat dat carried folks 'cross de water dat had to work on de mainland. It sho wasn't no easy job neither. He had to read de water and read de wind. He started work at dawn, and I used to make dese here cream biscuits for him to carry on his trips. He used to say dat with a piece of ham, six of dese biscuits would keep his belly full clear 'til lunch.*

## CREAM BISCUITS

**1 cup heavy cream**

**2 cups self-rising flour**

Yields 24 biscuits.

Preheat the oven to 450°. Beat the chilled cream until thick. Add the flour. Mix well; then knead lightly. Pat out to about ¾ inch thick and cut. Use a clean can or glass if you don't have a cutter. Place on a greased baking sheet and bake about 12 minutes until golden brown.

*I had dis aunt, Aunt Willa. Her was a fresh somethin' and she would tell me dese stories dat woulda set my mama's ears burnin' if she had a heard 'em. I remember one dat still makes me laugh when I think on it. Oh, was Aunt Willa good at tellin' de lie!*

*Aunt Willa told me dat dis woman went shoppin' and when her got home, her husband asked her what she bought. So she told him, "Two bras." Well, he called himself bein' smart and said to her, "What did you do dat for, you ain't got nothin' to put in 'em." Honey, dat woman ain't missed a beat. She looked over at him and said, "Well, you wear shorts, don't you?"*

*Chile, dere are some mens you jus' got to shut up every once in a while, and my aunt was good at handlin' anything in pants, I can tell you dat.*

*Well, dis here recipe is hers. I used to sit in her kitchen, watch her bake, and listen to her tell de lie. I don't know where de Lord sent her, but wherever she is, I know she's probably still running her mouth.*

## CORNBREAD SALAD

1 pan of cornbread

8 slices bacon, fried and crumbled

1 onion, chopped

1 green bell pepper, chopped

2 hard-cooked eggs, chopped

2 tomatoes, chopped

1 cup mayonnaise

Prepare the cornbread. Let cool. Then crumble into a bowl. Add the crumbled bacon, onion, bell pepper, and eggs. Add the tomatoes and stir in mayonnaise. Chill until served.

Yields 10 servings.

*Death has always been a strange time for my people. Us was always sad to lose somebody we loved, but we was sure dat dey was leaving bad times behind and going on to a better place. I remember my Aunt Bertha used to sing a song at de burying grounds whenever dere was a funeral. It went something like dis:*

> *Ain't you got somebody gone?*
> *Lay down a li'l while.*
> *Ain't you got somebody gone?*
> *Lay down a li'l while.*

> *Lay down body.*
> *Lay down a li'l.*
> *Lay down body.*
> *Lay down a li'l while.*

*I tell you, it seem like my family has always lived by de goodness of de water. My uncle was an oyster-man, his brother was a fisherman, and Aunt Bertha would sometimes shuck oysters at a cannery. Dey ate some kind of seafood, seem like, every day, and my Aunt Bertha always made her famous hush puppies every chance she got. You know, de Gullah folks believe dat when you put somebody away, and you want de spirit to rest easy, you got to leave somethin' with dem dat dey loved and was special to 'em. So when it come time to put Aunt Bertha away, I made a batch of hush puppies and put one in her pocket. We buried her close to de river so she could see de water, and I sang dat very song she loved so much. When you make her special hush puppies, do me a favor and think about her, please. She woulda liked dat.*

# SPICY HUSH PUPPIES

**1 cup cornmeal**
**½ cup all-purpose flour**
**½ cup corn flour**
**1 tablespoon baking powder**
**½ teaspoon salt**
**1 teaspoon cayenne pepper**
**½ teaspoon black pepper**
**½ cup onion, finely chopped**
**2 dashes hot sauce**
**2 eggs, slightly beaten**
**2 tablespoons vegetable oil**
**1 cup milk**
**Vegetable oil for deep frying**

Mix the cornmeal, all-purpose flour, corn flour, baking powder, salt, cayenne pepper, and black pepper together in a bowl. Add the chopped onion, hot sauce, and eggs, and mix well. Bring the 2 tablespoons of oil and the milk to a boil in a large saucepan. Add flour mixture and cook until thickened, stirring constantly. Chill for 1 hour.

Heat the vegetable oil to 350° in a large skillet or deep fryer. Drop the batter by tablespoons into the hot oil. Deep fry until dark brown. Drain on paper towels.

Yields 24 to 30 hush puppies.

*When my Aunt Bertha worked at shuckin' oysters like I was tellin' you 'bout, her was always gettin' hold of some recipe or another. Dese next two was two of my favorites.*

## OYSTER DRESSING

**1 medium onion**

**3 or 4 shallots**

**1 bell pepper**

**1½ pounds ground beef**

**½ pound ground pork**

**½ cup chopped parsley**

**2 to 2½ cups cooked rice**

**1 jar oysters (16 ounces)**

**Salt**

**Pepper**

Grind the onion, shallots, and bell pepper together and set aside. Brown the beef and pork together; add all ground ingredients and chopped parsley. Cook on medium to low fire for 1 hour. Add rice and cook for 20 minutes. Add oysters and cook for another 20 minutes. Salt and pepper to taste.

Yields 8 servings.

## OYSTER CLUB SANDWICH

**12 slices bacon**

**1 pint oysters**

**½ cup flour**

**½ teaspoon salt**

**⅛ teaspoon pepper**

**12 lettuce leaves**

**12 slices tomato**

**½ cup mayonnaise**

**18 slices buttered toast**

Fry the bacon and drain on absorbent paper. Drain oysters, roll in flour, and season with salt and pepper. Fry in the bacon fat. When brown on one side, turn and brown on the other side, cooking for about 5 minutes. Drain on absorbent paper. Arrange lettuce, oysters, bacon, tomatoes, and mayonnaise between three slices of toast. Fasten with a toothpick.

Yields 6 servings.

*Me and my husband jus' loved to go crabbin'. We'd go out with a net and some chicken backs and come back with a bucket-load. Dis here recipe is one I mixed up to use up a batch of crabmeat I had left over. My husband ate so much of it de first time I made it, he had a bellyache for two days after.*

## CRAB STUFFING

1 pound crabmeat,
  fresh or frozen

½ cup chopped onion

⅓ cup chopped celery

⅓ cup chopped green
  bell pepper

2 cloves garlic,
  finely chopped

⅓ cup melted fat

2 cups breadcrumbs

3 eggs, beaten

1 tablespoon chopped parsley

2 teaspoons salt

Pepper to taste

Preheat the oven to 350°. Drain crabmeat. Cook onion, celery, green pepper, and garlic in fat until tender. Combine breadcrumbs, eggs, parsley, salt, pepper, cooked vegetables, and crabmeat. Mix well. Fill crab shells with mixture; bake for about 30 minutes. This can be used as a casserole also.

Yields 4 cups.

# Cha-Wa-Ke
## (Sarah Emily Tell)

The house was cool, and the moon was full and bright. A good night to take a walk, Sarah thought to herself. But it had been a long day, and in truth, she was feeling a bit tired this evening. So a cup of tea, a little sweet, and some TV were really about all Sarah could handle. But there was supposed to be a great movie on at eight o'clock, at least that was what the newspaper said. "A splendor of history and adventure," the critic claimed. High praise from that one, too, because he gave the majority of television specials two thumbs down. However, this movie was supposed to be different, and Sarah was looking forward to it.

At five minutes to eight, Sarah lit a fire in the fireplace and grabbed a blanket to wrap up in. The old easy chair with its lumpy stuffing and ragged little rips and tears was just perfect for movie watching. You could sit on it for hours and hours, and you didn't have to worry about your bottom going numb. There was nothing worse, as far as Sarah was concerned, than a numb bottom halfway through a great show. So maybe the chair wasn't too much to look at, but Sarah had no intentions of getting rid of it. It fit her needs perfectly, especially from the waist down.

Well, things were beginning just fine. The opening music was good, and the pictures of the actors showed that they were handsome enough. Sarah sat back a little farther to get as comfortable as she could. Then the movie started, and sadly things went downhill from there. It was supposed to be a western, a good old-fashioned shoot-'em-up between two men in love with the same woman. The newspaper didn't say a thing about Indians anywhere, because if they had, Sarah wouldn't have even sat down. Hollywood didn't know a thing about Indians—never had and probably never would. They turned them all into something akin to circus clowns, whooping and hollering from mountaintops for no reason at all. Then when you tried to talk to them, the Indians couldn't even speak in complete sentences. Instead they grunted out replies that resembled a bear stuck in a hunter's trap.

Well, Sarah turned the television off before she even had a chance to see which man got the girl. Both of 'em seemed like losers to her. The child would be better served by going home to her mama and staying put until somebody worthwhile came along.

Sarah placed the dirty dishes in the sink to soak. She was too upset to even wash them. Cowboys and Indians—white folks and red folks. It was a battle that seemed as old as time, but thankfully, as truth made its way into the open, the battle did seem to be dying out, and there was even a chance that everybody could win in the end.

When Larissa had asked Sarah to tell her all about Indians, Sarah had been honest and told her that she surely couldn't speak for all native peoples. All Sarah could do was tell her own story and the story of her fiercely proud people.

# Cha-Wa-Ke's Story

## Ani-Yun-Wiya (The Principle People)

The Cherokee called themselves Ani-Yun-Wiya, the Principle People, and they have lived for many, many years in a place of high mountains and beautiful green spaces that today folks call Southern Appalachia. In the beginning, the Cherokee saw this place as kind of an island, the center of the world dropped down from the heavens by way of solid rock ropes, but it was not always that way. Before the island was made, everyone lived up in the sky and it was very crowded, so the water beetle went down to explore the vast sea below. He found no land, but he dived below the water and surfaced with mud that began to grow until it became an island named Earth. The buzzard who had been circling the sky became tired and his wings hit hard upon the ground. Everywhere that he hit that was soft became a valley, and when he lifted his wings back up again, he formed a mountain. Well, thank you, Mr. Buzzard and Mr. Beetle, because you gave us an incredible home.

For thousands of years the southern Appalachian Mountains belonged to the Cherokee Nation. We are a people of principle, but we are also a people of harmony and balance. When a Cherokee hunter killed a deer, tradition demanded that he pray over that deer, begging forgiveness from the deer spirit for having taken its life and explaining that hungry Cherokee families needed the deer for food and clothing. This balance was also important if a Cherokee took a human life. If we lost any of our people in combat, we were required to take an equal number of lives from the tribe who had attacked us. Also, if one Cherokee killed another, the murderer's life, or that of a family member, had to be taken to keep the balance.

Just as we balanced death, we also balanced living. Everyone had their place and their responsibilities. The men had to hunt, patrol the hunting grounds, and dance. The women really worked the hardest, though. They had to farm, gather food, cook, raise the children, and make all the clothes, baskets, and cookware. Now, because the women did so much of the work, we had to balance that by giving women more power in our society. When a woman decided who she wanted to marry, the intended either had to build a new home or come to live in the wife's home. In either case, the house was the woman's property, as were any children from their marriage. Also, the wife decided if a deformed newborn should live, and if the father killed the baby, he was determined to be guilty of murder and possibly executed.

And of course, no woman was expected to stay with a man who was making her crazy. She could divorce him very easily. All she had to do was stuff her husband's clothes in a sack and set it outside the door. I like that system—all the paperwork you need today seems far too complicated to simply end a bad marriage. Just put him out the front door and shut it right behind him, that's what I say.

When I was a little girl we lived in small houses; the walls were made by weaving saplings between large posts and then covering them with mud, and the roofs were made by weaving saplings and covering them with bark shingles. We lived in small communities with all the homes built around the square in town. There were seven clans in one village, and each one had its own leader, or chief. Everyone lived close together and everybody worked together, and I loved growing up that way.

I know that way back in the old days, the Cherokee were a lot more traditional than they are now. The men used to wear cotton trade shirts, loincloths, leggings, front seam moccasins, beaded belts, multiple piercings around the rim of the ear, and a blanket over one shoulder. The women wore feathers, skirts of leather or woven mulberry bark, front seam moccasins, and an earring in their earlobe. Then that changed, and the men started wearing shirts, pants, and trade coats with a special kind of Cherokee turban. The women wore calico skirts, blouses, and shawls. That's the way I remember it as a child, but today we dress like everybody else except on very special occasions.

My childhood was a good one. I had seven brothers and sisters to play with, and because I was also the youngest, I was a little spoiled. Mama let me do pretty much what I wanted to, and even when I did misbehave she refused to spank me. Instead she would give me a stern look or a pinch on one of my shoulders. I went to school with all the other children in the village, and we learned to read and write English and also Cherokee. We hadn't had a written Cherokee language all that long at the time, and every parent was anxious for their child to really understand it. Finally, we would be able not only to tell our stories but write them as well. They were destined to last forever that way.

I was a mischievous child and was always into something or another. I think that was why when I told my mother I wanted to get married at seventeen, she didn't say no. I think she was more than ready to pass her headache on to someone else. Well, my husband was a good man, but he could have his own way of doing things, and sometimes his way wasn't my way, so we had some very lively discussions in our home. But we never stayed mad for long. We loved each other too much. We had six children together, who all still live in the mountains of North Carolina, before my husband died at the young age of thirty. Once the children were raised and grown, I moved to the eastern part of Carolina and I just love it. I do go home two or three times a year to see my family and friends, but it feels less and less like home, as more and more tourists trample through what used to be private spaces. I am getting used to it, though, so I guess it isn't so bad. It brings money to the village, and our people so desperately need that.

The Cherokees are a proud people, and they are survivors as well. Driven out of their home by the U.S. government in the 1830s, they were forced to move in a brutal Trail of Tears, yet they still maintained their connectedness. Now we are scattered all over the place, but we are still Cherokee. We will always be Cherokee—fierce, proud, and beautiful.

> We have taught our children the earth is our mother.
> Whatever befalls the earth, befalls the sons of the earth.
> This we know.
> The earth does not belong to man. The man belongs to earth.
> This we know.
> All things are connected. Like the blood which unites our family.
> All things are connected.
> Whatever befalls the earth, befalls the sons of earth.
> Man did not weave the web of life. He's merely a strand in it.
> Whatever he does to the web, he does to himself.
>
> *AiSv Nv wa do hi ya do.*
> (Walk in peace.)

# Bread! Bread! Bread!

*According to the story that the elders tell, there is a very good reason that we have the corn and beans that we use to make these wonderful breads, and her name was Selu.*

*The Cherokees say that the first man and woman were called Kana'ti and Selu, and they only had one child, called Wild Boy, whom they had managed to capture when he sprang from the river one day. They tried to tame him, but he was very mischievous.*

*Kana'ti was the hunter and he always brought home lots of meat so no one would ever be hungry. Selu provided the vegetables for the family, and she kept the beans and the corn in a storehouse. Well, one day Wild Boy followed her there. He watched as Selu stood in front of a basket, rubbed her stomach, and corn appeared in the basket. Then she rubbed her armpits and beans dropped in. Oh my, thought Wild Boy, Selu is a witch. He decided he had to kill her. Well, Selu knew just what he was going to do, but before she died, she told him what to do. Wild Boy needed to clear the land in front of the cabin, drag her body around the clearing seven times, and stay awake all night. If he did just as she told him, there would be plenty of corn in the morning. But Wild Boy was lazy. He only cleared a few little spots, and he dragged his mother's body over the ground only twice. So corn grew only in a few places and required lots of cultivation. Well, the Cherokees cultivated corn and beans from that day forward for several thousand years, and these next recipes celebrate that history. Enjoy!*

## BEAN BREAD

**2 cups cornmeal**

**1 teaspoon baking powder**

**2 eggs**

**1½ cups milk**

**2 cups cooked brown beans, drained**

Preheat the oven to 450°. Mix together cornmeal and baking powder; then add eggs and milk, mixing well. Stir in beans and pour into a greased pan. Bake for 20 minutes or until brown. Do not add salt to this recipe as it will cause the bread to crumble during cooking.

Yields 1 pan.

# FRY PAN CORN/BEAN FORK BREAD

½ cup dry kidney or black
    beans, rinsed

I bay leaf

2½ cups water

I teaspoon salt

I large onion, chopped

2 to 6 cloves garlic, minced

2 tablespoons corn oil

I cup cornmeal

I egg, beaten

¾ cup bean stock

2 teaspoons baking powder

I to 4 tablespoons
    chili powder

¾ cup grated cheese

¼ cup black olives, sliced

A few green onions, diced

I tomato, cut up very fine

Yields 4 to 6 servings.

Combine beans and water in a pan and bring to a boil. Boil for 1 minute. Remove from heat and let stand 1 hour. Return to a simmer and cook until very tender, adding salt during the last 15 minutes of cooking. Drain and measure the cooking liquid. Add enough water to measure ¾ cup.

Preheat the oven to 350°. Fry onion and garlic in the corn oil in a skillet that can go in the oven. Take out half of the onion and garlic, and mix it with the cornmeal, egg, beans, bean stock, baking powder, and chili powder. Mix thoroughly and pour into the skillet on top of the onion and garlic. Bake for 12 minutes; then sprinkle cheese, olives, green onion, and tomato; bake for 5 minutes longer. This is a fork-eating, not a pick-up, cornbread.

Unlike Selu, the Cherokee could not rely on magic to fill their baskets. Instead they had to rely on their hardworking women. My grandmother was one of those women. She said that the men might help a little with clearing the land or maybe even with the harvesting, but the tending of those fields was not their business. The women planted crops with pointed digging sticks, and the old women who could not do such backbreaking work sat in the middle of the fields chasing away crows and raccoons that tried to steal their food. Believe it or not, these women had their children with them, too. The older ones helped, but the younger ones were bound to a cradle board and left under a cool shade tree.

When the corn was ready, the women presented it to the village in the most important celebration of my people, the Green Corn Festival. Naturally there had to be good food at such a happy time, especially wonderful breads made from hand-crushed cornmeal. The Cherokees had no butter back then, but they did use bear grease or oil from nuts to give the breads that little something extra. Well, these next three recipes are made with cornmeal and they are easy to make, so I encourage you to give them a try. If you have a little bear grease, use it; if not, a little butter is just fine.

## CHEROKEE CORN PONES

**2 cups cornmeal**
**¼ teaspoon baking soda**
**I teaspoon salt**
**½ cup shortening**
**¾ cup buttermilk**
**¾ cup milk**
**Butter**

Yields 8 corn pones.

Preheat the oven to 400°. In a medium-sized bowl, combine cornmeal, baking soda, and salt. Cut in shortening with a pastry blender until mixture resembles coarse meal. Add buttermilk and milk, stirring just until dry ingredients are moistened. Form batter into eight ½-inch-thick cakes. Place on a greased pan and bake for 15 minutes. Turn cakes over and bake an additional 15 minutes. Serve hot with butter.

## LUMBEE CORN PATTIES

**I cup yellow cornmeal**
**I cup milk**
**½ teaspoon salt**
**I tablespoon shortening**

Yields 12 patties.

Combine cornmeal and milk in a medium-sized bowl. Add salt and shortening. Mix again. Drop batter by tablespoonfuls onto a hot, lightly greased griddle or frying pan. Turn when corners are brown and center is bubbly. Serve hot with butter.

# SQUAW BREAD

2 cups water
⅓ cup oil
¼ cup honey
¼ cup raisins
5 tablespoons brown sugar,
    divided
2 packages active dry yeast
¼ cup warm water
2½ cups unbleached
    all-purpose flour, divided
3 cups whole wheat flour,
    divided
½ cup nonfat dry
    milk powder
2½ teaspoons salt
1½ cups rye flour
Cornmeal
Melted butter

Yields 4 loaves.

Combine 2 cups water, oil, honey, raisins, and 4 tablespoons brown sugar in a blender; liquefy. Soften the yeast in ¼ cup warm water with the remaining 1 tablespoon brown sugar. Sift together 1 cup all-purpose flour, 2 cups whole wheat flour, powdered milk, and the salt in a large bowl. Add honey and yeast mixtures. Beat at medium speed until smooth (2 minutes).

Gradually stir in enough of the remaining flours to make a soft dough that leaves the sides of the bowl. Turn out onto floured surface and knead until smooth and satiny (10 to 12 minutes). Place dough in lightly greased bowl and turn to grease surface. Cover and let rise until doubled in bulk, about 1½ hours.

Punch down and let rest 10 minutes. Divide dough into 4 round loaves, and place on greased cookie sheets sprinkled with cornmeal. Cover and let rise in warm place until doubled in bulk (1 hour).

Preheat the oven to 375°. Bake loaves for about 30 to 35 minutes. Brush with melted butter and cool on wire racks when done.

*If you eat our breads, you should also understand our hearts and our souls. Cherokees are wise people who try to live in harmony and truth.*

## INDIAN FRY BREAD

**2 cups flour**

**½ teaspoon salt**

**4 teaspoons baking powder**

**I egg, beaten**

**½ cup warm milk**

**I¾ cups shortening or lard for frying**

Sift together flour, salt, and baking powder. Stir in beaten egg. Add milk to make a soft dough. On a lightly floured board, knead dough mixture lightly. Roll or pat out ¼ inch thick. Fry in about an inch of shortening or lard in skillet, turning once, until brown. Drain on paper towels. Serve hot.

Yields 1 loaf.

*This bread is so quick and easy that I can whip it up at the last minute when I have unexpected company for dinner.*

## INAGAMI-PAKWEJIGAN (SOFT BREAD)

**I¾ cups water**

**⅔ cup white corn flour**

**¾ teaspoon salt**

**Margarine or shortening**

**Sunflower seeds**

Bring the water to a boil. In a medium bowl, mix together the flour and salt. Pour boiling water onto the dry ingredients while stirring. Continue to stir until the mixture becomes thick and uniform. Serve in a bowl topped with margarine and sunflower seeds.

Yields 1 loaf.

*This is a great bread to make for the little ones. It has just enough sweet to keep them coming back for more.*

## CHIPPEWA INDIAN FRIED BREAD

**2½ cups all-purpose flour**
**1½ tablespoons**
**baking powder**
**1 teaspoon salt**
**¾ cup warm water**
**1 tablespoon vegetable oil**
**1 tablespoon nonfat**
**dry milk powder**
**Vegetable oil**
**(for deep frying)**
**Cinnamon sugar**

Yields 8 servings.

Combine flour, baking powder, and salt in a large bowl. Combine water, oil, and dry milk, and stir into flour mixture until smooth dough forms. Turn out onto lightly floured surface. Knead 4 times into smooth ball. Cover and let rest 10 minutes.

Divide dough into 8 balls. Flatten with fingertips or roll out each ball to form an 8-to-10-inch round. Make a small hole in the center of each with finger or handle of wooden spoon. Lightly flour rounds, stack, and cover with towel or plastic wrap. Heat about 1 inch oil to 375° in large skillet. Gently place 1 bread round in hot fat, and cook until golden and crisp, 1 to 2 minutes on each side. Drain on paper towels. Repeat with remaining dough. Serve bread hot or at room temperature, sprinkled with cinnamon sugar.

*The Cherokee world in western North Carolina is a lot different from when I was a little girl. Now the tourists come from all over to see what we are all about. Unfortunately, to appease these folks, the Cherokee sometimes show off things that were never a part of us—things like big feather headdresses and teepees. There is a little restaurant there now that's run by a friend of mine, and thank goodness, her delicacies are as true blue as it gets. This next recipe is hers, and she claims that folks from everywhere just love this pudding and eat it almost as fast as she can make it.*

## INDIAN PUDDING

**4 cups whole milk**

**½ cup yellow cornmeal**

**½ cup maple syrup**

**¼ cup molasses, light**

**2 eggs, slightly beaten**

**2 tablespoons butter or margarine, melted**

**⅓ cup brown sugar, packed**

**I teaspoon salt**

**¼ teaspoon cinnamon**

**¾ teaspoon ginger**

**½ cup whole milk, cold**

Yields 8 servings.

Heat the milk in the top of a double boiler; slowly stir in cornmeal. Cook over boiling water, stirring occasionally, about 20 minutes.

Preheat the oven to 300°. Lightly grease a 2-quart baking dish. In a small bowl, combine maple syrup, molasses, eggs, melted butter or margarine, brown sugar, salt, cinnamon, and ginger. Add this mixture to the cornmeal mixture; mix well.

Turn into a greased baking dish; pour cold milk on top but do not stir. Bake uncovered for 2 hours, or just until set but quivery on top. Do not overbake. Let stand 30 minutes before serving. Serve warm, with vanilla ice cream or light cream.

*I have a sweet tooth that must be a mile long and just as high, because I love dessert. Either of these next two recipes will do in a pinch when I need a little pick-me-up.*

## GOOSEBERRY COBBLER

**2 cups flour**
**½ cup cornmeal plus 2**
   **tablespoons**
**½ teaspoon baking powder**
**I teaspoon salt**
**¾ cup butter or margarine**
**¾ cup boiling water**
**2 (15-ounce) cans sweetened**
   **whole gooseberries,**
   **divided**
**I tablespoon honey**
**Juice of ½ lemon**

Yields 1 pan.

Preheat the oven to 425°. In a medium-sized bowl, sift the flour with ½ cup cornmeal, baking powder, and salt. Using a pastry blender, cut in butter or margarine. Add the boiling water, mixing quickly but thoroughly. Divide the dough in half, and pat half of it into a greased 8x8x2-inch pan. Sprinkle with 1 tablespoon cornmeal. Mash half of the gooseberries in their syrup; then stir in remaining gooseberries, honey, and lemon juice; pour over the dough. Pat the remaining dough into a square and place on top of the filling. Sprinkle with remaining tablespoon of cornmeal.

Bake for 30 minutes or until top is lightly browned. To serve, cut into squares.

## GRAPE DUMPLINGS

I cup water

I cup flour

I teaspoon baking powder

2 tablespoons shortening,
   melted

Grapes, enough to make
   2 quarts juice, or use
   2 quarts pure grape juice

Yields 1 large pot of
dumplings.

Mix together the water, flour, and baking powder. Add melted shortening; continue mixing until it reaches the consistency of a stiff dough. On a lightly floured surface, roll out dough to ¼ inch thick. Cut into small strips about ½ inch by 1 inch.

Stem and wash grapes. Place them in a saucepan with enough water to barely cover them. Cook over medium heat until they are very soft, and mash with a potato masher. Put a piece of cheese-cloth over the pan, and pour the juice through. Add sugar to suit your taste, and bring the juice to a boil in a large pan.

Drop dumplings, one at a time, into the boiling juice. Cook for about 5 minutes; then reduce heat and simmer for 10 minutes or more, until the dumplings are done.

*My sister gave me this recipe when she was here last year. I took these cookies to a tea with the ladies at the center, and they ate every single one.*

# PUMPKIN COOKIES

½ cup shortening

I cup sugar

2 eggs

I½ cups cooked pumpkin

½ teaspoon salt

½ teaspoon nutmeg

¼ teaspoon ginger

½ teaspoon cinnamon

2½ cups flour, less 2 teaspoons

4 teaspoons baking powder

I cup raisins or dates

I cup nuts, chopped

I teaspoon lemon extract

Preheat the oven to 400°. In a large mixing bowl, cream shortening and sugar. Add eggs, pumpkin, salt, nutmeg, ginger, and cinnamon. Blend well. Sift flour and baking powder and add to pumpkin mixture. Blend until smooth. Stir in raisins, nuts, and lemon extract. Drop by teaspoons onto greased cookie sheets and bake for 15 minutes.

Yields 3 dozen.

*The world is a different place from what it used to be, and I for one am glad of it. Now people who are different are at least trying to understand one another. Now we can feel free to share our food and our stories, making new friends all the while. I made this bread for the ladies at the center the very first month I moved here. They were strangers to me then, but now they're like family. I really believe that food just brings people together, don't you?*

## ANISH-NAH-BE PAKWEJIGAN
## (REAL INDIAN BREAD)

**1 recipe of**
  **Inagami-Pakwejigan**
  **(Soft Bread; see page 106)**
**⅔ cup sunflower oil**
**½ cup blueberries or raisins**

Yields 1 loaf.

Let the soft bread dough cool to room temperature. Mix in the blueberries or raisins and put the dough into a bowl. Chill until it thickens. When the dough is firm, cut it into ½-inch slices, and fry in sunflower oil until it is a golden color. Serve hot with maple syrup.

# Annie Lee Watkins

The sun was bright and pretty that Saturday afternoon, but last night had been a sleepless one for Annie Lee Watkins. So instead of finding the endlessly bright beams warm and comforting, they were now punctuating her migraine headache with annoying little punctuation marks. But she was headed to a wedding, and any hint of love in the air usually picked up her spirits. She was certain she'd be feeling better in no time, so Annie stepped a little livelier. It was almost two, and the invitation had read two o'clock sharp and it sounded as if these folks meant business.

She really didn't know any of these people that well, so Annie was surprised that she was included in such a personal occasion. She didn't know the groom at all and she barely knew the bride, Susan, or her family. They owned a little shop downtown where folks often stopped in to get a cup of coffee and a newspaper, but Annie hadn't been in there as of late. The last time she had stopped in, she'd complained about the splintery wood floor. Well, instead of fixing it, those crazy folks had simply covered the entire place with newspaper. It was scattered from hither to yonder. Why not a rug? Annie Lee wanted to know. They did have a Sears in town after all. Who wants to sip their coffee with newspaper rustling under their feet? Well, Annie Lee hadn't been back since, nor had she heard a word from them, at least not until the invitation came in the mail a week ago. But despite it all, Annie had decided to join in the festivities, and she had even bought the couple a gift. She'd started to buy 'em a rug, but that might have hurt their feelings, so she'd gotten 'em a clock instead. It had taken a good while to decide—what would be perfect to give, that is—but a clock seemed pretty good. Of course, these were some strange folks, so who could really know what would be perfect for them.

Annie had assumed that the ceremony was going to be in some kind of church or reception hall, but the directions were, surprisingly, taking her into a residential area. It wasn't very far, but Annie had to pay careful attention because she had never been in this part of town before. Well, two short blocks and ten minutes later, Annie had arrived. But what kind of place was this to hold a wedding? she wondered. Somebody had hung laundry out in the front of the house instead of in the back, like anybody with good sense was supposed to, and that wasn't the worst of it. There was a raggedy old sofa between a near-dead rosebush and the left side of the house. There were also an easy chair and four old coffee tables right nearby, where two big dogs were sitting as bold as you please. Not too long ago the county had passed a "beautiful home and garden" ordinance that required residents to remove all junk from their front yards. Well, apparently no one that lived here was paying the ordinance any attention.

The dogs seem to be harmless, but Annie wasn't taking any chances. She pushed the gate open slowly to see what their reaction would be, but they didn't even look in her direction. Annie made it to the front door and knocked. In a moment, it opened up just wide enough for a hairy arm to stick itself out and wave her inside. Once in the living room, she was greeted by a barefoot woman in a calico dress (the invitation did say casual, but surely they meant shoes), who then pointed to a table lined with buckets of chicken wings (the buffet) and a cooler full of beer (the open bar) and invited Annie to help herself, but Annie decided to pass. After that, everything kind of all ran together, fading into one huge chaotic blur.

The guests were seated in hard folding chairs and waited endlessly for the wedding to begin. There was no preacher; they had bribed a notary instead and he was late. When he finally got there, Susan's brother had desperately tried to fix the cassette player in order to play their dime-store copy of "Here Comes the Bride." But it had obviously been around for a while and stubbornly refused to work. It was then that Susan's father had come racing down the steps to lend a hand, but it did absolutely no good, so the two finally gave up in frustration. However, they were evidently not without options because with the father directing all the while, the brother proceeded to jump in his pickup and drive it through the open sliding glass doors, playing the bridal march at full volume on the truck stereo.

The bride didn't wait for the father to come up and get her. Instead she raced down the steps wearing a cheap white dress and bright purple plastic shoes. The groom walked stiffly to the front as if someone was holding a gun to his back, and with a muddy blue pickup for a centerpiece and twenty very hot and very tired witnesses, exchanged vows with his bride. Annie never did actually hear anybody say "I do" because they both mumbled so badly. But then again, the notary didn't seem to know what he was suppose to say either, because he read some, misquoted the rest, and completely skipped whole sections in the middle. When questioned by the father, he swore the marrying was legal because he did get in all the important parts, but Dad wasn't completely satisfied. So he only paid the notary ten dollars instead of twenty, since he felt he had only gotten half of what he was supposed to. The notary protested, but Dad stuck to his guns, insisting that ten dollars was all a partial marrying was worth. "And the groom is worth less than that," he'd added laughingly.

Well, when Annie Lee Watkins had seen enough, she handed the couple their clock, wished them all the best, and grabbed a chicken wing to snack on while walking to the bus stop. When she got home, she undressed quickly, got into bed, and put a cool cloth on her head. She had lived in the North Carolina mountains for sixty years and here in the eastern part for almost fifteen. She really thought she had seen it all, but clearly that was not true. Annie closed her eyes for a moment and thought back to the craziness of the day. "And folks call my people backwards," she muttered in disbelief. "Well, if we are indeed the ignorant hillbillies they label us, I wonder what in the world they call those people that I saw today?"

# Annie Lee Watkins's Story

## Just Plain Mountain Folk

Back where I come from, the mountains of North Carolina seem to jes' rise up outta nowhere and knock right at God's front door. When you're there, it's jes' like you a-settin' on top of the world. I done stood on my porch many a day and looked out as far as my eyes could see. I declare I could see clear to Tennessee, but my mama said there wasn't no way I could see that far. I don't know, though, it sure looked like Tennessee to me.

My people were them good-natured, rowdy Scotch-Irish folks, who came from way 'cross the seas lookin' for a place to lay down their hats and call their new home. They was wanderers, but they ain't jes' wander for nothin'. They was lookin'—lookin' for land and lots of it. They found it, too. They settled themselves in the valley between the pretty Blue Ridge Mountains and the great big North Mountain. But they wasn't alone. The French, Germans, English, and Irish came here, too, and they was looking for pretty much the same thing my people was lookin' for. 'Course the Indians was already around and had been for quite some time, but there was more than enough room for everybody, so we all hung around. At first we musta all got along, 'cause there's a whole lot of mixed-up folks there today—Irish, Scotch-Irish, French, German, and Cherokee. I figure couldn't none of 'em help but stay put once they got to that pretty, pretty place. The land is so green and the sky is so blue that it looks jes' like somebody come along and painted it all in place. Oh, you ought to see it!

My daddy used to stick out his chest and tell anybody who would listen that our people done been here since America first came to be America. In fact, we helped to make it happen. Them Scotch-Irish—fearless, determined, and stubborn—hated that English government more than anything, so when it come time to fight, they fought harder than jes' 'bout anybody. Even George Washington hisself said so.

After that we don't know too much 'bout our kin 'til sometime 'round the Civil War. Oh, we know some names and such, but that's 'bout all. My great-grandmother was the first one I remembered hearing 'bout. She was one of my mama's people, but we don't know a whole lot 'bout Daddy's 'cause they was down near Georgia somewhere. But this here great-grandmother, her name was Laurel, and I think people always gonna have a little something to say 'bout her 'cause that woman was a case and a half.

My daddy used to say that the Civil War wasn't our fight. I mean we ain't had slaves, nobody up in the hills did. We could barely feed ourselves, so we sure didn't have no money to be buying or feeding nobody extra. We was working farmers, and if there was anything that needed doing, we was the one to do it. But you know men: the fact that they ain't had no business in something don't mean they gonna stay the heck out of it—'specially a good fight. Well, my great-grandpa was a man like any man, so when the war came to pass, off he went like Johnny-got-his-gun and joined up with the Union. Well, folks might not have had slaves, but they sure had plenty of opinions and 'bout half of 'em said the Union was right, and the others, well, they settled their hearts with the Confederacy. People 'round them mountains 'bout tore themselves in two over that mess. One church even had one door for the Union folks and one door for the Confederates. I guess if you didn't care for either, you couldn't get in.

Well, off my great-grandpa went to fight, leaving my great-grandma all by her lonesome, well 'cept for a few babies and a goat or two. Things was sure tough, but my folks ain't ones to roll over and jes' die. That woman worked that place good as any man. She took care of everybody she needed to and even sold moonshine to get a little extra. One time, some of the men who lived the next farm over thought they could jes' take them some moonshine. Jes' take it! Well, they was messin' with the wrong woman. When they climbed over that fence one night, ready for mayhem and mischief, Great-grandma Laurel was waiting for 'em. She filled their britches with so much buckshot, they didn't sit for a year without thinkin' of her first. Well, didn't nobody mess with her after that.

My grandma said that her daddy didn't come home for years and years. She figures she was 'bout six 'fore she laid eyes on him again. Even then, it took a good while before he was made to feel welcome, but he must of wormed his way back into his wife's heart some kind of way 'cause they had five more babies after that!

My grandma was a quiet little lady, who kind of kept to herself and spent her time taking care of my grandpa. We used to go 'round their place on the weekends when I was little, and she would feed us pie and sweet tea until we had so much sugar in us we didn't act like we had a lick of sense. She died when I was 'bout ten, and I remember my mama cried every day after for almost a month. I didn't think she would ever stop, but I missed my grandma, too, so I know how she felt.

My mother was sweet like her mama, but she had a strong backbone like my great-grandma! She'd smile at you one minute, but grab hold and shake you 'til your teeth rattled in the next. Didn't none of us try to trouble her too much, so even though there was ten of us, things was pretty peaceful 'round our place. Besides, by the time you cleaned the house, weeded the garden, milked the cows, and fed the hogs, you didn't have enough strength to fight nobody too much. If idleness is the devil's workshop, then he must of never come near us, 'cause I don't remember too many free moments, but I have fond memories of those days and I tell you, I wouldn't change a thing.

I met my husband when he came to the hills to work the coal mines. It was dirty, dangerous work that paid almost nothing, but it was the job my husband chose to do, so I went along with it. Seem like every week, almost, there was an explosion of some kind, and the women would gather together then and wait to hear if their men were among the dead or near dead. I was scared everyday my James went to work. So I prayed and I prayed, but it wasn't God's will that we have a long life together. My James was killed five years after we was married. We never had no babies, so I was all alone after we buried him. I never married again. I moved back home with my mama and did a little of this and a little of that for the next thirty years or so, just to keep a good meal on the table and a decent dress on my back. After my mama and daddy died, I moved here to the coast so I could look at something a little different, and I like it, at least I think so.

Folks call my people a little bit of everything—Appalachian, hillbillies, and mountain people. Some talk 'bout us like we haven't got a lick of good sense, and others say we are the best folks in all the world. We are simple, I agree with that. We don't like nothin' that's hard to understand. We ain't got time for no whole lot of figuring, but we sure ain't stupid. We're just plain folks, good folks, who love good clean living and lots of good food.

# Mountain-High Goodies

*Little Larissa couldn't believe that when I was a child there was never a dull moment, but there wasn't. When I was a little girl, there wasn't nothin' easy 'bout nothin'—not even a pan of cornbread. You see, the work ain't never begun when you pulled out that pan to make it. No sir, it all started way long before that, out in the fields.*

*See, like just 'bout everybody else 'round there, we grew our own corn and lots of it. Well, you couldn't handle all that corn by yourself; you had to get some folks to help you, so you had you a corn shucking—sometimes a great big one. Now, when it come time to shuck, my mama and my daddy would go out early one morning when that corn was ready, and they would pick as much as they could. Then they'd put it in great big piles right by the corncrib. That's when you bring all your family and friends in. Folks gather 'round them piles, shuck that corn, toss them shucks on behind 'em, and then pitch that corn in the crib. You get you a good group and you could shuck a mess of corn in no time.*

*Of course, after all that shucking, you had to feed them suckers. So the women got busy in the kitchen and fixed up more food than you ever seen in your life.*

*After the corn shucking, we would fill up the feed house for the cows, hogs, and horses, and then we would take the rest of it down the road to the mill. It had a big old wheel that the water turned 'round and 'round. You gave them your corn, and after a while they gave you back some meal. Now you was ready to make bread.*

*Corn fritters are so versatile, they go with just about anything. I used to take a few, wrap them in a napkin, and shove them in my pocket. By the time I got to where I was going, I had a big grin on my face and nobody knew why.*

## CORN FRITTERS

**1 egg**
**¼ cup milk**
**1¼ cups flour**
**½ teaspoon salt**
**1 tablespoon unsalted butter, melted**
**1 cup creamed corn**
**Oil for deep frying**

Combine all ingredients except the oil. Drop by the tablespoonful into deep oil and fry until golden brown.

Yields 24 small fritters.

*When we made gritted cornbread, we always used the white cornmeal. Now the young folks will use the yellow or the white. My mama used to say white cornmeal is for folks and the yellow was what you fed to critters. I still hold to that today. You make cornbread with white cornmeal, and for goodness sakes, don't add sugar. If you do, it ain't good gritted cornbread!*

## GRITTED CORNBREAD

1 ¼ cups gritted cornmeal
½ cup all-purpose flour
1 teaspoon salt
2½ teaspoons baking powder
2 tablespoons bacon grease
Water as needed

Preheat the oven to 450°. Combine cornmeal, flour, salt, and baking powder in a bowl. Add bacon grease and enough water to form a soft dough. Mix ingredients thoroughly, stirring until mixture is smooth and creamy, the consistency of gravy. Pour into an 8-inch square pan; bake approximately 25 minutes.

Yields 1 pan.

*When Mama whipped up these cornmeal batter cakes, no one went away hungry. I still fix these for myself because they're so quick and easy.*

## CORNMEAL BATTER CAKES

1 cup cornmeal
½ teaspoon baking soda
¼ teaspoon salt
2 eggs, beaten
1½ cups buttermilk
2 teaspoons bacon drippings

Sift together cornmeal, baking soda, and salt. Add beaten eggs and buttermilk. Stir until smooth; then add bacon drippings and mix well. Drop a tablespoon of batter onto a hot greased skillet. Let brown on bottom, turn quickly, and brown on the other side. Serve with butter and syrup.

Yields 20 cakes.

*Mama never made these unless she had a little fatback or bacon to go along with them. She usually made them on Sunday mornings so that way we could carry 'em with us on down the hill to church. She even carried a rag in her pocket so she could wipe our greasy hands and mouths right before the service started.*

## CORNMEAL ROLLS

1¼ cups flour
¾ cup cornmeal
½ teaspoon salt
4 teaspoons baking powder
1 tablespoon sugar
2 tablespoons Crisco
1 egg, well beaten
½ cup milk

Preheat the oven to 450°. In a large mixing bowl, sift together flour, cornmeal, salt, baking powder, and sugar. Rub in Crisco with fingertips, then add well-beaten egg and milk. Roll out and cut into rounds with a large cutter. Place on a baking sheet. Brush over with melted Crisco, fold over, and brush tops with beaten egg or milk. Bake for 10 minutes.

Yields 15 rolls.

*We had cornmeal dumplings whenever we had soup or stew. It gave the meal that little bit extra that would keep you good and full for quite a while.*

## CORNMEAL DUMPLINGS

8 cups vegetable, greens, or
  beef stock liquid
1 cup all-purpose cornmeal
¼ cup flour
1 teaspoon baking powder
½ teaspoon salt
2 eggs
½ cup milk
1 tablespoon butter, melted

Have the liquid hot and simmering. Mix together cornmeal, flour, baking powder, and salt. In a separate bowl, beat the eggs to a froth and add milk; blend in cornmeal mixture. Stir in melted butter. Drop batter from a teaspoon into boiling vegetable liquid, cover, and cook 12 minutes. Remove dumplings from pot.

Yields 4 to 6 servings.

*Fall was always a time when the land lit up like magic. It was so beautiful that all you wanted to do was climb up in the crook of a big old tree and just watch the leaves turn red and yellow, one by one. But there was just too much to do—smoking, salting, drying, and spicing the meat, and of course, putting up the summer fruits and vegetables. My mama used to can anything and everything she could find, but her favorite was apples. By the time Mama was through, we had enough apples for months to come. These dumplings were her specialty and I still make 'em when I want a little sweet.*

# APPLE DUMPLINGS

**3 cups flour**
**2 teaspoons baking powder**
**¼ teaspoon salt**
**4 tablespoons Crisco**
**¾ cup milk**
**5 apples**
**Sugar**
**Cinnamon**

Yields 5 dumplings.

Preheat the oven to 375°. In a large mixing bowl, sift flour, baking powder, and salt together. Work in Crisco with fingertips. Gradually add milk, mixing with a knife, to form a nice dough. Roll ½ inch thick, cut into squares, and lay in the center of each square an apple, peeled and cored. Fill up centers of apples with sugar and cinnamon; take corners of the dough and pinch together. Place in greased baking pan, dot over with sugar and Crisco, and bake for 25 minutes or until nicely browned. Serve hot with milk.

# A Touch of the Irish

*The plain folks have always had a whole lot of good sense. Listen to them and you'll start to understand a few things:*

> *The Lord stands between us and all harm.*
> *Marry a woman from the mountain, and you marry the mountain.*
> *A mother's love is a blessing.*

*And finally:*

> *God's help is nearer than the door.*

## IRISH SODA BREAD

**2 cups all-purpose flour**
**2 tablespoons white sugar**
**½ teaspoon soda**
**½ teaspoon baking powder**
**½ teaspoon salt**
**2 tablespoons butter**
**1 cup buttermilk**
**½ cup dried currants**

Yields 8 servings.

Preheat the oven to 375°. Combine flour, sugar, baking soda, baking powder, and salt. Cut butter into flour mixture with pastry cutter. Add buttermilk until dough is soft. Stir in currants.

Turn dough out onto a lightly floured surface. Knead for 5 minutes or until smooth. Form dough into a 7-inch round. Place on a lightly oiled cake pan or cookie sheet. Score with a cross ½ inch deep on the top. Bake for 40 minutes.

*My daddy used to also grow wheat and rye, so naturally we had breads that used wheat flour. This is one of the easiest.*

## IRISH WHEATEN BREAD

**I cup all-purpose flour**

**2 tablespoons sugar**

**I package Rapid Rise yeast**

**¾ teaspoon salt**

**½ teaspoon baking soda**

**3 tablespoons butter, softened**

**I cup buttermilk**

**¼ cup warm water**

**2¼ cups whole wheat flour**

Yields 1 loaf.

Combine all dry ingredients in a large bowl, except the whole wheat flour. Heat butter, buttermilk, and water until very warm (125°); the mixture will curdle, so not to worry. Stir liquids into dry ingredients. Stir in enough whole wheat flour to make a stiff dough. Remove dough to lightly floured surface and form into a smooth 5-inch ball, adding more wheat flour if necessary.

Place in a 9-inch pan. Cover and let rise until doubled in bulk for about 45 minutes in a warm, draft-free place.

Preheat the oven to 375°. With a sharp knife, cut an "X" in the top of the dough (about ½ inch deep). Bake for about 35 minutes, until done. Remove from pan and cool on a wire rack.

*Once a year at the church, we'd have a foot washing on a Communion Sunday. They'd stack white towels at the end of each pew, and after the bread, the wine, and the prayers, you would wash your friends' feet and they would wash yours. This was our way of humbling ourselves like Christ done. After the service there was always food, and this bread was always one Mama would bring.*

# IRISH BATTER BREAD

**3 cups all-purpose flour**

**½ cup sugar**

**4 teaspoons baking powder**

**2 teaspoons cinnamon**

**1 teaspoon salt**

**2 tablespoons shortening, melted**

**1 egg, well beaten**

**1½ cups milk**

**3 tablespoons grated orange peel**

**1 cup (5 ounces) currants or raisins**

Yields 1 loaf.

Sift together flour, sugar, baking powder, cinnamon, and salt. Blend in shortening. Make a well in the center of ingredients and add egg, milk, orange peel, and currants or raisins all at one time. Beat until smooth. Turn dough into a greased 9x5x3-inch loaf pan. Let stand at room temperature for 20 minutes. Meanwhile preheat the oven to 325°; then bake the loaf for 1 to 1¼ hours until done.

NOTE: This bread should be stored in plastic wrap for 12 to 24 hours before serving so it will slice properly and have a moist texture.

*Up until the turn of the last century, my mama and all the women that come before her always made their bread in the fireplace. They used this little oven that sat on three legs. You put coals on top of that oven and under it, and Mama says it was the best bread ever. Well, the day I was born she got her first four-eye cast-iron wood stove. It was something else. She used to say she didn't know which she was happier to see, me or that contraption, but she always laughed when she said it, so I know it was me.*

*I learned how to cook on a wood stove, and for the longest time I couldn't figure out these modern ovens, but I can work them now. Well, you can make this next bread no matter what kind of oven you have—long as it works.*

# SOUR CREAM SODA BREAD

**4 cups all-purpose flour**

**I cup white sugar**

**I teaspoon baking soda**

**2 teaspoons baking powder**

**½ teaspoon salt**

**3 eggs**

**I pint sour cream**

**1½ cups raisins**

Yields 2 loaves.

Preheat the oven to 325°. Mix the flour, sugar, baking soda, baking powder, and salt in a large bowl. Add the eggs, sour cream, and raisins and mix until just combined. Distribute batter evenly between two 8x4x3-inch loaf pans. Bake for 1 hour.

*There's a whole lot a ways to enjoy spoonbread. You can butter it, dip it in syrup, or dab it with a little jam. But me, I like mine with buttermilk, or better yet, crumbled right up in the buttermilk. You can mash it up in the glass and then eat it spoon by spoon. Well, no matter how you eat it, I just know you'll love this spoonbread!*

# MOUNTAIN SPOONBREAD

**2 cups milk**

**¾ cup sifted white cornmeal**

**I teaspoon salt**

**3 tablespoons butter**

**3 eggs, separated**

Yields 1 pan.

Preheat the oven to 350°. Heat milk in a double boiler until steaming. Add cornmeal slowly. Stir and cook until it becomes a thick white sauce. Add salt and butter. Beat egg yolks and stir into cornmeal mixture. Then fold in stiffly beaten egg whites. Pour into buttered baking dish and bake for 30 minutes.

*I take these muffins to the senior center to our weekly checkers game. It makes that beating I give 'em a little easier to take, I reckon.*

## BLACK MUFFINS

¾ cup hot water

½ cup molasses

¼ cup milk

2 cups whole wheat flour

I cup all-purpose flour

¾ cup sugar

3 tablespoons baking powder

I teaspoon baking soda

I teaspoon salt

I½ cups chopped dry-roasted pecans

Preheat the oven to 300°. In a medium-sized bowl, combine the hot water and molasses, stirring until well blended. Stir in the milk until blended. In a large bowl, sift together the flours, sugar, baking powder, baking soda, and salt. With a rubber spatula, fold the liquid mixture and the pecans into the dry ingredients just until the flour is thoroughly incorporated; do not overmix. Spoon into 12 greased muffin cups. Bake until done, 45 minutes to 1 hour. Remove from pan immediately and serve while hot.

Yields 12 muffins.

*This recipe is a new one I've learned in the last few years. Mama didn't like anything spicy, but I do and this bread is one of my favorites.*

## SPICY CORNBREAD

2 cups all-purpose flour

I cup yellow cornmeal

⅓ cup white sugar

4½ teaspoons baking powder

I½ teaspoons salt

I½ teaspoons cayenne pepper

½ cup shortening

I½ cups milk

2 eggs, beaten

4½ teaspoons hot pepper sauce

Preheat the oven and skillet to 400°. In a large bowl, mix together flour, cornmeal, sugar, baking powder, salt, and cayenne pepper. Cut in shortening until the mixture resembles coarse breadcrumbs. In a small bowl, beat together milk, eggs, and hot pepper sauce. Stir milk mixture into the flour mixture until just blended. Remove hot skillet from oven, spray with nonstick cooking spray, and pour batter into skillet. Bake for 20 to 25 minutes, or until a toothpick inserted into center of loaf comes out clean.

Yields 12 servings.

*Here is another bread with a little zing, but it isn't as hot as that last recipe, so if you couldn't handle that spicy cornbread, maybe this one will go a little easier on you.*

# SPICE BREAD

1¼ cups flour

2 teaspoons baking powder

½ teaspoon baking soda

1 teaspoon mixed spices
  (equal parts cinnamon,
  nutmeg, and allspice)

½ teaspoon ginger

½ cup light brown sugar

¼ cup candied peel, chopped

¾ cup raisins, plain or golden

½ cup butter

¾ cup dark corn syrup

1 large egg, beaten

4 tablespoons milk

Yields 1 loaf.

Preheat the oven to 325°. In a large bowl, sift together flour, baking powder, baking soda, mixed spices, and ginger. Add brown sugar, chopped peel, and raisins; mix well. Make a well in the center. Melt the butter with the syrup over low heat and then pour into the well. Add the beaten egg and milk; mix well. Pour into a greased 8-inch loaf pan and bake for 40 to 50 minutes, or until it tests done.

*This tasty bread is loaded with fruit and flavor. It was one of Mama's favorite recipes, and she used to make it for special occasions.*

## BARM BRACK BREAD

**I package active dry yeast**

**¼ cup lukewarm milk**

**2 tablespoons sugar**

**3½ cups flour**

**½ teaspoon salt**

**½ teaspoon nutmeg**

**½ teaspoon cinnamon**

**I cup lukewarm milk**

**3 tablespoons butter,**
    **softened**

**2 eggs**

**I cup white raisins**

**½ cup dried currants**

**½ cup candied lemon peel,**
    **chopped**

Yields 1 loaf.

Preheat the oven to 375°. Combine yeast, milk, and sugar. Let stand 5 minutes till bubbly. In a large bowl, blend the flour, salt, nutmeg, and cinnamon. Add the yeast mixture, 1 cup milk, butter, and eggs. Beat until smooth. Add the raisins, currants, and peel; blend well into the dough.

Place dough in a buttered 10-inch tube pan and cover; let it rise in a warm place for an hour.

Bake the bread for 1 hour, or until it has a light brown color and sounds hollow when tapped. If the bread seems to brown too quickly, cover the top with a piece of aluminum foil. Remove from oven; let bread stand in the pan for 10 minutes before removing. Cool on a wire rack. Can be served warm with butter.

# Mrs. Rachel Cohen

Zoe was having a bad night, and she let Rachel know it as soon as she walked through the door.

"My act went completely flat tonight. I could just feel it. I threw it all out there as best I could, but the whole routine took a nose dive somewhere around the middle, and then just stubbornly resisted any attempts on my part to lift it up and get it moving again. That audience just sat there and stared at me with that same pitiful look my mother does whenever I show up at a family shindig with six more strands of gray hair and still no man on my arm."

Zoe was a thirty-five-year-old comedian from up north who was making her first performance tour through the South. Rachel didn't know her personally, but her mother was the distant cousin of a dear friend, so Rachel had promised faithfully that she would keep an eye on the child. At the time, the request hadn't appeared as if it would be very much trouble, and it hadn't been. Rachel had always loved comedy, from vaudeville to Milton Berle, so the chance to have a few laughs seemed like it might be fun. Truthfully, looking back on the evening, she had enjoyed herself. Zoe was really quite funny, but she was also strange. Very strange!

Rachel watched Zoe move around the tiny dressing room rather nervously for five full minutes before finally settling herself down in front of the mirror to begin the daunting task of removing all that eye makeup that made her look like a member of the Addams family. Zoe was a carefully dyed blonde, about five foot four, and weighed no more than maybe one hundred pounds. But despite her slight figure, she seemed to be always obsessing about that body of hers. During the show, it had been her sagging boobs, but Rachel had taken an opportunity, on the sly, to take a closer look at them; she herself couldn't see enough flesh sitting on the girl's chest for anybody to worry about. Given the fact that the child didn't have as much cleavage as Rachel did when she was ten, Rachel failed to see how two things so obviously insignificant could be a source of obsession for anyone, but what did she know? Her own boobs had gone south a very long time ago. They were just waiting for the rest of her to catch up. Now the child was complaining about her thighs. They simply weren't shaped right, Zoe complained, so Rachel looked at them as well—alas, the rest of the body, including the thighs, didn't look as if it had any more going for it than the boobs did. Oh, maybe some of those Northerners might find Zoe petite and pretty, but by Southern standards, the child didn't even have enough meat on her for a man to even grab hold good. Maybe dinner tonight would help her out some.

"But they loved my Sophie, the Jewish mama, joke." Zoe's eyes were now shining in remembrance of her greatest moment during the evening. (What kind of telegram does a Jewish mother send? Bad news coming so start worrying now.) "That one always gets a laugh," Zoe announced proudly as she moved behind the screen to change into jeans and a sweater. Rachel then looked around at the place. The Noname Café was new in town, but it was long overdue. When Rachel was growing up in Charleston, there were always plenty of good shows coming in and out of town and comedy was a local favorite. But this was a smaller town, and things usually took a little longer to come about here, but from the look of things, the place was doing pretty well. It sure had been packed tonight.

Even Sarah Weinstein had come out this evening. She was new to town—an out and out Northerner who was a "come here" to the South, and not a native, or a "from here." Her journey south had been a monumental move in more ways than one, and she was still desperately trying to figure it all out—like, for instance, why the local Jewish people attended spiritual night at Pastor Brown's church, ever so proudly acknowledging how much they loved the music, or better yet, getting to their feet and joining on in. Sarah was troubled, too, by the fact that the local deli served turkey barbecue instead of tuna fish. But most confusing to Sarah was why old Miss Fine insisted on serving neck bones and cabbage with the potato latkes whenever she invited folks to dinner. It all seemed perfectly normal to those Jews who had enough grits in their voice and collards in their soul to call themselves Southern, but Sarah, on the other hand, was still struggling with "y'all."

Rachel had already decided to take Zoe to the Deli Diner for dinner because it was one of her favorites. When they arrived, there were already several people seated there and two of them had taken over Rachel's favorite table, so they had no choice but to take the one by the window. Boy, did something smell good, Rachel thought as she took her seat, but they didn't get to sit for long. There was no one to serve you here. You had to get yourself up, check out what was cooking, and wait patiently for one of the clerks to decide to feed you. Well, the special for the evening was chicken soup, but not ordinary chicken soup. No way. This pot of goodness was embellished with okra, tomatoes, and black-eyed peas. Zoe frowned momentarily, and Rachel could almost hear the "what in the world is that?" that was probably going off like rockets inside Zoe's head. After a while, Zoe smiled hesitantly and asked for a jumbo-sized bowl. She also requested a roll, but the deli clerk handed her a piece of cornbread as if she hadn't even spoken and then waved her away to their nearby table. Rachel decided on the special as well, but only a cup. She was going to need room and lots of it because she was having greens and fried chicken as a second course. Oh, and there was that bowl of banana pudding that had her name on it. Not your typical deli fare by Northern folks' standards, but down home this was as good as it got.

When Rachel dropped Zoe by her hotel room, she gave her a hug and wished her well. The child really did seem to be a good girl, even if she was a little strange. Well, this was one time Rachel was glad that she had the chance to play hostess. It had been a long time since she'd laughed so much. But there was really nothing better than smart humor—it did so much more than bring on just a chuckle or two. It made you think, it made you remember, and it helped to connect you to who you really were.

# Mrs. Rachel Cohen's Story

## Laughing Sometimes to Keep from Crying

When Larissa asked me to tell her my story, I couldn't help but smile; just remembering it all made me feel good. You see, from the time I was a little girl, laughter was a part of our home. My father was a wonderful storyteller, and he always made up his own, so his folktales were something else. Well, when Daddy wasn't telling us stories, Uncle Abraham took over. He talked very slowly, and sometimes he just stopped in the middle of the telling like he had forgotten what he was going to say. I learned later that was all done for effect. It built up the suspense until you couldn't wait for the punch line, and neither the joke nor the punch line was carelessly chosen. It always revealed just a little something more about being a Jew, and what better learning is that?

> A group of elderly, retired men gather each morning at a café. They drink their coffee and sit for hours discussing the world situation. Given the state of things, their talks are usually depressing. One day, one of the men startles the others by announcing, "You know what? I am an optimist."
>
> The others are shocked, but then one of them notices something fishy. "Wait a minute, if you're an optimist, why do you look so worried?"
>
> "What? You think it's easy being an optimist?"

Every time that I hear that joke, I laugh, but I also want to scream out that it isn't easy being an optimist, and if you're a Jew whose family has a long history in Charleston, South Carolina, you would know that, I am sure of it.

Jews came to Charleston sometime around the 1690s. For years, more Jews lived in that city than in any other city in North America. In the beginning, most of these Jews were Sephardic Jews, whose homeland had once been Spain and Portugal. However, as time went on, more and more

Ashkenazic Jews, those who had lived in Central Europe, came to the city, and eventually there were more of them than there were Sephardic Jews.

In Charleston, the Jews gained rights earlier than anywhere else in the Western world. Some of them even grew rich and powerful. Over and over again, they referred to their new home as "the Happy Land" (can you get any more optimistic?). But nothing comes to anyone that is not hard earned. From the beginning, the Charleston Jews knew that if they could become citizens, they could be prosperous, so in the late 1690s four of them requested citizenship. The assembly passed a law intended to give all aliens, including wives and children, their rightful place regardless of where they had originally come from. Strangely enough, the assembly worded this law so that full freedom of conscience and worship would be granted to all Christians, except for Roman Catholics. At first, it appeared as if all this excluded the Jews, but those folks apparently just lumped the Jews in with the Protestants. Obviously, the Jews didn't mind, though, because they became citizens. Well, that was the beginning of Jews living in Charleston, South Carolina, and my ancestors were among the very first.

Once upon a time an old man who was Jewish by birth was walking along the road with a new friend who had a hunchback. After a few moments of silence, the old man says to his friend, "You know, I used to be a Jew." His new friend then replied, "And I used to be a hunchback."

My dad would tell this joke and finish up with the line "A Jew is a Jew is a Jew," and I think that is probably true. It was certainly true for the Jews of Charleston, but make no mistake about it, they became Southern in every way possible. They had white skin and they gladly joined in with all the other whites. They even owned slaves and many supported the Confederacy to maintain that right. Yes, the Charleston Jews were Jews, but they were also Southern, moved by the beauty of the language and the land and just as tangled up in the turbulence of its politics as other Southerners. To this day, the Southern Jew holds fiercely to both those identities—

Southern and Jew—and I am no different. You're as likely to find fried chicken on my table for dinner and grits there for breakfast as you will any of the "traditional" Jewish delicacies, and I'm as proud as I can be about that.

A Christian and a Jewish woman get into a fight in a post office line. The argument escalates, and the Christian woman yells at the Jew, "Christ killer."

"You're right," the Jewish woman says. "And if we could kill your God, imagine what I could do to you."

There is something sad about that joke, and I think it's because it shows how much misunderstanding can exist between the people who are all supposed to be God's children. This was especially true in the South. Although Charleston was fairly good to the Jewish people, this was not the case everywhere, especially in small towns and rural places. My husband came from such a place, and he speaks often of his painful childhood memories. His father had been an immigrant from Eastern Europe who wanted nothing more than to be an American and for his children to learn to act, speak, and think like Americans. If they did, perhaps they would have a chance at a decent living. But he and his wife found out quickly that nothing is ever as easy as it sounds when it's running around in your head.

With so few Jews in their new hometown, they were lonely and hard-pressed to hold on to their old ways. There was no synagogue for miles and miles, and that was the hardest for my mother-in-law to accept. They owned a store that catered to blacks as well as whites, and that didn't sit too well with the poor whites who weren't used to such things—so they gave my in-laws a hard time. Yes, they were considered to be white, but they were outsiders as far as everyone else was concerned. And then there were times when people could be so hateful, like the time my husband's baby sister was born. Several of the rich local women stopped in to see the baby because they wanted to see if a Jew baby looked anything at all like other babies; they wanted to find out if you could see the devil in the baby's face. We still go back to that small town in Mississippi from time to time so that my husband can see family, and things are better, thank goodness, but there is still something about that joke that makes me kind of sad.

A new rabbi comes to a well-established congregation every week on the Sabbath, and a fight erupts during the service. When it comes time to recite the Shema, "Hear, o Israel, the Lord is our God, the Lord is One," half the congregation sits and the other half stands, and the people who are standing yell at those who are sitting, and those who are sitting yell back. Well, it was driving the rabbi absolutely crazy.

Finally it's brought to the rabbi's attention that at a nearby home for the aged is a ninety-eight-year-old man who was a founding member of the congregation. So, in accordance with Talmudic tradition, the rabbi appoints a delegation of three—one who stands for the Shema, one who sits, and the rabbi himself—to go see the man. Well, they enter the room and the one who sits rushes over to him yelling all the while, "Wasn't it the tradition in our congregation to stand for the Shema?"

"No," the old man answers. "That wasn't the tradition."

The other man then jumps up and asks, "So we used to sit?"

"No," the old man says. "That wasn't the tradition."

At this point the rabbi cannot control himself. He is clearly very angry. "Right now I don't care what the tradition was—just tell them one or the other. Do you have any idea what goes on in services every week? The people who are standing yell at the people who are sitting; the people who are sitting yell at the people who are standing."

"That was the tradition," the old man says.

Jews are always taught that their concern for other Jews is most important. Despite any differences we may have, we feel a kinship to one another because we know that a Jew does not join the group—we are born into it. Nevertheless, the Jews of Charleston had major differences within their group and those differences were not easily resolved.

By the 1700s there were enough Jews in the city to begin to organize themselves into social institutions, so in 1749 the Sephardic Jews established Beth Elohim, the very first synagogue. It was strictly orthodox in its obedience of the law and anyone who violated the Sabbath or any of the religious holidays could expect a loss of membership in the synagogue.

Well, in the 1820s a group of men got together in order to bring changes to the worship service. They wanted the service shorter, easier to understand, completely in English, and less strict. Those men played a leading role in changing all of American Judaism by eventually making Beth Elohim a reform synagogue in the mid-1830s. However, by the 1840s and 1850s, there was a great deal of tension in Charleston because there were two congregations with greatly opposed practices. But a Jew is a Jew is a Jew, and over the years I am proud to say that we have worked out these differences. Now what is most important to us is to keep our Jewish community together. So many have left Judaism for one reason or another, and we certainly don't want to lose ourselves now, not after all we've been through just to be who we are.

Age is strictly a case of mind over matter;
if you don't mind, it doesn't matter.

Jack Benny was so right about that. I'm an old lady now, but it doesn't matter because I am so proud of who I am and all my people have been. A Southern Jew—a whole lot of people still don't understand how those words could possibly fit together, but believe me, they do. I go back to Charleston and I am reminded that my people were here before America was even America. I go back to King Street and I look at all those shops that used to be ours, and I can't forget that we contributed heavily to the success of that place. I walk by the synagogue and I remember that we were a community—loving each other one minute and fighting the next, but connected all the same. And of course, I can't leave until I go by the cemetery and look in on my loved ones, especially my parents.

My daddy was a shopkeeper and my mother worked as a clerk in his store. We lived right above our place like most Jews did then, and we weren't the richest, but we weren't the poorest folks either. After they died, my brothers and sisters and I decided to sell that old place to a family corporation that owned shoe shops all over the country. It was so much money that it was hard to say no, and we were able to do so much for our children and grandchildren. But sometimes I wonder if we did the right thing—that building was such a part of our history. But my husband says you don't need a building to hold on to your history; you do that by clinging to the memories you have in your heart. So now I cling and I cook. I cook because food is a sacred blessing, especially the bread that is so important to my people. My father used to say that when Jews make their bread, they are never just making bread. They are mixing together all the old stories, all the old faces, and all the old places. We are celebrating our history with each and every loaf. So as long as I can bake, there isn't a chance that I will ever forget.

# Sacred Blessings from Rachel Cohen's Kitchen

## Passover

*Passover was an important holiday in our house, as it was for any Jew. My father used to say that it was a celebration about remembering, so at our seder, each and every year, he told us the story of Passover even though we knew it as well as he did. Well, you don't have to be Jewish to appreciate the beauty of this story, but you may appreciate these next recipes even more if you take the time to enjoy it as I do.*

*About three thousand years ago, the Israelites were enslaved by the Egyptians under the rule of the pharaoh, Ramses II. According to the Book of Exodus, Moses, a simple Jewish shepherd, was told by God to go to the pharaoh and demand the freedom of his people, but Moses' plea of "let my people go" was ignored. Moses warned the pharaoh that God would send severe punishments to the people of Egypt if the Israelites were not set free. Again the pharaoh did nothing, so God then unleashed a series of ten terrible plagues on the people of Egypt.*

1 *Blood*
2 *Frogs*
3 *Vermin (lice)*
4 *Wild beasts (flies)*
5 *Blight (cattle disease)*
6 *Boils*
7 *Hail*
8 *Locusts*
9 *Darkness*
10 *Slaying of the firstborn*

*The holiday name* **Pesach***, meaning "passing over" or "protection" in Hebrew, came from the instructions given to Moses by God. In order to encourage the pharaoh to free the Israelites, God intended to kill the firstborn of both man and beast. To protect themselves, the Israelites were told to mark their dwellings with lamb's blood so that God would know them and "pass over" their homes.*

*But the pharaoh was still unconvinced and refused to free the Jewish slaves until the very last plague. Well, when the pharaoh did agree to their freedom, the Israelites left their homes so quickly that there wasn't even time to bake their bread. They simply packed up all the raw, unleavened dough and took it with them on their journey. As they fled through the desert, they had to bake their bread in a hurry, so they cooked it under the hot blazing sun into hard crackers called matzos.*

*Even though the Jews were now free, their liberation was still incomplete. The pharaoh's army had chased them through the desert toward the Red Sea. When the Jews reached the water, they thought they were trapped, but that was when the miracle happened. The Lord parted the Red Sea so that they were able to safely cross over to the other side, but the Pharaoh's army was not so fortunate. The waves closed upon them, and it was then that the Israelites realized that finally they were free. Passover celebrates all of that important history.*

*These next recipes are some of my favorites to make during the Passover holiday season.*

## PASSOVER MANDELBREAD

**3 eggs**
**¾ cup sugar**
**¾ cup oil**
**¾ cup matzo cake meal**
**2 tablespoons potato starch**
**1 teaspoon cinnamon**
**½ teaspoon salt**
**¼ cup matzo meal**
**¾ cup chopped walnuts or almonds**

Yields 36 cookies.

Beat together the eggs and sugar and then beat in the oil. Sift together the cake meal, potato starch, cinnamon, and salt and add the matzo meal. Add the nuts and then combine this mixture with the wet ingredients. Refrigerate for 24 hours.

Preheat the oven to 350°. With oiled hands, form mixture into rolls and place on a lightly greased cookie sheet. Bake for 30 minutes. Cut slowly into slices while slightly warm, and dip each slice into sugar and cinnamon mixture. Place cut side up on a cookie sheet, and return to the oven to crisp for about 10 minutes. Keeps well in a closed container.

## PASSOVER FARFEL MUFFINS

**1½ cups Passover farfel (pellet-sized noodles)**
**4 eggs**
**1 tablespoon schmaltz (liquid chicken fat) or vegetable oil**
**Salt and pepper to taste**

Yields 8 muffins.

Preheat the oven to 400°. Put farfel in colander and put the colander in a bowl. Pour boiling water over it—the farfel should be immersed in the water. Let stand till soggy, about 5 minutes. Drain well; add eggs, schmaltz or vegetable oil, and seasonings. Put dab of schmaltz or vegetable oil in bottom of muffin tin. Heat pan in oven; then take out and fill with mixture. Bake for 30 minutes. The muffins will come out big and puffy, and as they cool, they will flop.

## PASSOVER POPOVERS

**1 stick margarine**
**¼ teaspoon salt**
**1 cup water**
**½ cup matzo cake meal**
**½ cup matzo meal**
**4 large eggs**

Yields 12 popovers.

Preheat the oven to 450°. Boil together margarine, salt, and water. Add ½ cup cake meal and turn off the heat. Add in ½ cup matzo meal and cool for 5 minutes. Beat in eggs, one at a time. Fill greased muffin tins three-quarters full. Bake 20 minutes. Reduce oven temperature to 350° and bake an additional 20 minutes.

## PASSOVER LADYFINGERS

**6 egg yolks**
**¾ cup sugar, divided**
**4 egg whites**
**½ cup matzo cake meal**
**¼ cup potato starch**
**Superfine sugar**

Yields 24 ladyfingers.

In a large mixing bowl, beat the egg yolks with ¼ cup sugar until light and creamy. In a separate bowl, beat the egg whites until foamy; then gradually add ½ cup sugar, beating well after each addition until stiff. Fold the egg whites into the yolk mixture.

On a piece of waxed paper, sift the cake meal and the potato starch. Sprinkle the cake meal mixture over the batter and fold in gently. Line a large cookie sheet with brown paper. Using a pastry bag fitted with a round tube, pipe the batter onto the paper to form finger shapes about 1 inch wide and 4 inches long. Dust with superfine sugar shaken through a small sieve.

Preheat the oven to 375°. Bake for 10 to 12 minutes. Using a spatula, loosen from paper immediately.

TIPS: Use the ladyfingers to line a springform pan, and fill it with your favorite mousse recipe. They also can be served with a fruit topping.

*These matzo balls are served in chicken soup at the beginning of the Passover meal. They're so delicious, it's hard to save room for the rest of the meal.*

# FLUFFY MATZO BALLS

**4 eggs, separated**
**½ cup cold water**
**⅓ cup peanut oil**
**1 teaspoon salt**
**Dash of pepper**
**1¼ cups matzo meal**

Yields 10 balls.

Beat the egg whites with a rotary beater until slightly fluffy. Beat or mix the egg yolks with the cold water until foamy. Combine the egg whites and the egg yolk mixture, and beat until foamy. Add the oil, salt, and pepper to the egg mixture and beat well. Add the matzo meal and stir with a fork until thoroughly combined. Let stand overnight or at least 2 hours in the refrigerator.

Lightly grease your hands with a little oil and form balls. Do not try to form perfect balls; just shuffle the matzo ball from one hand to another like a hot potato or it will fall apart. Drop into 1½ quarts or more of simmering salted water. If the water is boiling too rapidly, the matzo balls will fall apart. Cover the pot and cook for 20 minutes. Do not lift the top off the pot or you will have matzo rocks.

*After Passover, if you're wondering what to do with all that leftover matzo, crush it up into meal and make this tasty recipe.*

## MATZO STUFFING

**4 matzos**
**¼ cup water**
**1 tablespoon parsley, chopped**
**Celery, chopped, to taste (optional)**
**2 eggs, beaten**
**2 tablespoons onion, chopped**
**¼ teaspoon ginger**

Crumble matzos and sprinkle with water. Add other ingredients. This stuffing may be used for any meat or poultry.

Yields 1½ cups stuffing.

*Today, to commemorate Passover, Jews eat matzo in place of bread, but I make this bread at other times of the year just to remember the spirit of the Jewish people during that difficult time in history.*

## FAVORITE UNLEAVENED BREAD

**⅓ cup hot water**
**½ cup butter**
**1 ⅓ cups whole wheat flour**
**2 cups oatmeal flour**
**2 to 4 tablespoons brown sugar**
**1 teaspoon salt**
**½ cup nut meats**
**Sesame seeds (optional)**

Preheat the oven to 350° to 375°. Mix hot water and butter. Add remaining ingredients. Form into a ball and chill about 3 hours. Roll out very thin and cut with cookie cutters, or score into squares. Bake until light brown, about 12 minutes.

Yields 36 pieces.

# *The Sabbath*

*And they gathered it morning by morning, every man according to his eating, and as the sun waxed hot, it melted. And it came to pass that on the sixth day they gathered twice as much bread, two omers for each one; and all the rulers of the congregation came and told Moses. And he said unto them, "This is that which the Lord hath spoken: Tomorrow is a solemn rest, a holy sabbath unto the Lord. Bake that which ye will bake, and seethe that which you will seethe; and all that remaineth over lay up for you to be kept until the morning.*

*—Exodus 16:21–23*

*When I was a little girl, the bread was baked on Friday, just as the Torah said it should be, but it was our black cook that made it. She had worked for another Jewish family before coming to us so she had her own way of doing things, and we knew better than to get in her way. Her name was Harriet, and I was sixteen at the time she started with us. Because I was always home early on Friday, I got to be in the kitchen every Friday afternoon when she made the bread for the Sabbath. She was something else, and I could talk to her about things I couldn't even mention to my mother, so it was Harriet that instructed me on the ways of men and how best to make it out in the world. I think that's why I have such spunk today.*

*But as important as Harriet was to our family, the relationship was not without questions for me. I would look at Harriet and her husband, Israel, our gardener (it was common for blacks to name their children with names from the Old Testament), and listen to them sing songs as they worked. Those songs told their story, but they told mine as well.*

> *Go down Moses*
> *Way down to Egypt*
> *And tell ole*
> *Pharaoh*
> *To let my people go.*

*Harriet and Israel's people had created those songs during slavery as a plea for freedom, just as my people had struggled for freedom many, many years ago. Yet my people had owned slaves once upon a time, and Harriet's people were still not really free. I didn't know at the time how I was supposed to feel about all of that, and I still don't. I do know Harriet was a good woman who worked hard for all of us, and I wouldn't know how to bake bread today if it had not been for her. I admit I've taken a few of her recipes and changed them somewhat, but she's not here to see me do it, so I'm safe.*

*Harriet used to say that she would never really be free until she passed on through the Lord's pearly gates. I just hope that now she is indeed free at last.*

## QUICK CHALLAH

1½ cups warm water (110°)

1 cup butter or margarine, melted

¾ cup white sugar or honey

3 eggs, beaten

2 packages Rapid Rise yeast

1 teaspoon salt

7 to 8 cups bread flour

1 egg, beaten

Poppy seeds to taste (optional)

Sesame seeds to taste (optional)

Yields 2 loaves.

In a medium bowl blend together warm water, melted butter or margarine, sugar or honey, and 3 beaten eggs. In a large bowl, mix together yeast, salt, and 7 cups of the flour. Slowly stir liquid ingredients into the flour mixture, and mix until the dough holds together.

Knead dough on a floured surface with remaining flour as needed until smooth. Split dough into 2 pieces. Then split each large piece into 3 pieces. Roll each piece into a ¾-inch-thick rope and braid 3 strands together. Repeat with the other 3 pieces. Place dough on greased baking sheets. Brush dough with remaining beaten egg. Poppy or sesame seeds can be sprinkled on top (optional). Let rise in a warm place until doubled in size. Bake in a 325° preheated oven for 20 to 30 minutes.

*This recipe is a great way to use up any leftover challah.*

# BREAD KUGEL

¾ pound challah, broken in
    pieces, soaked in hot
    water and drained
¾ cup sugar
4 eggs, beaten
1 teaspoon vanilla
½ teaspoon baking powder
½ cup golden raisins
2 apples, peeled and chopped

Preheat the oven to 350°. Mix together challah pieces, ¾ cup sugar, eggs, vanilla, baking powder, raisins, and apples. Lightly grease a 9x11-inch baking dish and pour mixture in. Mix together topping ingredients: ¼ cup sugar, cinnamon, and walnuts. Sprinkle the topping on the kugel and bake for 45 minutes.

Yields 1 pan.

## TOPPING
¼ cup sugar
1 teaspoon cinnamon
½ cup chopped walnuts

*The Jewish New Year is the anniversary of the creation, and it is a time that one examines oneself and repents. It comes ten days before Yom Kippur, the day on which divine judgment is sealed. During Rosh Hashanah the table is filled with delicacies that represent hope for a sweet future: we serve round challah with raisins, apples dipped in honey, and other sweet dishes. This recipe for brown bread with raisins is perfect for this holiday or anytime you want a great-tasting bread.*

# BROWN BREAD

1½ cups raisins
1½ cups water
3 tablespoons shortening
2¾ cups flour
1 cup sugar
1 teaspoon soda
1 teaspoon salt
1 tablespoon molasses
1 egg

Preheat the oven to 350°. Boil raisins and water for 15 minutes. Cool, leaving raisins in the water. To the water and raisins, add shortening, flour, sugar, soda, salt, molasses; and egg; mix together. Bake in two 16-ounce cans (sprayed with nonstick cooking spray) or in 9x5-inch loaf pan (sprayed with nonstick cooking spray). Bake for 1 hour or until done.

Yields 1 loaf.

RECIPES

*These next two recipes were Harriet's specialties. I think of her every time I make them.*

# POPPY SEED ROLL

## DOUGH

**2 teaspoons sugar**

**2 packages active dry yeast**

**1 cup lukewarm water**

**6 cups flour**

**¼ cup sugar**

**1½ teaspoons baking soda**

**½ teaspoon salt**

**1 cup margarine (oil can be substituted)**

**4 eggs, beaten until foamy**

## FILLING

**3 cups poppy seeds**

**1½ cups sugar**

**2 teaspoons vanilla**

**1½ cups hot water**

**¼ cup flour**

## EGG GLAZE

**1 egg**

**1 tablespoon water**

**1 teaspoon sugar**

Yields 1 roll.

DOUGH: Dissolve sugar and yeast in the lukewarm water and set aside. Sift all dry dough ingredients together in a large bowl. Cut in margarine (or blend in oil). The mixture should be crumbly. Make a well in the center. Add the yeast mixture and eggs into the well. Slowly mix ingredients together. Blend until you have formed a soft dough. Remove the dough from the bowl and lightly grease the bowl. Return dough to the bowl, cover, and set aside in a warm place to let the dough rise until doubled in size.

FILLING: Grind poppy seeds. You can use a mechanical grinder, coffee grinder, blender, or food processor. Add the remaining filling ingredients to the ground poppy seeds; mix well.

On a lightly floured pastry board, roll out the dough to ¼-inch thick. Spread the poppy seed mixture over the dough, keeping away from the edges. Roll the dough and mixture in a jelly roll fashion. Place roll on a greased cookie sheet. Cover and let rise for 1 hour.

EGG GLAZE: Beat the egg with the water and sugar in a small dish. With a pastry brush, brush the roll with the egg mixture. Sprinkle a few whole poppy seeds on top of the egg glaze.

Bake in a preheated 325° oven for 45 minutes. Remove from pan and cool on a wire rack. Slice and serve when cooled.

# CHEESE BLINTZES (ROLLED CHEESE PANCAKES)

## CHEESE FILLING
- **I cup dry cottage cheese**
- **I cup pot cheese or low-fat ricotta cheese**
- **I egg**
- **I tablespoon sugar**

## PANCAKE BATTER
- **I cup flour**
- **I cup low-fat milk**
- **3 eggs**

**Vegetable oil for frying**
**2 tablespoons margarine**
**8 ounces plain low-fat yogurt**

Yields 6 servings

CHEESE FILLING: In a medium-sized bowl, beat together cottage cheese, pot cheese, 1 egg, and sugar.

PANCAKE BATTER: In a medium-sized bowl, combine the flour, milk, and 3 eggs. Beat until the batter is smooth.

Heat a 6- or 8-inch skillet. Coat with vegetable oil and pour in 2 to 3 tablespoons of batter. Tilt the pan to distribute the batter over the bottom of the skillet. Cook until the dough is firm and browned. Remove from pan and place on a lightly oiled plate with browned side up. Spoon 1 tablespoon of cheese filling onto the edge of the pancake. To roll up, bring the edge with the filling to the center of the pancake, fold in each side, and fold over once more to make a sealed pouch. Continue with the rest of the batter.

When ready to serve, heat the margarine in the skillet. Fry the blintzes until golden brown on all sides. Serve with yogurt.

*I got this next recipe from the bakery here in town, but it wasn't easy. I had to eat there every morning for a month before the owner finally gave it to me. I gained five pounds in the process!*

## CHOCOLATE CHIP MANDELBREAD

**4 eggs**

**I cup sugar**

**½ cup oil**

**I teaspoon vanilla**

**3 cups flour**

**2 teaspoons baking powder**

**Dash of salt**

**I cup semisweet chocolate chips**

**½ cup nuts, optional**

Yields 2 long loaves or 4 short loaves for slicing into cookies.

Preheat the oven to 350°. In a large bowl, beat eggs and sugar until whipped. Add oil and vanilla to this mixture. Mix well. Then add flour, baking powder, salt, chocolate chips, and nuts. Mixture will be sticky.

Place on cookie sheets by plopping spoonfuls of batter to form a large long loaf. You can either have 2 long loaves or turn the cookie sheet and get 4 short loaves.

Bake for 20 minutes. Use two spatulas and pick up the loaf and place on a cutting board. Slice the loaf on an angle to cut cookies. Replace the cookies on the cookie sheet and heat another 5 minutes. This allows the cookies to get brown and crunchy. Remove from heat and cool on a wire rack.

*This Hanukkah recipe has been in my husband's family for years. When I make it now, I make it with one or two of my grandchildren, laughing and telling stories all the while.*

# SUFGANIYOT (ISRAELI DOUGHNUTS)

**l package active dry yeast**

**4 tablespoons sugar, divided**

**¾ cup lukewarm milk or warm water**

**2½ cups all-purpose flour**

**l pinch salt**

**l teaspoon cinnamon**

**2 eggs, separated**

**2 tablespoons butter or margarine, softened**

**Apricot or strawberry preserves**

**Oil for deep frying**

**Sugar**

Yields 12 doughnuts.

In a medium-sized bowl, mix together the yeast, 2 tablespoons sugar, and the milk. Let sit to make sure it bubbles. Sift the flour and mix it with the remaining sugar, salt, cinnamon, egg yolks, and the yeast mixture.

Knead the dough until it forms a ball. Add the butter or margarine. Knead some more, until the butter is well absorbed. Cover with a towel and let rise overnight in the refrigerator. Roll out the dough to a thickness of ⅛ inch. With a juice glass or cookie cutter, cut out the dough into 24 rounds, approximately 2 inches in diameter. Take ½ teaspoon preserves and place in center of 12 rounds. Top with the other 12 rounds. Press down the edges, sealing with egg whites. Crimping with the thumb and second finger works the best. Let rise for about 30 minutes.

Heat 2 inches of oil in a frying pan. Drop doughnuts into the hot oil, about 5 at a time. Turn to brown on both sides. Drain on paper towels. Roll the doughnuts in sugar.

When my husband and I were first married, I became friends with a young Jewish woman named Ada Wernick, who had recently moved with her husband to Charleston from Tennessee. They opened up a ladies' hat shop not too far from my home, and although my head was always way too big to look decent in a hat, I used to stop in all the time. She and I would talk for hours, and I was always amazed at how different her life in rural Tennessee had been from mine in Charleston.

To begin with, there were not many Jews in the small town where she grew up, and the few that were there had assimilated into the white Protestant culture as much as they possibly could while still remaining Jews. During their Friday night services, there was an organ, no hint of Hebrew, no skull caps, and no prayer shawls. Even the music sounded more like Christian hymns than ours was supposed to. Despite it all, Ada remembered the stories of Jewish struggle that her grandmother loved to tell, and she tried her best to hold on to as much of herself as she could. She even closed her eyes in school when they were supposed to be reciting the Lord's Prayer.

In Charleston, she said she was finally able to reclaim her identity as a Jew, and she was happy about that. We were friends for a long time. She died about ten years ago, right before I moved here to North Carolina, but these next recipes are hers and I still make them from time to time. I think of her every time I do.

## CRANBERRY BREAD

2 cups flour, divided

½ teaspoon baking soda

½ teaspoon salt

5½ teaspoons baking powder

⅞ cup granulated sugar

¾ cup orange juice

1 egg, lightly beaten

3 tablespoons oil or melted shortening

1 teaspoon vanilla extract

1 teaspoon freshly grated orange rind (optional)

2 cups fresh cranberries

1 cup walnuts or pecans, chopped

Preheat the oven to 350°. Grease and flour a 9x5-inch loaf pan. In a large mixing bowl, combine the flour (reserving ¼ cup for later use), baking soda, salt, baking powder, and sugar. In a small bowl, mix the orange juice, egg, oil, vanilla, and orange rind (optional). With a spoon, stir the wet ingredients into the dry ingredients until combined. In a separate bowl, mix the cranberries with the ¼ cup flour and nuts. Fold the cranberry mixture into the batter. Pour into the prepared pan and bake for 45 minutes to 1 hour or until done. This bread freezes well.

Yields 1 loaf.

# Light Rye Bread

I cup lukewarm water

I teaspoon sugar

2 packages active dry yeast

1½ cups buttermilk

¼ cup butter or margarine, melted

¼ cup brown sugar

2 teaspoons salt

2 cups rye flour

4 to 6 cups unbleached white flour

Yields 2 loaves.

Combine lukewarm water, sugar, and yeast in a small bowl. Let stand for 10 minutes. In a large mixing bowl, combine buttermilk, melted butter, brown sugar, salt, and yeast mixture. Add rye flour and mix well. Add white flour until dough is stiff enough to be turned onto a floured board.

Knead for 10 minutes, place in greased bowl, cover, and let rise until doubled in size. Form into 2 round or oblong loaves on cookie sheet, and let rise until doubled in size. Bake in a 400° oven for 25 minutes.

*A friend brought these delicious Middle Eastern rolls to a potluck supper at the synagogue. I just had to get the recipe!*

# Yemenite Rolls

4 cups flour

2 tablespoons oil (or butter)

2 tablespoons vinegar

I teaspoon salt

I teaspoon sugar

2 cups water (or enough water to make a soft dough)

I stick margarine, room temperature

Yields 8 rolls.

Mix everything, except the margarine, together; knead a bit for smoothness. Then rest the dough and cover for 3 hours.

Preheat the oven to 350°. Divide the dough into 8 pieces. Flatten out one piece into a 6-inch diameter circle. Spread about 2 teaspoons of margarine into the dough circle by pushing and kneading while trying to maintain the circle. Cut a line open from the center of the circle to the outside edge. Take one end and roll it around counterclockwise into a small ball. This is the *ajin*, or bread dough. Prepare the remaining pieces the same way. Bake for 20 to 30 minutes or until done.

# Signora Josephine Morelli

Josephine Morelli clutched her Bible a little closer to her heart as Celeste D'Angelo sped along a back road she called a shortcut. Oh Lord! She was too old for this kind of chaos and so was Celeste D'Angelo. Of course, it was always an adventure to ride anywhere with Celeste, but today, given the nature of the occasion, a smoother ride would have been greatly appreciated. This was simply no way to carry on when one was on the way to a funeral. First of all, Celeste drove a Cadillac that made so much noise, you couldn't possibly talk to one another while you were in it. The windows rattled, the steering wheel had no sense of direction, and the brakes were fair at best. In the last few minutes, Celeste had barely managed to skirt a ditch, had come close to hitting a tree, and had surely scared Miss Johnson's milking cow almost to death.

They did eventually arrive at the church in one piece, and Josephine stepped unsteadily out of the car feeling every bit of her seventy-five years. Celeste however, looked calm and collected as she slammed the driver's door shut and strutted boldly into the church, high heels, fitted black dress, and all. But that was hardly surprising; Celeste was always beautifully coiffed and perfectly manicured. She was a striking woman with salt-and-pepper hair that barely grazed her shoulders. Her eyes were a beautiful blue, and Celeste accented them with just the right makeup. She even had her own teeth—all of them—and nobody else in the bingo game could make that claim, that was for sure.

Josephine would have been tempted to smile as Celeste's high heels clicked on the newly waxed floor, her generous hips jiggling a little more than necessary, but this afternoon was not a time for smiles. It was a time to say good-bye and it wasn't going to be easy.

The priest had already taken his place, and the organ was playing quietly. The pews were filling up, and it looked as if Leona was going to have a fairly nice send-off. It was time to take their seats, but Celeste never did what she was supposed to, so of course, she was now in the front of the church peering down at the deceased. Josephine tiptoed to her side and tried to gently lead her to where they were supposed to be, but naturally Celeste wouldn't budge.

"She looks good," Celeste choked out, "but they put lipstick on her. She would have never worn lipstick to the church. I should pull out my handkerchief and wipe it off—it just doesn't look natural." But thankfully, Josephine noticed that Celeste kept her handkerchief balled up in her hand. "But she looks like she's finally at peace. That Alzheimer's disease just seemed to pick her apart bit by bit. By the time I visited her last, she didn't know me. She didn't know herself and she didn't even know her grandbaby. My heart just about broke, and when they called and told me that she had a stroke, I didn't know what to pray for, but God always knows best, and my mother used to always say that He never makes a mistake." Celeste paused for a moment. "You know, we met at a bingo game many, many years ago. She won almost every week, and I thought she was cheating and I told her so. We yelled at each other for about fifteen minutes, then broke out in big grins, and we've been friends ever since. Two lost Italian women new to this place and looking for a little kindness. And oh, Josephine, she was an amazing cook! I know you haven't known her that long, but if you had ever had the pleasure of tasting her marinara sauce, you would have wept over your plate. Whenever we went to her house for dinner, my husband would clean his plate like he'd never had pasta before in his life. I would be so mad, I could have killed him, but in my heart I could not blame him. That woman had blessed hands when it came to a saucepan.

"The obituary is so short. There's so much it doesn't tell—that her mama and daddy were from Sicily, Italy, and they eked out a living picking oranges for years and years. It doesn't mention that she became a widow at a young age and raised good Catholic children all by herself, by cleaning floors at the hospital. She also drank too much and cussed when she thought nobody was listening, but God forgives us all and I think He understood.

"A good Catholic woman—gone too soon—who suffered far too much. But, Josephine, she persevered and I just know she's at heaven's door, probably knocking like a fool for somebody to let her in. No, this obituary really says nothing. I guess you just can't tell the story of a life on a single page. But how I worry, Josephine! I don't ever want my memories to dwindle away, the way they did for her. I am so afraid of forgetting one thing that I look at the family pictures over and over again to see how much I can remember. Yes, some things have slipped away, but not too much, not yet. Our lives, Josephine, after all is said and done, they're really all that we have that matters." Celeste was finished talking then, and the two ladies stood there for a moment longer before taking their seats. Celeste was right, Josephine thought sadly; the lives they had already lived were really all that mattered in the end, and memories were sometimes about the best gift an old lady could hope for.

# Signora Josephine Morelli's Story

## Memories, Memories, Memories

My grandfather always said that he came to America in 1875 because he heard the streets were paved with gold, but when he got here he found out three things. First, the streets weren't paved with gold; second, they weren't paved at all; and third, he was expected to pave them. He and my grandmother came from large families in a little village called Taormina in southern Italy, and their people worked the land to make a living, if you call near starvation making a living. In truth, they were little more than peasants, so they left for America where they hoped their children had more of a chance at a good life than bending their necks to the yoke of a mule and never being able to lift their eyes off the very land that imprisoned them. So often, my grandfather said, they prayed for something better and America seemed to be the place to get it.

They left by steamship, crammed in with others who carried with them everything they owned and every loved one they could manage. There they sat, day after day, on that boat for two weeks, eagerly awaiting the sight of America's shores. When they finally arrived, they say that a single tear rolled down my grandfather's cheek, but he said absolutely nothing. Not a single thing did he utter until he and my grandmother had made their way safely through the check gate and into New York City to a friend's house. They stayed there until they could move on. For a good while after, all he could manage to say was "thank you" over and over again. Grandmother said he seemed to be in a state of shock for at least a week, as if he simply couldn't believe that they had actually made it.

They didn't stay in New York too long. They were anxious to move on, to make a home, and get settled. They had big dreams then, of a big beautiful house, acres and acres of farmland, and all of the things they had wished for but could not possibly have back home in Italy. But America is no easy place, then or now, and my grandparents found out the hard way that life is pretty tough when you are starting out with nothing, even in the great land of America.

Grandfather and Grandmother didn't speak English very well, could barely read or write, and knew nothing about this country, but they were brave souls who left the comfort of a large Italian population in New York and headed south where Italians were not only unwelcome but were also very misunderstood. Their first stop was St. Helena, South Carolina, a pretty place where the farmland bumped up to the ocean and where Grandpa thought the laps of the waves would bring him peace and contentment. But that place offered Grandpa little more than Italy had given him. Although they stayed there almost fifteen years, it was a very long fifteen years.

They couldn't get land because they had no money, and nobody trusted "the foreigners" enough to even let them sharecrop for a living, so they worked odd jobs and moved, it seemed to Grandmother, "every time the sun set." Grandfather did anything he could to make a dime—dug ditches, cleaned graveyards, slaughtered chickens, and even hauled dead bodies for the funeral parlor. Mama made lace for rich ladies, who thought that she was dirty just because she was ragged and secretly feared that she was a witch because of her strange homemade altars, rosary beads, and foreign prayers. The black folks hated them because the few Italians who lived there wanted to do the same backbreaking, low-paying jobs they did. They were used to maintaining a grudging respect for the white landowners who controlled everything, but "the dirty foreigners," the blacks decided, deserved nothing at all. There were also a few Jews in town, but they stayed to themselves, speaking to Grandmother only when they wanted her fine lace to sell in their stores. So Grandmother and Grandfather kept to themselves and worked every moment they could to take care of each other and my mother, Grace. She couldn't go to school because she also had to work, but she taught herself to speak English better than her parents, and one summer a nearby friend taught her how to read and write by scratching letters and numbers in the dirt whenever they played together.

After South Carolina, they went to Louisiana for a little while, where they heard there was plenty of work for Italians with strong backs and a love of the land. So off they went in a wagon pulled by a mule to a little town outside of New Orleans. Mother, Grandmother, and Grandfather worked the cotton fields right alongside the other "foreigners," the poor white trash, and the down-and-out blacks. But the place was so hot and so humid, and filled with so many insects that carried diseases, that many Italians died. The climate was nothing like they were used to in Italy, and they just couldn't seem to adjust. Mother and her parents did fairly well because the coast of South Carolina had prepared them for such conditions. Still, they were unhappy there and decided to move on.

They ended up in Chicot County, Arkansas, in the 1890s, living on Sunnyside, a plantation that was worked by immigrants and blacks. The owners of the place had decided to experiment by using immigrants, but it didn't work out so well. With the harsh climate, dirty water, and dilapidated housing, a lot of them passed away pretty quickly. Our family was one of the lucky few who were able to get together enough money to buy our own farm, but even with our newfound success, we were still hated by the Southern whites. Other Italians came to the area, mostly from Louisiana, and so there was some companionship—someone to pray with, someone to feast with, and someone to court with—but the living was still very, very hard. The Italian children went to school, but they were bullied and beaten.

When they did fight back, the local people said they were violent criminals like members of the Mafia. I never did understand that kind of thinking. I mean, if we had been part of the Mafia, we surely would have had a good deal more than we had, but I guess there is just no reasoning with some people, so why bother?

Not too far from Sunnyside, Father Pietro Bandini, an Italian priest, came to organize a group of Italian men into what they called a cooperative. He bought about nine hundred acres and they all called it Tonitown in memory of Enrico Toni, an Italian explorer who had come to the area three hundred years before. But others tried to drive them away, even burning their church to the ground. The men rebuilt it and once again a mob tried to torch it. This time, Father Bandini stood his ground and told the mob that they, too, were men, many of them trained in the Italian army, and anyone who came among them with malice in their heart would be shot right where they stood. Well, that got everyone's attention and there wasn't too much trouble after that.

Mother and Father met when Mother was afraid that maybe she would be alone all of her life, but blessed Mary, she did find love at the age of thirty. Father was much older, almost forty-five years old then, and he was more than ready to end his lonely years. I came along quickly, almost too quickly, according to my grandmother; she did the count and although it was close, it was within the limits of respectability. I smile whenever I imagine my grandmother sitting there counting back all those days. She never was too good at figures, so all that counting must have taken her a good while. Well, maybe Mother and Father did wait until the priest said yes or maybe they didn't, but they were both so passionate, I wouldn't be surprised if they had a little moonlit madness before they made it to the church. Hugging and kissing all the time is how I remember them, and I wished as a girl for love such as theirs when it was my turn. Thankfully, I did find a good man of my own.

I was born at a time when the boll weevil was tearing up the South, and extreme climates were killing what was left. I am the oldest of four: three girls and one boy, who was so spoiled and well taken care of that his wife blames us to this day for his sometimes selfish ways. Of the three girls, I was the only one who married, and my husband, Christopher, always claims that the famous folktale I love so much should have been called "Christopher Who Married Three Sisters" and not "The Devil Who Married Three Sisters." But there are times, I tell you, that I am convinced that my Christopher and the devil are one and the same. That man! Lord!

I think my favorite memories of growing up were waiting on la Befana. She comes in the first week of January and marks the end of the Christmas season. It is the day that the three wise men arrived at the manger of the Christ child, and it is even more special to me than Christmas. The story goes that the three wise men were in search of the Christ child when they decided to stop at a home to ask for directions. When they knocked, an old lady answered the door holding a broom. She didn't know who the three men were and really couldn't give them any help. Well, they asked her to join them on their journey, but she said no, there was just too much to do. Later, however, she changed her mind and decided to try to catch up to them, but she couldn't find them. She truly hated that she had missed the chance to see the Christ child. So every year since, she sets out looking for baby Jesus. She stops at each child's house and leaves treats for the children who were good and a lump of coal for those who weren't. Of course, I kept my stocking hung by the chimney in hopes that la Befana would come by. She never let me down either. She left me a stocking full of Mary Janes each and every year. Oh, how I still adore stories and holidays. I guess in my heart I never, ever grew up. I will be a child until the day I die, I suppose, and that's fine with me. I still hang my stocking for la Befana, only now I get sugar-free treats instead of Mary Janes, but they are just as wonderful.

I was a good student all through school, and I even went to nursing school for a little while, but that didn't last long. I got married and the babies started coming fast and furious. We had eight all together, three girls and five boys. I met my husband when he was a farmhand for my father, but by the time we were married, he had a small farm of his own. We never got rich, but we had a nice big house, and we never went without, at least not too often.

After the children were grown and on their own, we decided to leave Arkansas and settle here in North Carolina, where the weather is a little kinder on old, tired bones. It wasn't easy leaving family, because as long as I can remember, family was pretty much all we had. But now we have new friends and some of them are *almost* like family. We go to a nice church and the priest is a good man, even if he does need a little meat on his bones. And, of course, there is bingo, and I am determined one day to be champ. My husband says I haven't got a prayer, but what does he know? He still wears brown socks with his black suit.

I told that sweet child Larissa that at this point in my life I don't need too much. My mother used to say, "The aged love what is practical, while the youth long for what is dazzling." Me? All I need is a firm mattress, a good kitchen, a few friends, a tolerable man, and perfectly ripe tomatoes for my pasta sauce. Anything else is extra and very well appreciated.

# A Glimpse into the Family Bread Book

*My mother believed that there were just some things every Italian woman needed to know, and two of them were how to make a basket of breadsticks and how to bake a perfect loaf of Italian bread.*

## ITALIANO BREADSTICKS

2¼ cups biscuit mix

½ cup grated Parmesan cheese

1 tablespoon melted butter or margarine

¼ teaspoon garlic powder

⅔ cup of milk

Preheat the oven to 400°. Combine first four ingredients in a large bowl. Stir in milk until blended.

Roll dough into a 10x9-inch rectangle on a lightly floured surface. Cut dough into 10 (1-inch) strips; place on a lightly greased baking sheet. Bake for 13 to 15 minutes.

Yields 10 breadsticks.

## ITALIAN BREAD

1 egg

1½ cups buttermilk

3 tablespoons olive oil

2½ cups all-purpose flour

2 tablespoons white sugar

2 teaspoons baking powder

½ teaspoon baking soda

¼ teaspoon salt

1 teaspoon dried rosemary

2 tablespoons dried parsley

1 cup shredded sharp cheddar cheese

¼ cup chopped green onions

1 clove garlic, chopped

¼ cup chopped sun-dried tomatoes

Preheat the oven to 350°. Grease a 9x5-inch loaf pan. Whisk together the egg, buttermilk, and oil in a small bowl. In a large bowl, whisk together flour, sugar, baking powder, soda, salt, and dried herbs. Stir in cheese and onions. Pour buttermilk mixture into the flour mixture, and stir to combine. Stir in garlic and tomatoes until evenly distributed. Spread batter into prepared pan. Smooth top and tap pan on counter to remove bubbles. Bake for 60 to 65 minutes until golden. Cool loaf on wire rack.

Yields 12 servings.

*This bread was my husband's favorite. I only made it, though, when he needed something special to pick up his dragging spirits. Oh, it was so hard to be different in the South. So hard to be Italian. So hard to be Catholic. And sadly, what people do not understand, they do not like and they do not trust. But we were determined to make our farm our home. We loved the big open spaces and the smell of the fruit trees after a rain. We even loved the way the dirt felt under our fingernails. I guess we never were meant to be big city people. This is where our hearts are, and this is where we will always be. But there were days when my love wondered if maybe we shouldn't try something new. It was then that I made him this bread and served it with big glasses of good wine. After a while, he felt blessed again and he could make it just a little while longer.*

*Volere è potere, my dear, volere è potere.*
*Where there's a will, there's a way, my dear.*
*Remember, where there's a will, there's a way.*

# SFINGI

**2 packages active dry yeast**

**2 cups warm water**

**½ cup sugar or to taste**

**5 cups flour**

**1 pound raisins**

**Powdered sugar**

Yields 48 cakes.

In a large bowl, dissolve yeast in warm water. Add sugar. Let this mixture stand until bubbly. Add flour and raisins. Stir to mix. Dough will be moist and very lumpy. Let rise in a warm place until doubled in size. Drop by tablespoonfuls into hot oil in a frying pan. Cook to a golden brown. Drain and cool on a brown paper bag. Roll in powdered sugar. These are best eaten the first day. They will get tough if eaten on day two.

*I remember that once when I was a young woman—still slim and pretty and my eyes filled with dreams—I went to the big city of New York. It was in July and, oh, it was so hot! I didn't get to stay too long, but I did get to go the annual Festa of the Madonna in a place they called Italian Harlem. Everyone there had taken weeks to prepare—cooking, cleaning, and sewing special things to wear. Then when the time came, the fiesta began with the sound of a great bell, which rang through everyone's heart. For days and days after, there was a grand celebration of God and family. People came from everywhere and the streets were crowded from one sunup to the next. All during the night there was prayer and mass given to la Madonna for her to please take care of us. After mass I bought a candle, a great big one, because times were tough back home and as bad as the crop was suffering, we didn't know how we would make it through another year. But la Madonna, she saved us—we made it through that year and many more after that.*

*Well, when I was in New York, I had just enough money after buying my candle to get myself some bread from the vendor who was selling baked goods next to the candle cart. Oh, it was so good, I ate the crumbs. Of course, I begged and I begged for the recipe, and the handsome man was good enough to give it to me. I still make this bread each and every July at the time of the Festa of the Madonna to remind me that she continues to bless and protect.*

# GARDEN HERB LOAF

**4¼ cups all-purpose flour, divided**

**3 tablespoons white sugar**

**2 packages Rapid Rise yeast**

**1½ teaspoons salt**

**1 teaspoon dried marjoram**

**1 teaspoon dried thyme**

**1 teaspoon dried rosemary**

**¾ cup milk**

**½ cup water**

**¼ cup butter**

**1 egg**

**1 tablespoon melted butter**

Yields 1 loaf.

In a large mixing bowl, combine 1½ cups flour, sugar, undissolved yeast, salt, marjoram, thyme, and rosemary. Heat milk, water, and ¼ cup butter until very warm (120° to 130°). Stir into dry ingredients. Stir in egg and enough remaining flour to make a soft dough.

On a lightly floured surface, knead dough until smooth and elastic, approximately 4 to 6 minutes. Cover and let rest on floured surface 10 minutes. Divide dough into 3 equal pieces. Roll each piece to 30 inches in length. Braid ropes and pinch ends to seal. Tie knot in center of braid and wrap ends around knot, in opposite directions. Tuck under ends to make a round loaf. Place on a greased baking sheet. Cover and let rise in a warm, draft-free place until it doubles in size. This will take approximately 20 to 40 minutes.

Bake in a 375° oven for 30 to 35 minutes or until done, covering with foil during the last 10 minutes of baking to prevent excessive browning. Brush with remaining butter. Sprinkle with additional herbs, if desired. Remove from sheet and let cool on a wire rack.

*Once I had tasted one fabulous herb bread, I was instantly on the look out for another. Here is the other that I just love, love, love.*

## PARMESAN HERB BREAD

**1 package active dry yeast**

**2 cups warm water (110°)**

**2 tablespoons white sugar**

**2 teaspoons salt**

**2 tablespoons margarine, softened**

**½ cup grated Parmesan cheese**

**1½ tablespoons dried oregano**

**4½ cups all-purpose flour, divided**

**1 tablespoon grated Parmesan cheese**

Yields 1 loaf.

In a large bowl, sprinkle yeast over water. Let stand for a few minutes and then stir to dissolve yeast. Add sugar, salt, margarine, ½ cup Parmesan cheese, oregano, and 3 cups of flour. Beat at a low speed for 2 minutes. Beat in remaining flour and cover bowl with a sheet of wax paper and a kitchen towel. Let rise in a warm place for 45 minutes or until doubled in size.

Preheat the oven to 350°. Lightly grease a round 2-quart casserole dish. Stir batter down for 30 seconds. Turn batter into casserole dish. Sprinkle with the 1 tablespoon Parmesan cheese. Bake for 55 minutes.

*My Aunt Geraldine came over from Italy to America around the turn of the last century. Oh, what a heartbreaking time it was—so many loved ones left behind, never to be seen again. In fact, she said they used to sing a song about it.*

He:　　I'm leaving for America,
　　　　Leaving on the boat.
　　　　I'm leaving you and I'm happy
　　　　never to see you again.

She:　　When you're gone,
　　　　You'll be sorry,
　　　　You'll be sorry,
　　　　You let me go.

He:　　When I'm in America
　　　　I'll marry an American
　　　　And then I'll abandon
　　　　The beautiful Italian.

She:　　I've trampled
　　　　The ring you gave me.
　　　　If you don't believe me, handsome,
　　　　I'll show it to you.

He:　　Oh, woman, you're so changeable,
　　　　Oh, woman without a heart,
　　　　You vowed your love,
　　　　But it was a lie.

She:　　Give me my letters.
　　　　Give me my picture.
　　　　Traitor, I will never
　　　　Love you again.

He:　　I'm leaving for America,
　　　　I'm leaving on the boat.
　　　　One day we will meet again
　　　　And I will love you again.

*Oh, my aunt said that when she was leaving, she had a lump in her throat as big as a biscuit. She was going on to a new place without her sweetheart, but he had promised to join her soon and that would be the dream* that she would hold on to as long as she could. Well, as she stood on the train, all of the immigrants raised their white handkerchiefs when the locomotive pulled away, but all of a sudden, as if out of nowhere, a woman on the platform began to cry and scream as if her soul was being torn in two. "Say hello to my husband," she begged. "Remind him that I am still waiting for the money so I can get my ticket. Please tell him that I feel like if I stay here one more day, I'm going to die." And then the woman fell to her knees and wept like a baby.

Well, with God's good grace, Aunt Geraldine came to America to live in New York, breaking her back over a sewing machine in a factory for fourteen hours a day. Her love never did come, and she never married. She did come to visit us, though, at least once a year and sometimes if I listened at the kitchen door while she baked, I could hear her singing that sad, sad song. Still, she was a wonderful cook and these bread recipes were her favorites.

# DILLY BREAD

1 package active dry yeast
¼ cup warm water
1 pinch white sugar
1 cup cottage cheese
1 tablespoon margarine
2 tablespoons white sugar
1 teaspoon dried minced
   onion
2 teaspoons dill seed
1 teaspoon salt
¼ teaspoon baking soda
1 egg
2¼ cups all-purpose flour
1 tablespoon margarine,
   melted
1 teaspoon kosher salt

Stir the yeast into the warm water and add a pinch of sugar. Set aside. In a large saucepan, warm the cottage cheese and margarine until the fat is melted. Remove from heat and add sugar, onion flakes, dill seed, salt, and baking soda. Mix in egg and dissolved yeast. Stir in flour for a stiff dough. Place dough in an oiled bowl, and turn several times to thoroughly coat. Let rise in a warm place until doubled in size, usually 50 to 60 minutes.

Stir the dough until it is deflated. Place into a buttered 8-inch round, 2-quart casserole dish. Let rise 30 to 40 minutes in a warm place. Bake in a 350° oven for 40 to 50 minutes until golden brown. Brush top with melted margarine. Sprinkle lightly with salt.

Yields 1 loaf.

# TOMATO PESTO BATTER BREAD

1 package active dry yeast

2 tablespoons white sugar

1 cup warm water (110°)

1 cup coarsely chopped fresh basil

2 tablespoons olive oil

3 cups all-purpose flour

½ teaspoon salt

½ cup chopped sun-dried tomatoes

2 tablespoons butter, melted

Yields 1 loaf.

In a small mixing bowl, dissolve yeast and sugar in warm water. Let stand until creamy, about 10 minutes. Place the basil leaves and the olive oil in a blender or food processor and purée until smooth.

In a large mixing bowl, combine flour with the salt. Add the yeast mixture, basil mixture, and sun-dried tomatoes; beat together until well combined, approximately 3 minutes. Cover the bowl with a damp cloth, and let rise in a warm place until doubled in size, approximately 30 minutes.

Lightly grease a 2-quart casserole dish or a 5x9-inch loaf pan. Gently remix the batter with about 20 strokes, and pour into the prepared pan. Let rise in a warm place until doubled in size, approximately 30 minutes.

Preheat the oven to 375°. Bake for 40 to 45 minutes, or until bottom of the loaf sounds hollow when tapped. Remove loaf from pan, place on a wire rack to cool, and brush with melted butter.

# ONION BREAD

2 cups milk

2 packages active dry yeast

¾ cup warm water

3 tablespoons white sugar, divided

2½ teaspoons salt

3 tablespoons margarine or butter

1 (1-ounce) package dry onion soup mix

6¼ cups all-purpose flour

Yields 2 loaves.

In a small saucepan, warm the milk until it bubbles and then remove from heat. Let cool until luke-warm. In a large bowl, stir in yeast, warm water, and 1 teaspoon sugar. Add milk, the remaining sugar, salt, margarine or butter, and soup mix to the yeast. Add flour and combine until dough forms, and then turn out on a lightly floured sur-face. Knead until dough is elastic. Oil a large bowl. Place the dough in the bowl and turn several times to coat. Cover the bowl with a damp cloth and set aside in a warm place to rise for 30 minutes.

Divide dough in half. Shape into loaves and place in two greased 8x4-inch bread pans. Set aside for 30 minutes to rise. Bake in a 375° oven for 40 minutes. When done, loaf will sound hollow when tapped.

*My grandmother had been born in the old country, and I know she must have missed it a great deal. I think that was why she never learned English very well. She held on to her Italian as if it were the very last thing she had of the place she loved so dearly. Still, she knew America was a better place, and she had a good, but not always easy, life here. It is because of her that I speak Italian as I do, and every once in a while, only an Italian phrase will do.*

Finché c'è speranza.
*(Where there's life, there's hope.)*

Freddo di mano, caldo di cuore
*(Cold hands, warm heart.)*

Scopa nuova scopa bene.
*(A new broom sweeps clean.)*

*With this next bread recipe, then, there is only one thing to say when my husband and five boys come to the table, and that is*

Si salvi chi può.
*(Every man for himself.)*

# EASY FOCACCIA

1½ cups bread flour

1½ cups unbleached
  all-purpose flour

2 teaspoons salt

1 tablespoon white sugar

1 package active dry yeast

1⅓ cups warm water (110°)

3 tablespoons extra virgin
  olive oil, divided

2 tablespoons chopped fresh
  rosemary

2 tablespoons grated
  Parmesan cheese

Yields 15 servings.

In a large stoneware bowl, stir together the flours and salt. Make a well in the center of the flour mixture. Sprinkle the sugar and yeast into that well. Carefully pour the water into the well. Let stand until the yeast begins to act, about 5 minutes. Pour 2 tablespoons of the oil into the well. With a wooden spoon, stir the mixture in the center of the bowl. Gradually widen the circle of stirring to take in all of the flour at the sides of the well.

Turn out on a floured surface, and knead just until smooth. Keep the dough soft. Pour ½ teaspoon of the oil into a clean bowl. Place the dough in the bowl, turning once to oil the top. Cover. Let rise until doubled, 30 to 45 minutes.

Punch the dough down. Use 1 teaspoon of the oil to coat a baking sheet, and place the dough on the baking sheet. Gently press the dough out to about ½ inch thick. Pour the remaining 1½ teaspoons oil over the top of the dough. Use the handle end of a wooden spoon to dimple the dough at 1½-inch intervals. Sprinkle with the rosemary and the cheese. Place in a cold oven on the center shelf. Place a flat pan of hot water on the shelf below the bread. Let rise until doubled, 20 to 25 minutes.

Turn on the oven to 375°. Bake the focaccia for 20 to 25 minutes, or until browned on top. Remove from the pan and cool on a wire rack. Serve warm.

*Risparmiare è guadagnare, or a penny saved is a penny earned, as my mama used to say. Oh, how she could stretch a little and make so much. We didn't have a lot, but we never went hungry. Well, Mama wouldn't throw anything out, not even day-old or stale bread. Croutons are a wonderful way to use that little you would normally throw away, and besides, who would dare make a salad without them?*

## GARLIC AND OREGANO CROUTONS

**2 tablespoons olive oil**

**3 garlic cloves,**
  **finely chopped**

**2 tablespoons grated**
  **Romano cheese**

**½ teaspoon dried oregano,**
  **crumbled**

**⅛ teaspoon pepper**

**6 (⅓ inch thick) slices of**
  **French bread baguette**

Preheat the oven to 350°. Heat olive oil in heavy small skillet over low heat. Add garlic and sauté until garlic is just golden, about 2 minutes. Drain immediately. (Reserve oil for another use.) Combine garlic with Romano cheese, oregano, and pepper in small bowl. Place bread slices on small baking sheet. Sprinkle garlic mixture evenly over bread. Bake until cheese melts and croutons are golden brown on edges, approximately 10 minutes.

Yields 6 servings.

## GARLIC LEMON CROUTONS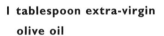

**1 tablespoon extra-virgin**
  **olive oil**

**1 tablespoon chopped garlic**

**1 tablespoon chopped fresh**
  **parsley**

**1 teaspoon grated lemon peel**

**12 thin baguette bread slices**

Preheat the oven to 425°. Mix first 4 ingredients in small bowl. Spread over baguette slices; arrange on baking sheet. Bake croutons until crisp, about 5 minutes.

Yields 12 servings.

# CORNBREAD CROUTONS

I tablespoon olive oil
2 Thomas's corn Toast-R-
   Cakes or I corn muffin,
   cut into ⅓-inch cubes
Salt and pepper

Yields 1 cup.

In a skillet (preferably nonstick), heat oil over moderately high heat until hot but not smoking, and toast cornbread until golden brown and crisp. Season croutons with salt and pepper. Croutons may be made one day ahead and kept in a sealable plastic bag at room temperature.

# GOAT CHEESE PITA CROUTONS

7-inch pita pocket, halved
   crosswise and separated
   to form 4 semicircles
Salt and pepper
2½ ounces (about ⅓ cup)
   soft goat cheese,
   such as Montrachet
¼ cup walnuts, minced

Yields 1 cup.

Preheat the oven to 350°. Spread the rough sides of the pita evenly with goat cheese, season them with salt and pepper, and sprinkle the walnuts evenly over the cheese, pressing them in gently. Cut the pita into 1-inch pieces, and bake the croutons on a baking sheet in the middle of the oven for 15 to 25 minutes, until golden brown.

*When the croutons get stale, don't throw them away either. Now it's time to make breadcrumbs.*

# BREADCRUMBS FOR PASTA

3 cups (I-inch) cubes of day-old
   bread (preferably whole grain)
I tablespoon extra-virgin
   olive oil
Salt to taste

Yields 2 cups.

In a blender, pulse bread in 2 batches until coarsely ground. In a dry large cast-iron skillet, toast bread over moderately low heat, stirring constantly, until golden and crisp, 10 to 20 minutes. In a bowl, toss breadcrumbs with oil and salt. Break crumbs and keep in an airtight container at room temperature about one week.

## FRIED BREADCRUMBS

**½ cup butter or margarine**

**2 cups fine, soft breadcrumbs**

Melt butter over high heat. Sauté crumbs until golden brown, stirring occasionally. Drain.

Yields 2 cups.

We always celebrated St. Joseph's Day because my Aunt Geraldine insisted. St. Joseph is the patron of many places and many trades, but most important to me is that he is the guardian of the Christian spiritual home and the church. March 19 is St. Joseph's Day and it has been around since the Middle Ages. It started with a drought when the farmers promised St. Joseph that if he brought rain, they would prepare a huge feast in his honor. Of course, their prayers were answered and in gratitude they set up, in public, big tables filled with wonderful food. Everyone was invited, especially the poor, and they ate as much as they wanted. When I was a little girl, we used to set up a small altar to St. Joseph with statues, flowers, and lace; it had three steps to it that represented the Holy Trinity.

The bread for this day is supposed to be shaped like a scepter or a beard, but mine always looked like a blob. It tasted good, though. We all go to mass on St. Joseph's Day, and after mass we head to the festive table filled with goodies and wait for the priest to bless the table. After he blesses, we all shout "Viva la tavola di San Giusè," and then we eat until we cannot eat anymore. Usually on St. Joseph's Day I serve a minestrone soup made with just about any vegetable that happens to be handy. But on St. Joseph's Day we do not eat cheese, so instead of grated Parmesan, I serve my minestrone with dry toasted breadcrumbs. At the end of the meal, I give everybody a gift, something small that I hope brings them blessings until the next St. Joseph's Day. Nowadays the family is more scattered than it ever was, so celebrations seem to get fewer and farther between. Still, I try to hold on to some of the old ways, and St. Joseph's Day is a must.

## SAUTÉED BREADCRUMBS FOR TOPPINGS

**1 teaspoon extra-virgin olive oil**

**1 cup fine, freshly ground breadcrumbs (2 to 3 slices of bread)**

**Salt and pepper to taste**

Heat olive oil in a skillet or sauté pan, add breadcrumbs, and toss. Cook until lightly browned. Season to taste and serve on top of pasta, salad greens, or with minestrone, as we do on St. Joseph's Day.

Yields 1 cup.

# Señora Chepita Cotera

**I**t was starting to rain even harder, Chepita noticed sadly as she gazed through the window and into the darkness. It would be dawn soon, yet there was still no hint of brightness. The sky remained somber and gray. Normally Chepita loved the rain. She usually found the sounds of bouncing droplets soothing and beautiful, but at the moment they sounded like rude little slaps, reminding her with a persistent pounding that there would be some who would be cold and wet as a result of their presence. She had tried to help though—had tried desperately to find lost souls a safe place to go, but she had run out of time. They had already disappeared into the thick trees along the fields before she had the slightest chance to offer them, at the very least, words of comfort.

They were the migrant workers, Mexican farm laborers whose efforts fed so many but who themselves often had far too little to eat. Most lived in dilapidated one-room family cabins in camps with no running water or working toilets. They worked in conditions that were strenuous and deforming, shortening their lives to less than fifty years. Sadly, they spent those years in poverty. And the children—child labor was so common that a high school education was rare, because the little ones had to work as soon as they were strong enough to help. It was a miserable existence, yet many Americans sat down day after day to their fruits and their vegetables with no thought whatsoever as to who really provided them. The help center did all it could, but there were simply limits to what they could manage. At seventy-five years of age, Chepita had prayed that things might be better before she died, but now she didn't know if she would ever see that day. Still, they had angels, good people like the ladies at the senior center who came and graciously helped out so very much. Even Larissa and her mother had come out just before Easter and given all the children candy and toys. It had been a very festive afternoon.

Chepita was a good Catholic woman, she knew that. She had followed Jesus on a journey of faith that meant she was to finish His saving grace here on earth. No, she was not a nun or a priest, she was just a woman. But a woman could do a great deal when she put her mind to it, and for years Chepita had been able to think of little else. She worked so hard, but things had not changed very much. Still, Jesus had promised his children material blessings along with spiritual ones, so there was no doubt that her people would have what they needed one day. But when was that day? Nobody seemed to know.

Chepita's thoughts were interrupted as she felt a heavy arm rest itself on her shoulders. Her husband, Jorge. He always seemed to know when she needed him most. After fifty years of marriage, they could comfort each other without saying a single word. The two of them stared into the wet, stormy morning in silence for a few moments before either of them had anything to say. "They will be all right, you know," her husband assured her. "They were both good, strong men. They can stand getting a little wet. After a night outdoors, they'll be back at the help center first thing in the morning, and then you can mother them until your heart breaks in two." He made an attempt at a lighthearted laugh, but it quickly gave way to a sigh. "At least they didn't have women or children with them, I mean none that we know of. We can be thankful for that, Chepita. Learn to take hold of God's goodness whenever you can."

But Jorge didn't have to tell Chepita that. Chepita thanked God each and every day for her husband, her children, her friends, and all the helpers down at the center. She didn't know what she would do without them. They worked tirelessly giving out clothes, blankets, food, and when they were lucky, books for the children. They helped teach reading and writing to the few who could afford to stop working long enough to learn a little bit. But for the most part, the needy were just nameless faces looking for a moment of hospitality before ultimately moving on. But Chepita had accepted a long time ago that a person could do only what a person could do.

Tomorrow she would be raising hell again. She was demanding that the new corporate farms do better by her people than they had been. It used to be that her fight was with men, individual men who owned land and were looking for the cheapest help possible, but now the battle was with business, big business. Today the fights might seem almost impossible, but they sure weren't finished. Chepita had been battling for almost fifty years, but she still had a little fight left. Her people had been living here in eastern North Carolina for almost a century, and it was past time they were made to feel welcome. Those businessmen, they probably thought that they were up against some feeble old lady, but they would learn differently, and soon. She came from a long line of strong women, and they had been carrying the world on their backs for as long as Chepita could remember.

# *Señora Chepita Cotera's Story*
## *Las Tejanas*

*For as long as Chepita's people could remember, the lives of las Tejanas, or the Mexican women of Texas, made an incredible story, and Chepita made it a point to tell anyone who would sit still long enough to listen.*

In the mid-1600s, Mexican pioneers founded a province called Tejas. It was a hard thing to do because the Mexican government offered them no help, and the American Indians were constantly trying to kill them. Still, along with their men, las Tejanas held their own. They nurtured children and maintained homes. They also cleaned missions, made candles, tended the sick, fed the livestock, and tended to the crops.

For the next one hundred fifty years, the Mexican pioneers tried to hold on, but there were too few of them, and they still received no help from the Mexican government and were still the victims of constant Indian raids. Finally, in the early 1800s, the Mexican government invited Anglos (white

Americans) to come and join the Mexican pioneers. At first, everyone seemed to get along and las Tejanas offered their new friends help and hospitality. But as more and more Anglos arrived, things changed and soon the Anglos began to see the Mexicans as inferior. The men were said to be lazy, sneaky, and dumb, and our women were seen as immoral because they bared their arms and showed their necks.

Well, it wasn't too long before the Anglos pushed and Tejas (now known as Texas) became independent—the Lone Star Republic it was called. That didn't last long because a few years later, with one Mexican-American war thrown in, Texas became part of the United States of America. Now the Anglos truly made life miserable for the Mexicans, and some took property and possessions as they desired. My people, well, they got no help from the law at all. It was then that my family pretty much lost everything they had and suddenly became laborers to survive. But my great-grandmother and great-grandfather were among the first Mexicans

to be Americans, and of course, they were also among the first to be Southerners. That's something, I suppose.

My grandmother talked very little about her childhood, so I know very little about my great-grandparents. I do know that my grandmother met my grandfather in the early 1900s. You see, my grandmother had to work because her mother could not. Right about that time the Spanish newspaper in Brownsville, *El Cronista*, decided that allowing married women to work outside the home was dangerous to the well-being of the family. Unmarried daughters could work and many of them did as maids or clerks. It was a sudden change in thinking, but a lot of Mexicans accepted it as truth and women began staying home. They did make a little money if they took in laundry, sewing, or even boarders, but my great-grandfather would not hear of any of that, so my grandmother (an unmarried daughter) went to work in a café where many of the handsome artists and musicians came in to eat during the day while other men were off working the land.

My grandmother said that the first time she saw my grandfather, he was tall and bronze with thick dark hair, a voice like silk, and shiny black boots. He was a *guitarrero* (singing guitarist) who played *música* Tejana (Tex-Mex music). In the dark of the night, he would go from cantina to cantina singing beautiful songs—sometimes telling old stories and sometimes the latest news or happenings in town. The other men would listen and discuss the songs, sometimes getting quite rowdy if they didn't like what they were hearing. Sometimes Grandfather would just play music without any words, and the music was different from what you would imagine. *La música* Tejana had been around since the 1700s, and over the years the Mexican sounds met up with German and French sounds, so many of the tunes my grandfather played sounded like polkas with a little Spanish beat thrown in. Some of the older musicians played the violin, and when I was a girl, some played the accordion. But Grandpa stuck with his guitar, and he did very well.

Grandmother said that she fell in love with my grandfather the very first time she heard him sing, so at twenty years old she married her twenty-five-year-old *guitarrero*. They decided to leave Texas and take their show on the road, following the trail of migrant workers as they made their way through the Piney Woods to North Carolina. Grandfather would play in the migrant camps, and the men would toss him coins if they liked his songs. My mama was born in one of those camps under the starlit skies between a Bible and a bottle of tequila. Maybe that was why my mother turned out to be the spirited woman that I knew and loved.

My mother spent her childhood bouncing all around, so when she met and fell in love with my father, she insisted that they settle down in one place no matter what. Now in the Mexican culture, it was unusual for a woman to speak up like that. Decisions are made by the husband, who is without question the head of the house, although the wife does have the final say in matters to do with the children. However, my mother always spoke her mind, and my father respected that, so they both took jobs on a tobacco farm not too far from here. They lived in a cabin the owner provided because my mother insisted. And not only did she insist on housing, but she fought and fought until she and my father got something close to decent wages. Of course, she couldn't stop there; she felt strongly that she had to make things better for other Mexican workers as well. So she collected money to send a young woman to nursing school; the nurse came back when she was finished and took good care of our people for years. Mother also organized a week-long strike once, to shorten the workday to twelve hours, and sadly it's still twelve hours to this day. In between all of that troublemaking, she did manage to have six children and I am the third of the set.

Mexicans are always taught that family is more important than anything, and that when there is little else, there are always loved ones. So as children we were taught to stick together, and when we had no one else to play with, we entertained each other. We went to school some of the time and we worked the rest. It seems to me like my childhood went by in a flash, and before I knew it, I was a young woman in love and preparing to marry. I had known my husband since we were three years old, and I think we'd known we were going to marry each other since we were twelve, so our love took no one by surprise.

Unlike most men, my husband didn't mind if I worked, so I was a clerk at a grocery store in town. The owners were good people, but some of the customers were another story. Many of the white men would see a Mexican woman, and they seemed to believe for some strange reason that we didn't deserve the same respect that their women did. But Mr. James would not allow them to be cruel, and I appreciated that.

My husband and I had three children, a small family by Mexican standards, but I had learned some things back then that kept a woman from having so many babies, and I used them, too. Because my husband and I were blessed enough to have steady jobs and make a decent living, we were able to send our children to the big city to get college educated. We couldn't go see them because nobody knew that they were Mexican, and we didn't want to ruin things for them, but they came home every chance they could. Of course, they have never forgotten where they came from, so they still come back often and help out at the center. They also send money, which we need very badly.

My granddaughter is now in law school, and every time I think about it, I get this silly grin on my face. She says that she is going to use her education to help our people, and I couldn't be more proud. Our people have lived in eastern North Carolina for a little more than a century, but we, the women, are still Tejanas at heart—working hard, raising hell, and loving well.

# Señora Chepita's Mexican Delights

*Tortillas are to us what sliced bread is to everyone else and I love to make them, especially for people who are non-Mexicans, because they remind us all how much we have given to America's food. People are constantly asking me where tortillas come from, and I tell them exactly what was told to me.*

*As my grandfather explained it to me, when the Spanish came to Mexico almost five hundred years ago, they came looking for gold, and they found it, too. But they also found food, really good food, and of course, most of that food begins with corn, our sacred plant. It gives us starch, protein, and a little bit of fat. Well, to make tortillas, you need the skinless kernels of corn called* **nixtamal***, mashed into* **masa** *(a dough to make tortillas), and in some parts of Mexico, you can still see some of the women making it the ancient way.*

*First, the woman will squat on the ground in front of a big stone called a* **metate***. Then she puts a handful of* **nixtamal** *on the flat part of the stone, and she scrubs back and forth with a stone roller. The* **masa** *may be white, yellow, or some other color depending on the corn, but for good tortillas, the woman must get the* **masa** *just right, not too wet or too dry. Then she takes a piece of* **masa** *(almost a handful, but not quite) between her wet hands and flattens it until it is just thick enough. After all that, the cooking is easy.*

*Luckily, we don't have to do all that to make tortillas toady. These next recipes are so simple that you can have tortillas in no time.*

## WHOLE WHEAT TORTILLAS

1½ **cups unbleached**
   **all-purpose flour**
1½ **cups whole wheat flour**
¼ **teaspoon baking powder**
1 **cup warm water (110°)**
2 **teaspoons vegetable oil**
¼ **teaspoon salt**
**Cornstarch**

Stir together all ingredients except cornstarch. On a floured board, knead dough until smooth. Divide the dough into 12 equal balls. Dust lightly with cornstarch. Roll into a circle as thin as possible on a lightly floured board. Drop onto a very hot ungreased griddle. Cook until brown spots appear on one side. Turn and cook on second side.

Yields 12 tortillas.

# Tortillas de Harina (Flour Tortillas)

2 cups flour

I teaspoon salt

3 tablespoons shortening

½ to ¾ cups lukewarm water

Yields 8 tortillas.

Sift together flour and salt. Add shortening, and using your fingertips, work shortening into the flour until it disappears. Add enough lukewarm water to make dough form a ball. If necessary, add more water until the bowl is clear of all dough. On a lightly floured surface, knead dough for 2 minutes. Using your hands to roll, shape into 1½-inch-diameter balls and let stand 15 minutes. On a floured surface, roll out dough into a circle about 7 inches in diameter. Bake in a hot ungreased griddle or skillet for 30 seconds on each side, or until bubbles appear on surface and they are lightly browned.

Tortillas may be cooked ahead of time and placed in a plastic bag for several days in the refrigerator.

*Here's that corn again, except this time it's fritters with a wonderful roasted tomato sauce. Enjoy!*

# Corn Fritters

½ recipe for Roasted Tomato Sauce (recipe follows)

Vegetable oil for frying

I cup unbleached flour

½ cup milk

I teaspoon baking powder

I teaspoon vegetable oil

2 eggs, large

I cup whole kernel corn

Yields 4 servings.

Prepare the Roasted Tomato Sauce (recipe follows) and set aside, keeping it warm. Heat the oil (1 inch deep) in a deep fryer or Dutch oven. Beat the remaining ingredients, except the corn, together until smooth; then add the corn. Drop by level tablespoonfuls into the hot oil. Fry until completely cooked through, about 5 minutes. Drain on paper towels. Serve with the warm Roasted Tomato Sauce.

## ROASTED TOMATO SAUCE

**4 pounds tomatoes, very red and fresh (approximately 12 to 16 medium)**

**1 pound sweet onions**

**5 large garlic cloves**

**2 tablespoons fruity green olive oil**

**1 teaspoon salt, or to taste**

**3 tablespoons coarsely chopped fresh basil**

Yields 2 cups.

To peel the tomatoes, cut a cross in the bottom of each one with a knife. Place them in boiling water for 1 minute. Remove them from the hot water and place into cold water; then slip off their skins and trim them over a bowl, catching all the juice. Cut the tomatoes into large chunks or wedges. Peel and chop the onions. Peel and slice the garlic cloves.

Toss all ingredients together, including the juice of the tomatoes, and spread evenly over a large baking sheet.

Put the tomatoes in a 375° oven and roast them for about 2 to 2½ hours, stirring once after the first hour, then once every 30 minutes. Most of the liquid will cook away, and the tomatoes will melt into a soft, thick, slightly caramelized marmalade. Can be served on corn fritters, pasta, rice, pizza, or in a quesadilla.

*These biscuit recipes are perfect for breakfast. I try to make them a least once a week for my husband and he loves them. I also make them for the migrant workers at the help center and they love them, too!*

# MASA BISCUITS

3¾ cups unbleached
   all-purpose flour, divided

1½ cups *masa harina*
   *de maíz*

2 tablespoons plus
   1 teaspoon baking powder

1 teaspoon salt

1 stick (4 ounces) unsalted
   butter, well chilled and
   cut into small pieces

½ cup vegetable shortening,
   well chilled and cut into
   small pieces

2 cups cultured buttermilk,
   chilled

Ham and Green Chili Gravy
   (recipe follows)

Yields 12 large biscuits.

Preheat the oven to 450°. In a large bowl, stir together 3½ cups of the flour, the *masa harina*, baking powder, and salt. With a pastry cutter, blend in the butter and shortening until the mixture resembles a coarse and slightly lumpy meal. Stir in the buttermilk until a soft, crumbly dough is formed. Sprinkle the work surface with half of the remaining flour. Turn the dough out, gather it into a ball, and briefly knead just till it holds together. Flatten the dough, sprinkle it with the rest of the flour, and roll it out about 1 inch thick. With a round 3-inch cutter, cut the biscuits, and then transfer them to 2 ungreased baking sheets, spacing them 2 inches apart. Gather the scraps into a ball, roll it out to 1 inch thick, and cut out the remaining biscuits. Put biscuits into the oven and bake about 15 minutes or until they are golden.

Split the biscuits and spoon Ham and Green Chili Gravy (see next page) on each biscuit.

# HAM AND GREEN CHILI GRAVY

5 long green chilies
   (Anaheims)
6 tablespoons unsalted
   butter
1 pound firm smoked ham,
   trimmed and cut into
   ¼-inch cubes
¼ cup unbleached
   all-purpose flour
5 cups milk (2 percent okay)
½ teaspoon salt
8 freshly baked
   Masa Biscuits, split

Yields 8 servings.

In the open flame of a gas burner, or under a pre-heated broiler, roast the long green chilies, turning them until they are lightly but evenly charred. Steam the chilies in a closed paper bag, or in a bowl covered with a plate, until cool. Rub away the burned peel. Stem and seed the chilies and coarsely chop them. There should be about ¾ cup.

In a large skillet over medium-low heat, melt the butter. Add the ham cubes and cook them, stirring constantly, until lightly browned, about 10 minutes. Sprinkle the flour over the ham cubes and cook, stirring constantly, for 5 minutes. Slowly whisk the milk into the ham mixture. Stir in the green chilies and salt. Raise the heat to medium and bring the mixture to a simmer. Cook, stirring occasionally and scraping the bottom of the pan, until thickened into a medium gravy, about 7 minutes.

Serve on Masa Biscuits that have been split.

VARIATION: Smoked turkey can be used in place of the ham.

# BOLILLOS (MEXICAN ROLLS)

### STARTER SPONGE
**3 tablespoons sugar**

**2½ cups warm water (110°)**

**I package active dry yeast**

**I½ cups unbleached all-purpose flour**

**¼ cup gluten flour**

### DOUGH
**I tablespoon salt**

**I tablespoon very soft butter**

**½ teaspoon cinnamon**

**3½ cups unbleached all-purpose flour, divided**

**½ cup gluten flour**

**½ cup warm water mixed with 2 teaspoons salt**

Yields 12 rolls.

Whisk together all starter sponge ingredients until well blended. Cover with plastic wrap or a damp towel, set in a warm place, and let rise, undisturbed, for 1 hour.

In a large mixing bowl, combine the starter sponge, salt, butter, cinnamon, 3 cups of the unbleached flour, and the gluten flour. Turn out dough onto a board and knead in the remaining ½ cup flour. Knead for at least 10 minutes (or if you have a heavy duty mixer with a paddle attachment, knead for 4 minutes). The dough tends to be sticky, so have patience. The finished dough should be on the softer-stickier side rather than being perfectly smooth. During the kneading process, the dough should develop long, stretchy strands, a sign the gluten has been well developed.

Place the dough in a greased bowl, turn to coat with grease, and cover with plastic wrap. Set in a warm place and let rise for 1 hour or until doubled in size.

Punch down the dough and turn out onto a floured board. Pinch off 12 equal-sized pieces of dough. With floured hands, roll each piece into an oblong, turning rough edges under with your fingers. To achieve pointed tips, gently pull the ends of each oblong, giving a slight twist as you pull. If the bolillos have sort of a rough surface, all the better.

Place *bolillos* on heavy baking sheets that have been greased or lined with parchment paper. Cover with a kitchen towel and let rise for 30 minutes, or until doubled in size.

Preheat the oven to 400°. Pour the salted water into a spray bottle. Bake *bolillos* for 10 minutes, misting with the salt water at least 3 or 4 times. This will produce a crusty exterior. Reduce oven temperature to 375° and bake for 20 minutes longer or until rolls are golden brown.

## Jalapeño Drop Biscuits

1 cup flour

½ cup yellow cornmeal

2 teaspoons baking powder

½ teaspoon baking soda

½ teaspoon salt

2 tablespoons cold unsalted
butter, cut into bits

1½ cups coarsely grated
Monterey Jack cheese

2 (2-inch) pickled jalapeño
peppers, seeded and
minced

2 (2-inch) fresh jalapeño
peppers, seeded and minced

⅔ cup milk

Preheat the oven to 425°. In a medium bowl, sift together the flour, cornmeal, baking powder, baking soda, and salt. Add the butter and blend the mixture until it resembles coarse meal. Stir in the Monterey Jack cheese and the peppers; add the milk. Stir the mixture until it just forms a soft, sticky dough. Drop the dough by rounded tablespoonfuls onto a greased baking sheet, and bake the biscuits for 15 to 17 minutes or until lightly golden.

Yields 16 biscuits.

*My good friend Carlita makes this bread for her Cinco de Mayo celebration, and she says she can never make enough.*

## Sopaipillas (Puffy Fried Bread)

4 cups all-purpose flour

1¼ teaspoons salt

3 teaspoons baking powder

3 tablespoons sugar

2 tablespoons shortening

1¼ cups milk (approximately)

Salad oil for deep frying

Yields 4 dozen.

In a large mixing bowl, sift together flour, salt, baking powder, and sugar. Cut in the shortening with a pastry cutter, and add enough milk to make a soft dough, just firm enough to roll. Cover bowl and let dough stand for 30 to 60 minutes. On a lightly floured board, roll out dough to ¼ inch thick and cut into diamond-shaped pieces. Heat about 1 inch of oil in a frying pan to about 370° to 375°. Add a few pieces at a time; turn at once so they will puff evenly, and turn back to brown both sides. Drain on paper towels.

*Each and every year on May 5 (Cinco de Mayo), my family has a great big dinner in celebration of that day in 1862 when the French were driven out of Mexico after they tried to set up a colony there. For Chicanos, or Mexican Americans, today Cinco de Mayo signifies that we can stand up to our enemies. Finally we can find ourselves again in the soul of our own heritage, and we can use this celebration to remind us to guard against those who would have us forget our roots.*

*At my house on this great day, there is music, food, and sometimes even speeches. At the end of the meal, we all lift our glasses and yell* "Viva la Raza" *(long live the race), and I can tell you that my dinner would not be complete without that wonderful spirit of pride or this tasty bread.*

Viva la Raza, *everyone!*
Viva la Raza!

# MEXICAN HOGAN BREAD

3 packages active dry yeast

I cup warm water (105° to 115°)

I tablespoon sugar

I teaspoon salt

I tablespoon butter or margarine, softened

I (2-ounce) jar diced pimientos, drained

I (4-ounce) can diced green chilies, drained

⅓ cup chopped green onions

½ cup shredded American cheese

I egg

½ cup creamed corn

I tablespoon honey

½ cup cornmeal plus more for sprinkling

5 to 6 cups all-purpose flour, divided

Yields 3 loaves.

Dissolve yeast in warm water in warmed bowl of mixer. Add sugar and stir; let stand 5 minutes. Add salt, butter, pimientos, chilies, onions, cheese, egg, corn, and honey. Attach bowl and dough hook to mixer. Turn to medium speed and mix 1 minute. Add cornmeal and 4 cups flour. On medium speed, mix 2 minutes. Continuing on medium speed, add remaining flour, ½ cup at a time, until dough clings to hook and cleans sides of bowl. Knead on medium speed for 2 minutes longer.

Place in greased bowl, and turn over to grease the other side. Cover; let rise in warm place, free from draft, until doubled in bulk, about 1 hour. Punch dough down and divide into thirds. Shape each third into a slightly flattened ball, and place on greased baking sheets. Cover again; let rise in warm place, free from draft, until doubled in bulk, about 1 hour.

Preheat the oven to 350°. Cut 2 slashes with a sharp knife in a cross pattern on top of each loaf. Sprinkle with cornmeal and bake for 45 minutes. Remove from baking sheets immediately and cool on wire racks.

When I was a little girl, my mother used to tell me a cute little story about the Jalapeño Cornbread Man. It seems that once upon a time, there was a Chicano woman who came to North Carolina many years ago with her husband and children to work at one of the large chicken farms. Well, she fell in love with the good Southern food, especially the bread, but like any good Mexican cook, she just couldn't leave well enough alone, and she simply had to spice things up her own way.

As the story goes, one night for supper she decided to make her husband a very special cornbread man. She added jalapeño after jalapeño until her husband finally yelled, "Enough! One more pepper and it will be too hot to handle." Of course, she didn't listen; she simply had to add that one more pep-per. Oh, that did it! That cornbread man came alive before their very eyes and hopped all around that kitchen for quite some time yelling all the while, "You can't catch me, I'm the Jalapeño Cornbread Man." I tell you, it took almost an hour before the husband could even get his hands on that cornbread man to eat him, and even then, the little cornbread man was still talking. So the lesson is, a few jalapeños make a good thing better, but be careful that you don't add too many, because you never know what may happen when you do.

## JALAPEÑO CORNBREAD (USE FOR STUFFING IN NEXT RECIPE)

**2 cups yellow cornmeal, preferably stone ground**

**2 cups creamed corn**

**2 cups grated sharp cheddar cheese**

**1 cup unsalted butter, melted**

**1 cup buttermilk**

**¼ cup drained, chopped green chilies**

**4 eggs, lightly beaten**

**2 teaspoons baking soda**

**Salt**

**2 tablespoons unsalted butter, divided**

Preheat the oven to 375°. Combine cornmeal, corn, and cheese in large bowl and blend well. Add melted butter, buttermilk, chilies, eggs, baking soda, and salt to taste and mix thoroughly.

Melt 1 tablespoon butter in each of two 9-inch cast-iron skillets or heavy 9-inch baking pans until very hot, but not browned. Divide batter between skillets, smoothing with spatula. Bake until done, about 45 minutes.

Yields 7 cups or 2 (9-inch) skillets

# JALAPEÑO CORNBREAD STUFFING

**7 cups crumbled Jalapeño Cornbread (see previous recipe)**

**4 cups toast cubes**

**3 hard-cooked eggs, chopped**

**¼ cup (½ stick) unsalted butter**

**2 cups finely chopped onion**

**I teaspoon finely minced garlic**

**I½ cups finely chopped green pepper**

**I cup finely chopped celery**

**Turkey gizzard, trimmed and finely chopped**

**Turkey liver, chopped**

**Turkey heart, chopped**

**Salt and pepper**

**3 eggs, lightly beaten**

**½ cup turkey broth (approximately)**

Combine crumbled Jalapeño Cornbread, toast cubes, and chopped eggs in a large bowl and toss lightly to mix well. Set aside. Melt butter in a large skillet over medium heat. Add onion and garlic and sauté until softened. Add green pepper and celery and cook until crisp-tender, about 3 minutes. Add gizzard, liver, and heart and sauté just until they lose raw color. Season with salt and a generous grinding of pepper. Let cool slightly. Add onion mixture to cornbread mixture and blend well. Stir in eggs. Blend in enough broth to moisten lightly.

Yields 8 cups.

# JALAPEÑO CUMIN BUTTER

**2 pickled jalapeños, finely chopped**

**½ teaspoon ground cumin**

**I stick unsalted butter, at room temperature**

In a bowl or food processor, beat the jalapeños and cumin into room temperature butter. Cover and refrigerate until ready to use. Serve at room temperature. Best if made at least one day in advance.

Yields ½ cup.

*When Larissa asked me for my favorite recipes, she also wanted me to share some of my family's often-used expressions. Of course, we have many, but my sister always had the very best ones. Some of the ones I remember are*

Las personas envidiosas nunca felicitian, ellas sólo tragan.
*(Envious people never compliment, they only swallow.)*

Los besos son primero, y los cusses vienen después.
*(Kisses come first, and cusses come later.)*

La verdadera amistad está como una sola raya del alma en dos llenar dos cuerpos.
*(True friendship is like a single soul split in two to fill two bodies.)*

*These next three recipes are my sister Lucia's.*

# RED BELL PEPPER AND CORIANDER PANCAKES

⅔ **cup all-purpose flour**

¼ **cup cornmeal**

½ **teaspoon red pepper flakes**

⅔ **cup milk**

⅔ **cup diced red bell pepper**

3 **tablespoons cilantro leaves**

2 **eggs, separated**

1 **tablespoon melted butter,**
  **plus butter for cooking**

Salt and pepper to taste

Sour cream

Guacamole (see page 202)

Yields 36 to 40 pancakes.

In a bowl mix together flour, cornmeal, red pepper flakes, milk, red bell pepper, cilantro, egg yolks, and melted butter. Season with salt and pepper. With an electric mixer, beat egg whites to soft peak and fold into batter.

In a nonstick pan over moderate heat, brush some melted butter. Drop batter by spoonful into pan so that pancakes are about 1½ inches in diameter. When bubbles appear on surface of pancakes, flip and allow undersides to cook until golden. Top each serving of pancakes with a ½ teaspoon sour cream and an equal amount of Guacamole (see page 202).

# STUFFED CORNMEAL PANCAKES

## BATTER

½ cup cornmeal

⅓ cup plain flour

I egg

¼ to ⅓ cup milk

2 tablespoons corn oil

Oil to grease

## FILLING

9 ounces dry white
    kidney beans or any
    small white bean

I teaspoon salt

3 tomatoes

3 garlic cloves

I ½ pounds spinach

2 tablespoons olive oil

I tablespoon tomato paste

¼ cup dry red wine

I tablespoon lemon juice

Yields 6 servings.

The day before, soak the beans in water overnight. Drain and rinse under running water. Place the soaked beans in a saucepan of boiling water and simmer, uncovered, for approximately 1¼ hours until the beans are tender, adding the salt after 45 minutes. Drain.

BATTER: In a medium-sized bowl, combine the cornmeal, flour, egg, milk, and corn oil. Whisk until the mixture is smooth, adding more milk if necessary until it reaches a pouring consistency. Allow the mixture to stand for 30 minutes.

FILLING: In a saucepan, boil water and blanch the tomatoes. Peel and dice. Peel and slice the garlic. Wash the spinach. Heat olive oil in the frying pan. Fry the sliced garlic on high heat for 2 minutes, until brown. Add the chopped tomatoes, tomato paste, red wine, lemon juice, and beans; simmer uncovered for 20 minutes. Add a little water if necessary. Add the spinach and stir until it has wilted; then set mixture aside, keeping it warm.

PANCAKE: Brush a nonstick frying pan with a little oil, and heat until the oil is hot. Using a ladle, spoon a little of the batter into the frying pan. Tilt the pan so that the batter evenly coats the bottom of the pan. Return any excess batter to the bowl. Cook the pancake for approximately 30 seconds, until it is evenly browned. Slip a spatula underneath the batter and carefully flip the pancake over. Cook another 20 seconds and slide the pancake onto a plate. Put some filling on pancake and roll up. Serve warm.

## Guacamole

1 avocado, peeled and finely
diced

2 tablespoons lime juice

1 jalapeño, seeded and diced

2 tablespoons chopped
cilantro

Salt and pepper to taste

3 Roma tomatoes, seeded
and diced

In a bowl combine avocado, lime juice, jalapeño, cilantro, salt, and pepper. Mash avocado with fork to smooth. Add tomatoes and mix well.

Yields 1 cup.

*My husband is one of those men who eats all the time but never gains a pound, so I am always looking for snacks I can make quickly for in-between meals. These next two recipes are delicious and filling. I use them, too, as a great way to say "welcome" to holiday guests who are passing through but cannot stay for dinner.*

## Queso Triángulos

3 cups cold water

1 cup coarse yellow cornmeal

1 envelope onion soup mix

4 ounces mild chopped
green chilies, drained

½ cup whole kernel corn

½ cup red pepper, roasted
and finely chopped

½ cup sharp cheddar cheese,
shredded

Bring the water to a boil in a 3-quart saucepan. With a wire whisk, stir in the cornmeal and onion soup mix. Simmer uncovered, stirring constantly, for 25 minutes or until thickened. Stir in the chilies, corn, and roasted red peppers.

Spread the mixture in a lightly greased 9-inch square pan and sprinkle with the cheddar cheese. Let stand for 20 minutes or until firm. Cut into triangles or squares. Serve as an appetizer.

Yields 8 servings.

# MEXICAN CHEESE MELTS

2½ cups (10 ounces)
  shredded hot pepper
  Monterey Jack cheese
10 (10-inch) flour tortillas
2½ teaspoons vegetable oil,
  divided

Yields 5 servings.

Sprinkle ½ cup of cheese each over 5 tortillas and top with the remaining tortillas. In a large skillet, heat ½ teaspoon oil over medium heat. Place 1 tortilla sandwich in the skillet at a time and cook for 3 to 4 minutes, or until the cheese is melted, turning over halfway through the cooking. Remove to a covered platter and repeat with the remaining sandwiches. Cut each melt into 4 wedges and serve.

TIP: You can top the wedges with sour cream, salsa, and onions.

*If you need a taste of Mexico that you can wrap up easily and take wherever you go, this sandwich is it.*

# MEXICAN CHICKEN SANDWICH

4 chicken cutlets
½ teaspoon chili powder
¼ teaspoon salt
¼ teaspoon ground cumin
⅛ teaspoon cayenne pepper
1 tablespoon vegetable oil
⅓ cup reduced-fat mayonnaise
¾ teaspoon grated lime peel
¾ teaspoon jalapeño hot sauce
⅛ teaspoon ground pepper
4 hard rolls, split
4 leaves green leaf lettuce
1 tomato, thinly sliced
1 avocado, pitted and sliced

Yields 4 servings.

Pound chicken between wax paper to ¼ inch thick. In small cup, combine chili powder, salt, cumin, and cayenne pepper. Sprinkle over both sides of chicken. In a large skillet, heat oil over medium-high heat. Cook chicken 1½ to 2 minutes per side, until cooked through; set aside.

Combine mayonnaise, lime peel, jalapeño sauce, and pepper. Spread mayonnaise on cut sides of rolls. Put lettuce, chicken, tomato slices, and avocado slices on bottoms of rolls; replace tops.

*So many Tex-Mexicans started their journey in the Southwest but traveled to other parts of the country looking for work. These transplanted Chicanos set up* barrios *(communities) wherever they went, and out of one of these* barrios *in Louisiana came this recipe. My* tia *Juanita made this for me one time when she came for a visit, and I've been making it ever since.*

## MEXICAN BREAD PUDDING

**I loaf good-quality white bread**

**2 sticks (½ pound) unsalted butter, melted (optional)**

**3 cups firmly packed dark brown sugar**

**I½ tablespoons whole cloves**

**5 (3-inch) cinnamon sticks**

**I½ teaspoons anise seeds**

**8 cups water**

**I cup unsalted shelled peanuts**

**I cup raisins**

**2 cups shredded white cheddar or Monterey Jack cheese**

**20 candied peanuts (optional)**

Yields 12 servings.

Slice bread into ½-inch-thick slices. Preheat the oven to 400°. Grease two cookie sheets. Arrange the bread on the cookie sheets and bake until golden. Turn and continue baking until both sides are toasted. Using a pastry brush, coat or drizzle the bread with melted butter, if desired.

Make the syrup. In a small pot combine the brown sugar, cloves, cinnamon sticks, and anise seeds with 8 cups of water. Bring to a boil and cook uncovered, stirring occasionally, until the sugar dissolves. Reduce the heat and simmer vigorously, uncovered, until the liquid reduces to a syrup, about 25 minutes. Strain out spices.

Prepare the casserole. Preheat the oven to 350°. Butter a 13x9x2-inch baking dish. Place a layer of bread on the bottom. Slowly pour 1 cup syrup evenly over the bread layer, and allow the bread to soak up the syrup. Sprinkle with a third of the peanuts, a third of the raisins, and a third of the cheese. Repeat the layers twice, ending with cheese. Pour the remaining syrup over the casserole.

Cover and bake for 30 to 45 minutes or until the cheese has melted. During the last 10 minutes, uncover the casserole and top it with additional candied peanuts, if desired.

*It would not be Christmas without pans and pans of great sweets for my grandbabies. These recipes are a great way to end a meal if you are an adult or to begin a meal if you are a little one. Either way, all of these desserts are incredible.*

# APPLE ENCHILADAS

I large can (21 ounces)
   apple pie filling
6 flour tortillas
⅓ cup butter or margarine
½ cup sugar
½ cup firmly packed light
   brown sugar
I teaspoon ground cinnamon
½ teaspoon nutmeg

Yields 6 servings.

Preheat the oven to 350°. Spoon fruit filling evenly down center of tortillas. Roll to enclose filling. Bring butter, sugar, brown sugar, cinnamon, and nutmeg to a boil in a saucepan at reduced heat. Reduce heat and stir constantly for 5 minutes. Pour over center of tortillas. Let stand 30 minutes. Bake for 20 minutes.

# CHURROS

I cup water
¾ stick butter
I pinch of salt
I cup white flour
3 eggs
½ teaspoon cinnamon
Corn oil for frying
I cup powdered sugar

Yields 18 *churros*.

Bring water to a boil. Add butter and salt. Add flour and remove from heat. Beat with a fork until well mixed. Beat in the eggs and cinnamon. Put the mixture into a pastry bag. Heat about 1 inch of oil in a pan, or use a deep fryer. Squeeze the mixture into the oil, making the *churros* about 7 inches long. Cook 3 to 5 at a time, turning occasionally, until they are a nice golden color. Drain on paper towels. Transfer to another dish; sprinkle with sifted powdered sugar. Serve immediately.

# PAN DULCE

**6 tablespoons butter or margarine**

**1 cup milk**

**1 package active dry yeast**

**1 teaspoon salt**

**⅓ cup white sugar**

**5 cups all-purpose flour, divided**

**2 eggs**

### STREUSEL

**½ cup white sugar**

**⅔ cup all-purpose flour**

**3½ tablespoons butter or margarine**

**2 egg yolks**

**2 tablespoons cocoa powder (optional)**

**1 egg**

**2 tablespoons milk**

Yields 14 servings.

In a small pan, combine 6 tablespoons butter or margarine and 1 cup milk; heat to 110°. In a large mixing bowl, combine yeast, salt, ⅓ cup sugar, and 2 cups of the flour. Pour in warmed milk mixture. Beat, scraping often, with an electric mixer on medium speed for 2 minutes. With a spoon, beat in enough of the remaining flour to form a stiff dough. Knead on a floured board until smooth, about 5 minutes. Place in a greased bowl, turn to grease the top, cover, and let rise until doubled.

STREUSEL: While the dough is rising, make streusel. Stir together ½ cup sugar and ⅔ cup flour. Mix in 3 ½ tablespoons cold butter or margarine. Mix to get fine crumbs. Blend in 2 egg yolks with a fork. (For chocolate streusel, mix 2 tablespoons cocoa powder with flour.)

Punch down dough and turn onto floured board. Divide into 14 pieces. Shape each into a ball. Shape 7 balls into seashells. For each round, squeeze ¼ cup streusel into a firm ball and press over the top. Score with slightly curved parallel lines to resemble a scallop shell. Shape the remaining 7 balls into crescents: roll balls into 7 (4x8-inch) ovals. Top each with 3 tablespoons streusel. Roll each oval from short end; stop halfway, fold in sides, and finish rolling. Curl ends in to form a crescent. Place buns (seashells and crescents) about 2 inches apart on a greased baking sheet. Cover lightly and allow to rise until doubled, about 45 minutes. In a small bowl, beat together 1 egg and 2 tablespoons milk.

Preheat the oven to 375°. Brush buns with egg mixture. Bake until lightly browned, about 15 to 17 minutes.

# TORTILLA FLATS

2 tablespoons sugar

I teaspoon ground
   cinnamon

Oil for frying

I wheat flour tortilla
   (do not substitute corn
   tortilla; it does not take
   on the texture of
   pastry when fried)

I tablespoon butter, melted

I scoop vanilla ice cream

Strawberries, sliced
   (or fresh peaches, sliced)

I tablespoon almonds,
   slivered and toasted

Yields 1 serving.

Combine sugar and cinnamon and set aside. Heat oil in a skillet and fry tortilla on both sides until golden brown and puffy. Drain on a paper towel. Brush tortilla with melted butter and sprinkle with cinnamon-sugar mixture. Top with ice cream and garnish with fruit and nuts.

# Ma Chère Elise

*Mais*, Elise had a bad pain today. It had started in the middle of her back and now was traveling down the right side into her leg. *Poo-yie,* she was still able to get around, but as her *grand-mère* would have said, "*C'est la vie,* what can you do? Still, I am jumping, just not so very high." Elise sat down on the hard-backed kitchen chair that offered her absolutely no relief, but that didn't matter. She was transfixed by the little bundle that rested itself in the middle of the table. It was a stack of letters—a stack that painfully reminded Elise that her life was now really more a collection of used-to-bes than new possibilities. Old age had caught up with her in a very big way, and there were times she would like to have forgotten that, but she couldn't—at least not today. Not with an aching right hip and a pile of tattered tales from long ago sitting right there in front of her.

She had pulled the letters out of her treasure box a few days ago to share some of them with Larissa because many of the notes had recipes attached to them. She and her sister Rita had written each other faithfully once upon a time (*Chère Soeur,* they had all lovingly began), and back then she had looked forward to the letters—rereading them sometimes over and over again. During that time she had tried her best to imagine what was happening in Shreveport, Louisiana, every single moment that her sister had been forced to stay away. Oh, how she had missed her. Still, Rita had managed to make a fairly fine home in north Louisiana, even if it wasn't the magical, mystical home of Cajun country. It turned out to be a fairly pleasant place, and her sister had made many, many friends there—wonderful friends that had helped her when she needed help the most.

Rita had even managed to find love there, even if that love hadn't lasted very long.

At the time, Elise could not imagine home being anywhere but the town of New Iberia, but she, too, eventually left it behind and moved on to this place. Yet all of these years later, the smell of the ocean never managed to equal in sweet fragrance the pungent aroma of the bayou. She had made a good life here, but it still wasn't home. Oh, there were times that she dreamed of moving back, but love had brought her here, and the memories of that love managed to keep her here. Now there was nobody left back in New Iberia to really call her own. Their family had been small from the beginning, and now sadly they were all gone. Every once in a while, though, she simply had to go back and look out over the levee and just remember all of those old used-to-bes.

# Elise's Story

## C'est la Vie

I was born in New Iberia, a pretty little southern Louisiana town located on Bayou Teche about twenty miles from the city of Lafayette. It's a place of vast coastal swamps; fierce alligators; lush, colorful gardens; elegant plantation homes; fiery red peppers; sweet, sweet sugar cane; good old rednecks; and accordions that magically come out to play in the moonlight. It's the place where exiled Acadians came two hundred fifty years ago looking for a safe haven and found a home. In New Iberia, Spanish, French, Native American, and African cultures mingle together in a wonderful mix, and in my mind there is nowhere like Cajun Louisiana in the world. Nowhere!

*Mais*, I really can't decide when New Iberia is prettier—in the springtime when the dangling strands of Spanish moss get the company of deeply hued wildflowers, or in the summer when it is hot, hot and there is a smoldering kind of beauty that thankfully gives way to warm afternoon rains. Or could it be the fall when the brightness begins to fade into a gray-brown sameness, and the sun starts to set early on marsh grasses that sway in the wind. But my mama would say that it was surely the winter when the beauty of the season goes indoors with family and friends awaiting the holiday season. Truly, I cannot decide. New Iberia is just beautiful no matter when you are lucky enough to be there.

I arrived in this world, the oldest of two girls, in 1927, during the flood. My mama used to say that just as the Spanish lake filled and overflowed, I decided I wanted to see it, so within hours there I was. My sister, Rita, was born three years later during the Mardi Gras. Oh, how she interrupted the party. Maybe that was why she seemed to have been looking for a party ever since. But if a good time is what you are looking for, New Iberia is the place to be. There was the Sugar Cane Festival that started when I was about ten

and still goes on today. With its pageants, parades, cooking competitions, and good food, the Sugar Cane Festival was the way we looked forward to ending the summer. There was also a crawfish festival—a tribute to the little mud bugs that we figured out how to cook every way that you can imagine. Legend has it that the crawfish started out as lobster all those years ago when the Acadians left Nova Scotia, but as the journey to South Louisiana went on and on, they got smaller and smaller until they became the crawfish they are today. But however they came to be, I just thank God for them, because I could eat them a bucket at a time.

And, of course, there was Mardi Gras, my favorite celebration of all—Catholics getting their last good times in before the beginning of the Lenten season. Oh, how I loved Mardi Gras! At that time, we always went to see Grand-mère and Grand-père. They lived in a small town that was not too far away.

I remember that early in the morning the *capitaine* (my *grand-père*) would gather together all the masked men and boys. Grand-père was not masked, so you could see clearly his handsome face. They would meet in the center of town and move to the outer edges. When they reached a farmhouse, the *capitaine* would stop the men at the road, and he would go up to the farmer's door and ask if his men could enter the yard. When the farmer said yes, Grand-père waved a flag to let the men know to come into the yard. Within moments the men would begin to sing and dance.

*C'est les Mardi Gras, c'est tout des bons jeunes gens.*
*Des bons jeunes gens, ça vient de toutes des bonnes familles.*
*C'est pas des malfaiteurs, c'est juste des guémandeurs.*

(The Mardi Gras, they are all good people.
Good people who all come from good families.
They are not evil doers. They are just beggars.)

After the men danced and begged, the farmer presented the *capitaine* with a chicken or two. The *capitaine* threw the chicken into the air, and the one who caught it was the winner. Then everybody celebrated by climbing trees and taunting the farmer to guess who they were. When the *capitaine* blew the whistle, off they would go from farmhouse to farmhouse. After they hit all the possible homes, they brought all the chickens back to town and everybody had big bowls of gumbo. The next day was Ash Wednesday, and if you did Mardi Gras right, you had plenty to pray about that morning. Oh, how I miss Mardi Gras. I can still taste the gumbo and oyster po' boys today, if I think hard enough.

We lived in a small house in the countryside outside town, but we did not farm. Our neighbors did—they grew sugar cane and during the harvest I could smell the sweet, sticky aroma from the nearby fields. Workers brought the cane in from the fields, and trucks lugged it to the mill to be processed. There it was turned into cane syrup, the very ingredient we needed to make the sweets I loved so much.

My daddy ran a butcher shop on Main Street, and Mama made cooked goodies that he could sell. Her specialty was *boudin* and I loved to stop in after school so I could get my share. When I was a young girl I even helped out, but when my mind turned to boys I found excuse after excuse to be anywhere but at that store. Not that we were allowed to keep company, but I could at least look and I did a lot of that. Unfortunately, my sister did more than look and that's when the trouble began.

Beautiful Cajun Louisiana—the place of good folks and good times. But it also is the place where the legend still exists of Evangeline, the young girl who lost her heart over two hundred years ago. So long ago it was that the poor girl waited for her love to come to her after fleeing Nova Scotia and ending up in Louisiana. *Mais*, she waited and she waited. Oh, after a time he did arrive, but then he had a new love and a new life. *Mais*, my Evangeline, he was *canaille*, no? The story goes that Evangeline died shortly thereafter from a broken heart. The old folks say that if you listen carefully when the rain blows, you can still hear her weeping away her sorrows. Oh, my sweet sister, Rita, did we lose you that way, too? Oh, how my heart breaks whenever I think that could be true.

# *Chère Soeur*

*Mon Dieu*, but Elise did not want to read those letters. She didn't want to know that an old lady could still feel homesick, sad, and lonely. She also didn't want to think about her sister today, that precious one that now existed nowhere but in her memories. No, she didn't want to be reminded of what used to be—that she used to be young, that New Iberia used to be home, that she used to be a daughter, and that for a short while she was an aunt. But there the letters lay, set so neatly in the middle of the table and so very easy to reach. *Poo-yie*, she did not want them because they always gave her the *frissons*. Still, she hesitated for a moment longer, and then she took hold of the little colorful pile and slowly untied the ribbon.

Some of these she had been able to share with Larissa, and others, she could not. They were just too personal. But she had showed a few of them to the *bébé*, and Larissa had copied down all the recipes she'd needed. The first letter unfolded almost by itself. Maybe that was a sign that it was due a reading. Miss Bessie down at the center always said that smart women grew in grace and with that grace came a wisdom that brought about acceptance for everything—the blessings and the curses. *Mon Dieu*, Elise hoped that Miss Bessie was right about that.

September 1947

*Chère Soeur* Elise,

*Comment ça va? Ça va bien*, so do not worry.

I am sending this letter to you through Tante Anita because I am sure that she will get it to you. *Mon Dieu*, I know by now that you are so *cagou* that your poor head is spinning. *Mais* you must understand that I didn't want to leave that way, sneaking out like a thief into the night. But I could not stand Papa's sad, angry eyes any longer. So I left, headed anywhere really, just hoping that somehow I would end up in the place I was supposed to be. And maybe I have.

I am in the big city of Shreveport. It is so far in north Louisiana that I feel as if I could just stick my toe out and I could touch Texas. Why Shreveport? Oh, I don't know. At the time I was surely *perdu comme un tchoc dans le brouillard, chère*, but there was a woman in front of me at the ticket office who was heading this way, so I decided to come here, too. It seemed as good a place as any.

The lady, she sat next to me on the bus and what an angel she was. Her name was Marian. With all of her easy chatter, I had no time to think on my own big troubles. I sat back and listened to her tell stories, and before I knew it, we were here in Shreveport. I cannot say that I like it or dislike it. I haven't been here long enough to decide, but we will see, no?

Marian knew of a lovely boardinghouse right in the middle of town. It is not too expensive and that is where I am. I have enough money to last a bit, but I will have to find work and soon! The house is run by a sweet older lady who was once a teacher here. She is a spinster with no family and nobody to love, so she shares her home and her heart with those who are merely passing her way. I look at her and there are times that I wonder if that will be me years from now. But if things go as I pray, hopefully it will not, for I will have *mon 'ti bebe,* who I hope will love me as much as I already love it. If that's all I ever have, then it will be enough.

Shreveport—the city built on tears, or the "weeping hill" as Marian called it. She told me that it was so nicknamed because of the Indians that first lived here. The story goes that once upon a time they lived in an underground cave. Well, one day they were led out of the darkness through this secret passageway, just by the light of the moon. On to the sunlit hill they climbed until an evil wolf rolled a big, heavy stone into the path of the passageway, trapping their loved ones inside. So sad were they for those they left behind that they wept for days and days.

*Mais,* I tell you, I can imagine their pain because I, too, have shed my tears for those I left behind. Oh, how I miss you, *chère.* I can just imagine you now in the kitchen baking something wonderful. And I have a gift for you from Marian. They are the recipes for the tasty jar bread and the delicious apple fritters that she shared with me during the long ride here. She said that you simply must try them and tell her what you think.

I have enclosed my address so that you may write me when you have time. Give my best to Tante Anita and tell her I am well. Tell Mama and Papa that I love them, especially Papa, even if he does act like he wants to pass me a slap when he hears it.

All my love,
Rita

And so it had all begun, remembered Elise, notes filled with love and food. Appropriate, too, since her family had never really been able to give one without the other.

## JAR BREAD

⅔ **cup shortening**

⅔ **cup sugar**

**4 eggs**

½ **cup water**

3½ **cups flour**

½ **teaspoon baking powder**

**2 teaspoons baking soda**

**1 teaspoon salt**

**1 teaspoon cinnamon**

½ **teaspoon brown sugar**

**1 dash allspice**

**1 teaspoon ground cloves**

⅔ **cup chopped nuts**

**2 cups canned pumpkin**

In a medium bowl, cream together shortening and sugar. Beat the eggs and water into the mixture and set aside. In a separate bowl, sift together the flour, baking powder, baking soda, salt, cinnamon, brown sugar, allspice, and cloves.

Add the dry ingredients to the creamed mixture and mix well. Add chopped nuts and pumpkin and mix well.

Grease pint canning jars with good wide mouths. Fill the jars halfway and place on a cooking sheet. Bake at 350° for 45 minutes. Allow them to cool slightly and seal with sterilized lids.

Yields 8 jars.

## APPLE FRITTERS

3 apples
3 tablespoons sugar, divided
1 lemon, juiced
1½ cups flour
2 teaspoons baking powder
¼ teaspoon salt
¾ cup milk
1 egg
1 tablespoon Crisco, melted
Shortening for frying

Yields 12 fritters.

Peel, core, and cut apples into ¼-inch slices; then in a bowl, sprinkle 2 tablespoons sugar and strained lemon juice over them. Sift flour, baking powder, remaining sugar, and salt into another bowl. Add milk to well-beaten egg and stir liquid gradually into dry ingredients, beating thoroughly. Add melted Crisco. Cover apple slices with batter. Heat 1 inch of shortening in a skillet or pan to 365°. To test the temperature, drop in some breadcrumbs—they should brown in 60 seconds. Drop ¼-cup portions of batter into the hot shortening. Fry for 4 to 5 minutes. Drain fritters. Apples or any combination of fruits can be used to make delicious fritters.

October 1947

*Chère Soeur* Elise,

*Comment ça va? Ça va bien.*

I am sorry that it has taken me so long to write, but I did receive your letter and I must have read it three times that day. I see that Papa is doing well. He and his hunt—grown men in a rotting old camp, getting up early in the morning and then hiding out in the marsh just to shoot down the ducks—so strange what a man will do for fun, but at least Mama has plenty to cook for the holidays.

I am surprised at you, *chère*, sneaking away from the house to go to a *fais-do-do*. I can just see you now in all of your *frou-frou* and dancing the night away. How lucky for you that Mama sleeps as if she is no longer in this world and that on Fridays Papa takes his whiskey for "medicinal purposes." They probably never heard a thing clear until morning. Oh, but you are a bad girl. And then to meet a man, a man I think you have snuck out to meet before because I could hear the big smile in your letter as you talked about him. But he is an army man! After my army man, I am afraid for you. And he is from this place we know nothing about—eastern North Carolina. That sounds as if it could be clear on the other side of the world. You could not go that far away—what would we do without you? I know you have said nothing about this in your letters, but oh, how I know so well that it takes no time at all to fall in love.

Last night I dreamed about my James, or should I say the James that I wish were mine. I woke to feel his baby move inside me for the first time, reminding me that I am *en famille,* and I wondered as I stared into the lonely darkness, where he might be at that moment. I also wondered what he would think about the baby if he had stayed around long enough to find out. *Mon Dieu,* I remind myself, he found his pleasure and I lost my heart. Do you believe, *chère,* that he ever even thinks of me? I know, probably not, but I can dream, can't I?

This morning Marian made us all the best banana bread. Oh, it was so good that I think it chased all the pain of love away. She says that you can also make banana biscuits. She has promised me some for tomorrow. I cannot wait. Marian was so happy that you enjoyed the jar bread and the apple fritters. Let me know about these, too, *chère.*

I am still not working. I have not been feeling that well, but it is surely nothing. The money you sent will help me, and also I am able to help out in the kitchen during breakfast so as to work off part of my rent.

> Believe me, all goes well.
> I love you,
> Rita

## Banana Tea Loaf

1½ cups flour

1 teaspoon baking powder

1 teaspoon baking soda

2 sticks butter

½ cup sugar

2 eggs

6 ripe bananas, mashed

1 cup chopped nuts

Yields 1 loaf.

Preheat the oven to 350°. Sift together the flour, baking powder, and baking soda. Cream the butter with the sugar until smooth and fluffy; then add the eggs one at a time, beating well after each addition. Alternately add the dry ingredients and the bananas a bit at a time, mixing with a spoon until all ingredients are well blended. Add the chopped nuts last.

Bake in a greased and floured loaf pan until a toothpick inserted in the center comes out clean (approximately 1 hour).

# Bayou Banana Biscuits

1 cup flour
3 teaspoons baking powder
1 teaspoon salt
1 teaspoon brown sugar
1 cup mashed bananas
2 tablespoons oil
½ cup milk

Preheat the oven to 350° to 400°. Sift all dry ingredients together. Add bananas and oil. Add milk so that it will make a soft dough. Roll out on a floured board. Cut out with the top of a drinking glass. Place biscuits on a greased pan. Bake for about 12 minutes.

Yields 14 to 16 biscuits.

November 1947

*Chère Soeur* Elise,

Again with the man from Carolina. Oh, I think I can hear your heart racing from here. I think I will soon have a new brother-in-law. You know for sure that it is love, no? Don't be shy. Tell me everything. *Comment s'appelle cet homme là?* If there is to be a wedding, I will find a way to be there, big belly and all, but you will *not* get married without me.

The boardinghouse family is really growing. There is even a Negro woman here and nobody seems to mind. Can you believe that? She is Creole from New Orleans, and she is here to get a job. Why she left home, she does not say. But I like her—she is such a big, beautiful black woman. Always in bright colors and wearing a smile. She makes me laugh when I need it, and she seems to know so many strange things. This morning she dangled a needle on a string over my belly and said that I was having a boy. A boy! Oh, how I would love a son.

Oh, and Elise, Satin is a wonderful cook and a great storyteller. Yesterday she made us all bread pudding for dessert. I had to watch her make it to get the recipe, but it was fun because she told stories all the while. I have enclosed the story that goes along with the recipe.

Satin told me that her mama taught her to cook and she could have made dirt taste good if she had put her mind to it. She also said Negroes used an unusual expression if something tasted good. They tell the cook that "it's so good, you must have put your toe in it." Well, Satin said that if you use one of the sauce recipes she gave me with her bread pudding recipes, people will think you put your whole foot in it.

Oh, how Mama will love both the story and the puddings. So get busy, *ma chère* Elise, you have some cooking to do and some tales to tell. Be sure to send me her smile the next time you write—I want every detail.

Please write soon. I get so lonely here during the day when everyone else is off minding their own business. The doctor still says no work, but if I take care, my baby will be here in the early spring—what a miracle that will be.

Last night I walked outside and looked up at the stars. I wondered if they were really angels like Grand-père used to say. Oh, how I hope so, I could use an angel looking over me right now. But *chère*, I looked around and I was not alone! There was a man not too far away. A young man who is now staying at the boardinghouse. I got a good look at him this morning over breakfast, and he looks harmless enough, maybe even handsome. Oh, and as I was watching him, he was watching me! I don't know why he is here, and really, I should not be so nosy. But if I find out anything, I'll let you know. Knowing you, you are curious already.

Well, enjoy the bread pudding, and remember to send me Mama's smile.

> All my love,
> Rita

## *Satin's Tale: Too Many Cooks*

Once upon a time there lived a woman named Marie Claire who had three daughters. Well, one day the priest announced that he was coming to dinner on Saturday evening. (In Louisiana many, many Afro-Creole people are Catholic, just like us in Cajun country.) Well, the priest was always inviting himself to somebody's house, so this really wasn't that unusual. Of course, Miss Marie wanted everything to be perfect, so she started early on Saturday morning, cooking and cleaning. At about noon she stopped and made her very special bread pudding, but at about three in the afternoon, while weeding the garden, she remembered that she didn't add any salt to the pudding. Now bread pudding doesn't need but a pinch, but that does make a difference, so Marie asked her oldest daughter to go and tend to it. But the oldest child said she had to find her new hair ribbon and she couldn't do it. When Marie asked the second child, she said that she really needed to iron her dress. Well, the third one yelled out that she couldn't do it either because she was in the tub.

After a while Miss Marie went and added that pinch of salt herself, and then she went up to her bedroom to get dressed. But not too long after, the oldest daughter found her hair ribbon, and she ran down to the kitchen to salt the pudding. Within minutes the second child finished ironing her dress, and she, too, went to salt the pudding. Of course the third child couldn't bathe forever, so as soon as she got dressed, she went into the kitchen and added a pinch of salt to the pudding.

Well, the priest came right on time. He was never late for a free meal. Once he was finished with his meal, he was ready for dessert, Miss Marie's famous bread pudding. But after he took one swallow, he choked and sputtered something awful. Holy water took on a brand new meaning, let me say that. Well, Miss Marie took one small spoonful and tasted it, and she knew immediately what had happened. "Who salted the pudding?" she asked. "I did," answered all three girls. "And so did I," said Miss Marie. "It looks like too many cooks sure enough spoiled the pudding."

## BREAD PUDDING

**2 cups stale bread cubes**

**I quart milk**

**3 eggs, beaten**

**⅛ teaspoon salt**

**¾ cup sugar**

**¼ teaspoon ground nutmeg**

**I tablespoon vanilla**

**½ cup raisins**

**2 tablespoons butter, softened**

Preheat the oven to 350°. Soak the bread in the milk until soft, about 5 minutes. Blend or mix together the eggs, salt, sugar, nutmeg, vanilla, and raisins thoroughly. Combine the bread with the egg mixture, add the butter, and mix thoroughly. Pour into a greased 13x9-inch baking pan and bake until golden brown, about 45 minutes. Allow to cool.

Yields 1 pan.

## Bread and Butter Pudding

I loaf white bread
Butter
I cup currants
4 eggs
½ cup sugar
I pint milk
Fresh nutmeg, grated

Preheat the oven to 350°. Cut a loaf of bread into thin slices, and butter each slice of bread. In a 1-quart mold or basin, put a layer of bread in the bottom; then sprinkle with currants. Beat the eggs and add the sugar, beating until light. Gradually add milk and grated nutmeg. Pour this mixture over the bread and let stand for 15 minutes. Bake for 30 minutes. Serve cold with cream sauce.

## Cream Sauce

I egg
⅓ cup milk
⅓ cup sugar
½ teaspoon vanilla
½ pint cream

Beat egg until stiff. Add milk, sugar, and vanilla, and lastly add the cream.

Yields 1 cup.

## Lemon Cream Sauce

I tablespoon flour
½ cup sugar
I cup boiling water
I lemon, juice and rind
I egg, beaten

Add flour and sugar to boiling water in a saucepan. Stir until boiling again; then add grated rind and juice of lemon. Pour while hot into beaten egg, constantly beating. For rich puddings, you can add a tablespoon of butter.

Yields 1 cup.

NOTE: Vanilla or orange extract can be used in place of lemon.

## Nutmeg Sauce

| | |
|---|---|
| **I cup sugar** | In a small bowl cream together sugar and butter. |
| **I tablespoon butter** | Put creamed mixture in medium saucepan and |
| **I cup water** | boil, gradually adding water. Boil for 10 minutes. |
| **Nutmeg to taste** | Add nutmeg for flavoring. |

Yields 1½ cups.


## Brandy Sauce

| | |
|---|---|
| **¼ cup butter** | Cream the butter and sugar in a large bowl. Add |
| **I cup sugar** | eggs, brandy, milk, and a little nutmeg. Cook in a |
| **2 eggs, well beaten** | double boiler until it thickens like custard. |
| **2 tablespoons brandy** | |
| **½ cup milk or cream** | |
| **¼ teaspoon nutmeg** | |

Yields 1 cup.


November 1947

*Chère Soeur* Elise,

I am not well this week. I just lie around *en plâtre*. I do not know what is wrong. The doctor has said that I am not gaining enough weight to keep the baby healthy. He wants me to gain ten pounds, but I don't see how that can happen. I am eating, but it does me no good, and I am cooking, too. Marian has taught me so much, and when I am not well she makes me something special. My favorite is French toast. Marian has many ways to make it, too, and she is another storyteller. Here is her tale to go along with the French toast:

> Down where I come from, French is still spoken here and there, and folks call this by the name *pain perdu*, or lost bread. They call it this because the bread would be lost if we couldn't find a good use for it, like French

toast or bread pudding. My mama had a special plate for the French toast. It was a big white platter with a big red chicken painted across it. She said it was a wedding present from her mama. That plate was all her parents could afford. Well, Mama would stack those pieces of French toast on that big plate, and I would count the minutes until the French toast was all gone, and we could see that big red chicken again. Ha! Ha! I don't believe I ever made it past three!

*Mais,* here are the recipes. I've also included some delicious beverage recipes to accompany the French toast. Why not try them out on Papa? Tell me, Elise, does he ever think of me? I know he and Mama know where I am, but does he ever think of me? It seems to me like I just keep giving my heart to men who take it for a while, then just toss it back. Maybe I should stay away from them altogether.

But seriously, Elise, make these for Papa and tell him I sent them with all my love. Maybe one day I will get up the nerve to write him a letter. But I don't think either of us is ready for that right now.

Oh, the baby is moving, but sadly he is dropping blood as he does. Elise, this baby just must be healthy. *Poo-yie,* I have given up everything for him, and I already love him. I don't think I could stand to lose yet another man I have come to adore.

All my love,
Rita

## FRENCH TOAST

¼ cup milk

2 tablespoons sugar

½ teaspoon vanilla

1 egg, slightly beaten

4 slices bread

2 tablespoons unsalted butter

Confectioners' sugar

Cane syrup for serving

Stir the milk, sugar, and vanilla into the egg. Dip the bread into the egg mixture. Make sure both sides are well coated. Melt the butter on a griddle. Brown the French toast lightly on both sides. Sprinkle with confectioners' sugar. Serve with cane syrup.

VARIATION: Sprinkle with pecan halves.

Yields 4 servings.

# BAKED CINNAMON TOAST

⅔ cup sugar

4 teaspoons cinnamon

6 (½-inch-thick) slices
   homemade bread, crusts
   removed, each slice cut
   into 4 strips

1 stick (½ cup) unsalted
   butter, melted

Yields 24 pieces.

Preheat the oven to 375°. In a wide, shallow bowl, stir together sugar and cinnamon. Working with one strip of bread at a time, turn strips quickly in butter, coating them on all sides and letting any excess drip off. Then turn them quickly in cinnamon-sugar, coating them on all sides. Bake strips in lightly buttered jelly roll pan in upper third of the oven for 10 minutes. Turn and bake 10 more minutes. Transfer with tongs to serving plate.

# STUFFED FRENCH TOAST

8 (1½-inch-thick) slices
   French bread

2 tablespoons butter or
   margarine, softened

4 breakfast sausages, cooked*

1 cup (4 ounces)
   shredded Swiss cheese

2 eggs

½ cup milk

1½ teaspoons sugar

¼ teaspoon ground cinnamon

Maple syrup, optional

Yields 4 servings.

Cut a pocket in the crust of each slice of bread. Butter the inside of pocket. Cut sausages into bite-size pieces; toss with cheese. Stuff into pockets. In a shallow bowl, beat eggs, milk, sugar, and cinnamon; dip both sides of bread in the batter. Cook on a greased hot griddle until golden brown on both sides. Serve with syrup if desired.

---

*Modern cooks can substitute 4 brown-and-serve sausage patties, cooked, for the 4 breakfast sausages, cooked.

# HAM-STUFFED FRENCH TOAST

½ pound breakfast sausage

6 to 8 ounces bacon

I loaf large-diameter French bread

½ cup milk

4 large eggs

¼ cup sugar

I teaspoon cinnamon

I ½ teaspoons vanilla

½ pound boiled ham (thinly sliced)

8 slices processed cheese

Yields 4 servings.

In a large skillet, fry the breakfast sausage and bacon until done. While the meat is cooking, slice the French bread into 8 slices, approximately 1½ to 2 inches thick. Then slice each slice ¾ of the way through again.

Mix the milk, eggs, sugar, cinnamon, and vanilla together into a batter in a deep bowl and set aside. Divide the bacon and sausage each into 8 equal parts and do the same with the ham. Dip each piece of bread into the batter and submerge it so that both sides and edges are coated. Open each piece and put in one portion of the meat, bacon, and ham, along with one slice of cheese, and close the bread again. Fry the stuffed, batter-coated bread slices in a greased skillet until golden brown on the outside and the cheese is melted on the inside. Serve 2 slices on each plate with your favorite side dishes and toppings (home fries, maple syrup, confectioners' sugar, etc.).

# Beverages

### Café Noir

*Café noir* is made by dripping. It is also called "drip coffee." For each 1 cup of water, use a heaping teaspoon of coffee, ground to a powder. Place this powder in a thick flannel cloth and lay in a strainer. Pour the boiling water over it and allow it to percolate into the pot. The flannel should not be porous, or the fine powder will also find its way through to the pot below. Like all other hot beverages, it should be served immediately.

### Boiled Coffee

To make boiled coffee, pour a sufficient quantity of finely ground coffee into the pot, and then pour the boiling water into the pot. Boil and then take from the fire, and add the beaten white of an egg and the crushed eggshells to the pot. Again, place coffee on the fire and let boil about 1 minute; remove and allow to stand a few minutes (not more than 5) and serve.

### Tea

Use freshly boiled water. Scald the teapot (earthen, granite, or china); for mild infusions allow ½ level teaspoon of tea for each cup. Pour the boiling water on the tea, cover closely, and let it stand and infuse, not boil, for 5 minutes. If you have a table teakettle, put the tea in a tea ball, fill two cups at a time with boiling water, and hold the ball in the water till the desired strength is secured. At afternoon teas and for iced tea, serve with lemon slices.

### Chocolate

Mix 2 rounded tablespoons of sugar, a few grains of salt, and ½ level teaspoon cornstarch in a granite saucepan; add 2 squares of unsweetened chocolate and ¼ cup of cold water. Stir over the fire until melted, thick, and smooth. Add 1 cup boiling water, and when ready to serve, add 3 cups scalded milk. Keep it hot over hot water until ready to serve.

December 1947

*Chère Soeur* Elise,

No time to write, but I saw these helpful hints in Wednesday's ladies page, as well as the recipe for coffee bread and shortcake biscuits. I have already tried out both and they are yummy. You wouldn't believe who I shared them with—yes, the handsome man I told you about who is staying here. He has been a real friend to me. Maybe he is one of those angels I wished for.

> All my love,
> Rita

## Helpful Hints

* Tough meat can be made tender by laying it a few minutes in vinegar.

* Remove black spots from dishes by rubbing salt on them.

* To take berry stains out of table linens, pour boiling water through the stains before wetting the linens with soapy water.

* To mend a crack in the side of the range, use a filling of equal parts of wood ashes and common salt, moistened with water. This will prove hard and lasting.

* To remove odors from a dish, fill it with boiling water and drop a piece of charcoal into it. A lump of charcoal left in a closed bottle or jar will keep it from becoming musty.

* A crust of bread put in the water in which spinach, beet tops, or dandelions are boiled not only prevents a disagreeable odor, but also adds delicacy to the vegetable.

* To get rid of ants, place lumps of gum camphor in their runways and near sweets infested by them.

## SHORTCAKE BISCUITS

Yield will vary with biscuit recipe used.

Make a standard biscuit using shortening to taste, but make biscuits rather larger than usual. Split and butter the biscuits while hot. Take any fruit, crush it, and add enough sugar to make plenty of juice. Strawberries, raspberries, blueberries, peaches, or any ripe or canned fruit can be used— just drain and reserve syrup and cut fruit into pieces. Pour the crushed fruit over and between the biscuits just before serving. Whipped cream, sweetened or flavored, can be added. To make flavored whipped cream, dilute cream with some of the reserved syrup before beating.

## COFFEE BREAD

¼ cup milk
2½ cups flour
1 package active dry yeast
½ cup Crisco, melted
2 eggs
1 cup sugar
1 teaspoon lemon extract
1 teaspoon salt
1 teaspoon cinnamon
¼ cup chopped English
  walnut meats

Yields 1 large loaf.

Heat milk just to lukewarm in a large pan; then add flour and yeast (dissolved in warm water) to make batter. Allow to rise until light; then add Crisco, well-beaten eggs, sugar, lemon, salt, and enough flour to make stiff dough. Knead 10 minutes and let rise until light. Place in a pan greased with Crisco and let rise again.

Preheat the oven to 375°. Spread dough with melted Crisco and sprinkle with sugar, cinnamon, and nuts. Bake for 30 minutes.

December 1947

*Chère Soeur* Elise,

Well, it looks like the last of autumn has come and gone, and winter has now said "good day" quite loud and clear. Soon it will be time for a visit from Papa Noël. *Mais,* what a wonderful time we always had! Friends in and out, out and in, all bringing love and greetings. Oh, and all the beautiful decorations, especially the ones along the levee. My favorite has always been the one of Papa Noël sitting up high and mighty in his fine sleigh that is pulled by alligators. I tell you, it is the only time you and I thought an alligator looked inviting, no? And then there is the boat ride along the bayou the night before Christmas. *Mais,* to sit back and enjoy the fantasy of Christmas in the still and breathtaking dark of the night. Do you remember that during the boat ride Mama would always remind us that we must be good or Papa Noël would simply pass us on by? Only those that were perfect got the pretty gifts, she would say. And, of course, I always promised to be good, in fact, better than good.

But I imagine that there will be no Papa Noël or pretty little gifts for me this year, except from you, Elise. But thank God for you and my new friends here at the house. I don't feel so alone anymore. Just yesterday, Christopher, the young man I told you about, took me for a ride in his car. We laughed a lot and even stopped to drink chocolate. And that's not all, just the other day he read me poems by Longfellow while we nibbled on French fritters and *beignets.* At the end of the evening, he even kissed me, his mouth still covered in powdered sugar, but, oh, Elise, that made it sweeter still. He does know all about the *bébé,* but still he does not care. I don't know what to do—is it not foolish to risk my heart again? Still, he is persistent, so we will simply see what is yet to be. That is all any of us can do.

Oh, Marian has sent you four new recipes—perfect for the holidays. She sent cinnamon bread, *beignets,* French fritters, and crêpes. With all these goodies in the house, Papa Noël will surely not pass you by. Enjoy!

All my love,
Rita

P. S. Oh, and Elise, the *bébé* still manages to hang on by what seems to be a thread. I am six months along now, and I just know if I can make it a bit longer, the *bébé* will be strong enough, even if he is born early. But still he bleeds, not so much anymore, just occasional drops of despair. I pray for him, Elise, every day and every night, and I want you to pray for him, too.

# CINNAMON BREAD

**2 cups all-purpose flour**
**I cup white sugar**
**2 teaspoons baking powder**
**½ teaspoon baking soda**
**I ½ teaspoons ground cinnamon**
**I teaspoon salt**
**I cup buttermilk**
**¼ cup vegetable oil**
**2 eggs**
**2 teaspoons vanilla**

## TOPPING
**2 tablespoons white sugar**
**I teaspoon ground cinnamon**
**2 teaspoons margarine**

Preheat the oven to 350°. Grease a 9x5x3-inch loaf pan. In a large mixing bowl, pour in flour, 1 cup sugar, baking powder, baking soda, cinnamon, salt, buttermilk, oil, eggs, and vanilla. Beat 3 minutes. Pour into the prepared loaf pan. Smooth top of batter.

Combine topping ingredients, mixing until crumbly. Sprinkle topping on batter. Using a knife, cut in a light swirling motion to achieve a marbled effect.

Bake for approximately 50 minutes. Test with a toothpick; when inserted, it should come out clean. Remove bread from pan and place on a wire rack to cool.

Yields 1 loaf.

# BEIGNETS

I package active dry yeast

1½ cups warm water (110°)

½ cup white sugar

I teaspoon salt

2 eggs

I cup evaporated milk

7 cups all-purpose flour,
  divided

¼ cup shortening

I quart vegetable oil for
  frying

¼ cup confectioners' sugar

In a large bowl, dissolve yeast in warm water. Add sugar, salt, eggs, evaporated milk, and blend well. Mix in 4 cups of the flour and beat until smooth. Add the shortening and then the remaining 3 cups of flour. Cover and chill for up to 24 hours.

Roll out dough ⅛ inch thick. Cut into 2½-inch squares. Fry in 360° oil. If *beignets* do not pop up, oil is not hot enough. Drain onto paper towels. Shake confectioners' sugar on hot *beignets*. Serve warm.

Yields 10 servings.

# FRENCH FRITTERS

I cup flour

½ teaspoon salt

1½ teaspoons baking powder

4 tablespoons sugar

2 eggs

2 tablespoons orange juice

I teaspoon melted butter

¼ cup milk

Vegetable oil for frying

Powdered sugar for sprinkling

Sift together flour, salt, baking powder, and sugar. In a medium bowl, mix together dry ingredients with eggs, orange juice, melted butter, and milk. Drop by large spoonfuls into hot oil and brown. Sprinkle with powdered sugar and serve for breakfast with preserves.

# CRÊPES

| | |
|---|---|
| **I cup flour** | Sift together flour, sugar, and salt in a medium bowl. |
| **¼ cup sugar** | Add eggs, one at a time, and mix with a whisk until |
| **⅛ teaspoon salt** | no lumps remain. Stir in melted butter. Slowly whisk |
| **3 eggs** | in milk until batter is the consistency of thin cream. |
| **2 tablespoons melted butter** | Let batter stand for 1 hour before making crêpes. |
| **I½ cups milk** | |
| **Butter or oil** | Heat a 6- or 10-inch pan and rub it with butter or |
| | oil. The butter or oil should sizzle when it touches |
| Yields 8 to 12 crêpes. | the pan. For each crêpe, pour a little batter in the |
| | pan, tilting the skillet so that the batter evenly |
| | coats the bottom of the pan. When lightly browned |
| | on the bottom, turn carefully with a spatula and |
| | brown the other side. Re-butter pan as needed. To |
| | serve, place fruit, whipped cream, or crabmeat on |
| | each crêpe and roll up the crêpe. |

Unfortunately there were no more letters after that last one. For a while, Elise thought that maybe Rita had found love with her young man and a touch of generosity from Papa Noël, and had simply been too busy to write. But during the first week of January, Elise received a telegram telling her that her wishes were not so.

January 1948

We regret to inform you that Rita is not well. You must come now.

Marian

And so Elise had jumped on the first bus headed to Shreveport, but she was too late. Her sister was gone. Elise remembered now how unreal it had all seemed. Just a few short weeks before, she had sounded like a woman filled with promise and then suddenly she was gone—a shell of a woman whose soul had already moved on to parts unknown. Elise could not understand how such a thing could have happened, but Marian quickly explained.

"About a week ago, Rita, she got a letter from that friend of hers, Claire, I think it is, who lives just outside of St. Martinville. Well, it seems like this Claire ran right into Rita's James at a party in town. He didn't recognize her, but she sure remembered him. She said he had this lady on his arm at the time—a pretty little thing with big brown eyes and long dark curls. Well, when Claire asked another man if he knew the couple, he said yes—that was James and his wife, Suzanne. They had just had a baby! Well, you never know what is truly in a woman's heart—me, I try not to judge. But still I cannot understand why Claire would send such news. Maybe she thought because of Christopher, Rita would not hurt so much at such a message. But I know a woman never really gets over a hurt such as that. Maybe that is the difference between the old and the young—we old ones are scarred enough to understand a great deal.

"Well, at first it seemed to me as if Rita would be all right despite it all. She had Christopher and the *bébé*. I hoped that if I were there for her, then all would be well, but that turned out not to be true. One night she started to bleed. I don't know when or how much because she did not call for me as she was supposed to. The bleeding must have started as a little and then grown heavier. Still, she lay there silent and alone. Maybe she believed that it would stop, that if any of God's goodness were anywhere near, it would do, or maybe she didn't care if it ever stopped at all. We will never know.

"By the time we found her, she was gone and the baby was, too. So we cleaned her up before we called anybody and once we did, they came quickly and carried her away to that place in town, you know where they have for such things. Poor Christopher, he is beside himself. I don't believe the boy will ever be the same."

And so Elise collected her sister and the last of her things and carried them all back to New Iberia, where the sun was setting early and the marsh grasses swayed in the wind. She, Mama, and Papa buried her quickly and many, many loved ones came by to say *adieu*. And after everyone was gone, the three of them just stood and stared at the ground as if looking long enough and hard enough would raise sweet Rita back up and into their arms.

Not one of them said a thing about the sadness of things left unsaid or feelings that ultimately had never been tended to. But after an hour, they accepted it all and moved on. Yes, there had been bitterness, but there had also been love. And there had been hope that, when all was said and done, Rita would be back home, *bébé* and all. Even Papa had continued to love and hope. Elise later found the cradle he had carved for the *bébé* in his workshop. Yes, there had been a daddy love for Rita up to the end, even if that love had been left sadly unattended.

The memories were now becoming too much for Elise. She slowly opened her farewell treasure box and dropped the letters inside. She called it her farewell box because everything inside said good-bye in one way or another.

"*Adieu*, my dear Rita, *adieu* . . . Oh, how I did love you."

## *Cajun Glossary*

*adieu*   farewell or good-bye
*bébé*   baby
*boudin*   blood sausage
*c'est la vie*   that's life
*Ça va bien.*   I am doing well.
*café noir*   black coffee
*cagou*   out of sorts, addled
*canaille*   tricky, shrewd
*chère*   dear
*Comment ça va?*   How are you?
*Comment s'appelle cet homme là?*   What is his name?
*en famille*   carrying a child, in the family way
*en plâtre*   lethargic, without energy
*fais-do-do*   a dance, often held outdoors
*frissons*   chills, shakes
*frou-frou*   a frilly or festive way of dressing

*mais*   well, but
*mon Dieu*   my God
*mon 'ti bebe*   my little baby
*perdu comme un tchoc dans le brouillard*   lost like a bird in a fog
*poo-yie*   wow! or oh!
*soeur*   sister
*tante*   aunt

# Recipe Index